O'er THE River Liffey

HEIDI ASHWORTH

O'er THE River Liffey

HEIDI ASHWORTH

POWER OF THE MATCHMAKER SERIES

Interior design by Heather Justesen
Edited by Kim Huther

Cover design by Rachael Anderson
Cover image credit: Christopher Bissell
Published by Dunhaven Place Publishing

This book is dedicated to Jami, my constant cheerleader,
Abbey, for gracing the cover
and especially Alacoque, for the inspiration

Pronunciation Guide

Aillil: *Al*-yil
Aobh: Eh or A
Aoife: *Ee*-fah
Bodb: Bow
Cairenn: *Care*-in
Conn: Kahn
Connacht: *Kahn*-ocht (the ch is soft)
Connla: *Kahn*-la
Daire mac Fiachna: *Dar*-ya mac *Fee*-uh
Deirdre: *Dear*-dra or *Dare*-druh
Doherty: *Dore*-ur-tee, *Dore*-tee, *Dar*-tee or *Dahk*-ur-tee
(Dougherty)
Eire: *A*-ruh
Eochaid: *Ock*-ey
Eoin: *O*-in
Geis: gesh, *g*-ice, or guise
Kiernan: *Keer*-nuhn
Lir: Leer
Maeve: Mayv
Mongfind: *Mon*-fin
Mullagh: *Mull*-ugh
Naoise: *Nee*-sha
Niall: Neal (original Irish) or *Nigh*-uhl (English)
Noígíallach: Noy-*gay*-letch
Shillelagh: Sh-*lay*-lah
Sidhe: Shee
Tuatha de Danaan: *Twa*-ha day *Dan*-uhn

The metal pedestrian bridge over the River Liffey is now known as the Ha'penny Bridge. It was opened to the public in May 1816 as the Wellington Bridge. At the time, it was one of only two metal bridges in the western hemisphere. There were originally turnstiles to collect the half penny at each end of the bridge. These have been dispensed with for this story.

Prologue

Ireland, July 1815

"Tell us a story, Niall," Pierre asked, his empty tankard dangling from his fingers.

"*Oui, donnez-nous!*" agreed Etienne.

Niall considered; which story should serve to keep the nightmares at bay tonight? "Have I told you about the children of Lir?"

"*Trop triste!* Too sad!" Michel insisted with a flash of pearly white teeth in his weathered face.

Niall looked into the eyes of the war-weary soldiers gathered around the fire of the taproom. Together, this trio of Napoleon's own had been imprisoned in Edinburgh Castle; together they had slipped away rather than board the ship bound for home after England's victory at Waterloo. Each had his reason to avoid the fate that awaited him in France. Their military service did not exonerate them; it merely delayed their penance. And yet, in the short time Niall had known them, they had always behaved honorably.

"Then, 'tis certain the tale of Deirdre and Naoise shall make you weep," Niall observed with a wry smile.

"As this shall be our last night with this ill-begotten band of deserters," Professor Luce said, his manner jovial, "perhaps you ought to give them a happier story."

"What is this?" Michel asked in surprise. "We thought to travel with you as far as Dublin."

"We do not go south, but west," Professor Luce replied; as mentor and benefactor, he dictated their schedule. "We go first to Belfast to call on Niall's mother and sisters. Then, he shall take himself off to Donegal, and I shall return to Cambridge and a victorious England."

"What waits for Niall in Donegal?" Michel asked.

Niall thought on his reply: loneliness; limited companionship, little to no chance he would be in the presence of an eligible young woman at any moment in the foreseeable future. He refused to speak his melancholy aloud, however. The Professor had acquired the post for him, as he had several others in the past. It would be selfish of Niall to deplore the solitary life of a tutor.

"It is in Dublin, not Donegal that your fate awaits."

All five men jerked their heads towards the shadows in the corner of the room from whence the voice, no doubt female, had come. She was alone; a rare circumstance, indeed.

The small figure cloaked in blue, her face concealed by a deep calash, rose to her feet. "If it is a story that you wish, I shall be most happy to oblige."

"'Tis always a good day when I might add a new story to my treasure-trove," Niall said. Despite his easy smile, he was wary. She was far too mysterious for his taste.

Unafraid, the small figure made her way to the men by the fire. "It is not a new story, nor is it old. It is your story," she said as she pushed back her hood.

The Frenchmen gasped in unison, a reaction Niall comprehended well. In all of his travels, he had never seen such a face save between the pages of a book. Her black eyes were exotic and fine, her skin dusky, and the bones of her face as delicate as a bird's. Her ebony hair, indistinguishable from the heavy shadows near the hearth, was twisted into a knot at the back of her head. He sat back against the wooden settle and stared, her words forgotten.

"Whose story?" Etienne asked gruffly.

"My message is for Mr. Niall Doherty," the woman replied in gently accented English.

For him? Niall rose to his feet. "Do be seated," Niall invited her as he fetched a chair. As he placed it next to that of Professor Luce, the two of them exchanged a look of consternation.

"Thank you," the woman said as she seated herself by the fire. "First, the story you know."

Niall's chest seized with apprehension; his was not a happy tale. How had she come to learn of it? Her words implied there to be a portion of his story of which even he was unaware. It could prove to be a tale worth listening to, he warranted, whether the first part were accurate or not.

"You were born in Donegal, a descendant of Niall Nóigiallach, long-ago High King of Ireland. Your father was a wealthy man, due primarily to your grandfather's cunning. His place as the Irish agent of an English landowner provided him with education and opportunity. He did well with the few coins he possessed, and eventually he became a man of leisure. Your father also invested wisely, and one day acquired enough wealth to move his family from Donegal to Dublin."

Uneasy, Niall shifted in his seat. How could this strange woman know so much about him? If the remainder of her tale was as accurate as the beginning, Niall could expect to feel the humiliation from which Professor Luce had so often protected him. Niall's stomach felt suddenly hollow.

"You were given every advantage," the woman continued. "The wealth of your family, however, was but a part of it. It was your wont to smile and your quickness to perceive and learn that endeared you to those around you. It was your black curls and light eyes the color of water that seem to see so much that made the women sigh after you; even those many years your senior. And then your father was cheated at a game of cards and everything was lost: the house, the cattle, the carriages, and the furniture."

"Cheated?" Niall urged, uncertain as to why her words gave rise to his anger. "He lost, pure and simple. He was bound to lose sooner or later. The only wonder is that we had not been cast out into the street all the sooner."

"In any event," she said tranquilly, "he died shortly thereafter. It had to do with his heart, did it not?"

Niall nodded, refusing to look at his companions to learn their reactions.

"Your mother and sisters," she said, her eyes full of compassion, "are now the poor relations of your aunt and uncle in Belfast. It was your teacher," she said with a nod for Professor Luce, "who funded the completion of your education at Cambridge. After which he procured several posts for you as tutor to boys not much younger than yourself." She looked at Niall, as if in want of a response.

4

"Please go on," Niall urged.

"As you know, there is little more. You have recently arrived from Scotland after having toured the Continent these last two years. These years abroad were made possible by your traveling companion," she said with another nod for Professor Luce, "so as to spare you the necessity of fighting a war for Ireland's oppressors."

Niall swallowed hard. "Who are you?"

The woman's smile was kind. "I am Miss Pearl, lately from Shanghai."

There was nothing in her reply that enlightened him in the least. Afraid to learn the answer, but certain he must, he asked, "And the part of the tale I do not know?"

She inclined her head, a Western gesture she made seem all the more exotic. "You must make a journey to Dublin. There you shall meet the one who shall make you the happiest of men."

"Our most charming Niall must journey to Dublin to meet a young lady willing to make him happy?" Michel exclaimed. "*Incroyable!*"

Miss Pearl ignored him. "Mr. Doherty, you shall be happy with whomever you choose. However, lasting joy can only be found with her of whom I speak. It is to tell you this that I have come to Ireland. Heed my words: you will meet her on a metal bridge that spans the River Liffey."

"Metal bridge! In Ireland?" Niall expostulated.

"She must refer to the footbridge meant to replace those decrepit old ferries," Professor Luce pointed out. "How she knows of it, I cannot say; it has not yet been completed."

Niall's thoughts had quickly moved on from footbridges to

lifelong felicity. "How shall I know 'tis her?" he asked the matchmaker.

"I am sorry to say that I do not see her with any clarity. All that I know is that she has blue eyes and that her name begins with the letter L."

"Would that be her given name or her family name?" Pierre asked with a sardonic smile. He seemed to know as well as Niall that the clues he had been given were no clues at all.

"Mr. Doherty, I am afraid there is no more that I can tell you. Regardless, I hope that you will act on my words. I have come far to deliver this message."

"I promise to remember your words, Miss Pearl, the next time I am in Dublin," Niall assured her. If only Dublin were in his future. For now, however, he was determined to be grateful. The war with Napoleon was over and Niall was free to return to Ireland. He was soon to see his mother and sisters, to live again in his native Donegal where the mighty Ben Bulben scraped the sky. And one day, if the mysterious matchmaker was to be believed, he was to meet the love of his life.

Chapter One

Caroline Fulton of The Hollows in Mullagh, County Cavan was on her way. She looked through the window glass and watched the scenery bounce along beside her. The travelling coach certainly afforded a smoother journey than did her jaunting car. Feeling a nudge in her side, she turned to look into the face of her dearest friend, Fiona O'Sullivan.

"Caro," she said, "I have been speaking to you this quarter hour and I am persuaded you have heard not a word." The red-haired beauty made a splendid moue, one that induced Caroline to fear her friend would be wed and carried off to parts unknown before the house party to which they journeyed was at an end.

"But, of course I have, *mon ami*. You have been speaking, at great length," Caroline said with an impish smile that would not be subdued, "on the subject of which of your white muslin gowns you should don in the morning."

Fiona *tsked*. "You sound for all the world as if such matters were not worthy of universal consideration. You are fully aware this house party is your one great hope, as well as mine. Where shall either of us find a husband in Mullagh? If it does not have the smallest population of eligible men in County Cavan, I couldn't say which does."

Caroline's papa, seated across from the girls, made a guttural sound deep in his throat.

"Papa is sore sensitive on the subject," Caroline whispered, "due to the sorrowful deaths of my brothers from the consumption. Imagine; they might have been twenty-five and three this year! Sure as not they would have been competing for your hand and you wed by now. To think, you might have been my sister," she added.

"To t'ink," her father echoed mournfully, "if I had not insisted you be handed off to a wet nurse when your brothers fell ill, you should have been buried in the same funerary box as your dear, sainted mother."

"Papa, you mustn't," Caroline asserted. "I know precisely where this talk leads. Pray, do not dampen the mood for Fiona; she finds her circumstances far enough straitened as 'tis."

"Straitened circumstances?" Fiona demanded with a lift of her chin. "I confess I am at a loss."

Caroline felt a lump rise in her throat; it would not do to offend one so dear. "I refer to the doleful dowry of a fourth daughter. That is not to say any man would dare to require a generous one," Caroline hastily added, "what with that hair and that skin and those eyes!" Truly, she had never encountered a pair of such piercing green.

"I?" Fiona asked with a hand to her throat. "It is you, Caro, who stands to woo every man to your side. It isn't only that you have the fairest locks of gold in all of Ireland, or that your eyes are bluer than a summer sky. You have the most pleasant disposition of any I have met. It shines in your face with every beat of your heart."

The lump that once again rose in Caroline's throat was more welcome than it had been prior. "Fiona," she said with a squeeze of her friend's hand, "where should I be without you? You are friend, sister, mother, all in one."

Fiona's eyes filled with tears. "I wish nothing more than for the pair of us to be suitably married, but, oh, what shall I do when we are parted?" she wailed.

Caroline shared Fiona's apprehension, but it was her father's loneliness that concerned her most. She stole a glance at him in hopes that she merely imagined the expression of despondency on his face.

"Regardless of whom we each shall marry," she said in cheery tones, "or where we shall land in all of Ireland, we shall come home to visit often and often, shall we not Fiona?"

"I suppose we shall," her friend said with a sigh. "Though I wonder if, come the day, Papa shall be glad to see me. He is always that irritable when my sisters and their little ones come to stay."

As Fiona had, perhaps, the most unruly clutch of nieces and nephews in all of Ireland, Caroline was far from astonished.

There was a bit of a gloomy silence before Fiona brightened and asked, "Caro?"

She was brusquely interrupted by Mr. Fulton. "That is not what she is called," he growled.

"Never you mind, Fiona," Caroline hastened to assure her friend. "Papa merely has the fidgets. He is intolerant of long journeys." She turned to her father. "Fiona has called me thus since the day we met at Mrs. Hill's Finishing School for the Gentlewomen of Ireland. To expect her to do otherwise at this late date is unwarranted."

9

Mr. Fulton sniffed, closed his eyes, and pressed his chin into his cravat.

"Well, then, Fiona," Caroline said briskly, "Papa is to nap. I daresay he shall ignore us," she emphasized for her father's ears as much as Fiona's, "and we may speak of whatever you please. I do believe you were about to pose a question."

"Yes. As you have clearly grown weary of conversing on which of my morning gowns I should wear on the morrow," she said with a playful lift of her nose, "I was venturing to ask which of yours you have determined to wear."

Caroline stifled a laugh and considered the question carefully. "If it is a day such as today, I suppose nothing shall do but the blue sprigged muslin."

"And the chipped straw bonnet with the cherries!" Fiona said with approval. "Yes, that promises to be enticing, indeed. I shall do your hair up smartly, and you shall do the same with mine."

"But of course!" Caroline insisted. "Such talk reminds me; shall our hostess disdain our lack of maidservant? I had not the heart to urge Bess to leave her poor mother at such a time." She paused to listen for her papa's gentle snores; she had no wish to distress him with her words. "We are bound for so grand a house, I wonder if we shall perish from the shame."

"Pish! We shall do for one another, just as we did at Mrs. Hill's. The lady of the house will doubtless be too distracted to notice. I fear I do not recall how she should be addressed," Fiona fretted.

"She is Nancy, Lady Bissell. It has been little more than a year since her husband, the baron, has gone to his final reward.

That has left his son, Arthur, the new Lord Bissell, to inherit all," Caroline explained.

"I admire your composure with which you speak his name, Caro. I should shake like a blancmange were I about to meet my future husband."

"You mustn't refer to Lord Bissell in such a way," Caroline insisted. "Perhaps Papa has intentions for him, but I should prefer first to clap eyes on the man before I agree to marry him. What is more," she said with a playful smile, "there is the small matter of his asking for my hand. There is naught to say that he intends to do so."

"Then why has he invited you to his home if he does not mean to make you known to his family?"

"Why, indeed?" Caroline drawled. "Should we not also wonder why you have received an invitation, as well?"

"That is simple enough to deduce. It would not do for him to appear wholly as if the house party is but an excuse to invite you to Oak View. What if the two of you should not suit?"

"O'course, they shall suit!" Mr. Fulton insisted. "For what other reason should we be gadding about the countryside?"

"Papa! I thought you dreaming already!" Caroline said with a merry laugh. "What he means is that none of the Irish lads would have me," she explained to her friend, "and he cherishes a hope that the English shall have standards lower than my countrymen."

"You know well enough, m'dear, 'tis not that a-tall." Uneasy, Mr. Fulton shifted about. "A man of education, money and sophistication is better placed to appreciate yer charms."

"Charms, is it now, Papa?" Caroline asked with a saucy

11

smile. "I do believe you referred to them as quirks when last you held forth on the subject."

"Ah, yes," Fiona said wittingly. "We all know it to be a fact that Caro is full to bursting with eccentricities. Why any Irish lad should wish to marry a woman who sings like a lark, paints like a Gainsborough, and is as good gold, I couldn't say."

"Whisht, now, Miss O'Sullivan," Mr. Fulton scoffed. "We must take care not to herald her headstrong ways. 'Tis hoped the baron shall take me daughter's Irishness in stride. For what else should I have spent me blunt on all t'at schooling if not to soften her countrified airs?"

"Papa! Never say that the Irish lads rebuffed me for my 'headstrong ways,' for we both know it is far from the truth."

"Aye," Mr. Fulton said with a finger to the side of his nose. "T'ose aren't the lads ye are after, me heart."

Fiona laughed. "No one is good enough for your papa, Caro, but a man with property and a title."

Caroline released her frustration in a sigh. "Why I should be compelled to marry an Englishman for his title and possessions, I cannot reckon. My dowry should be more than enough for myself and my husband."

Mr. Fulton coughed his displeasure. "It shall not be your money once the wedding vows are said. Should ye marry a poor man who is fond of betting at the races, how shall ye come by the coins to pay the dressmaker and the chandler, me heart? Besides which, yer funds shall be put to use in the purchase of sheep. The baron has a mind to grow rich on mutton, as has your father."

Caroline rather resented these plans for her dowry. "I should never choose to marry such a man."

"Ye shall not be doing the choosing," her father scolded.

Stung, she turned away to peer through the glass and hide her distress. When she felt her friend's hand on hers, she took courage. Fiona knew better than any how much Caroline had endured as the daughter of Padraig Fulton. He was an affectionate father but, like most Irishman, he felt too much. The death of her mother and brothers was a crushing blow and she the sole buttress to his sorrow. That he should be willing to marry her off to anyone at all was a notion at which to be marveled.

As for Caroline, she was desperate to get out from under his roof. A life of her own was all that she desired, one in which she was mistress of her own household. A doting husband and a parcel of children, ones better behaved than Fiona's nieces and nephews, were all for which Caroline's heart yearned. That and a man for whom she was capable of feeling some affection.

After a prolonged and awkward silence, her papa gave a cry. "'Tis Oak View! We have arrived!"

Caroline looked through the window glass as a grand gatehouse burst into view through the trees. Her stomach rose and fell as if she had jumped her horse over a barrier. She had not expected to be in the least apprehensive over a matter so slight, but she was rattled by the thought that Oak View would become her home should she marry Lord Bissell.

Her heartbeat quickened as they passed under the gatehouse and the main house became visible at the end of a long drive bordered by massive oak trees. The soaring edifice was punctuated by large tracery windows set above a generous portico. There was a wing to each side of the central building, each adorned with a row of classical columns. She thought it entirely lovely. However, it was even larger than she had anticipated, and her courage somewhat failed her at the sight.

"Only the best for me darling daughter," her father crooned. "Have ye yet seen a finer house?"

"No, Papa. You know I have not," Caroline said quietly despite the wild pounding of her heart. "Do you suppose he has erred? Surely, my dowry cannot be sufficient to render me worthy of such a house as this."

"Ach, me girl! There is no use filling yer head with sums and figures," her father insisted. "Be assured that it is sufficient to make ye worthy of Oak View and more."

"It is simply divine," Fiona breathed. "I should not care if the baron had a crook for a nose and a humped back if I were mistress of this house!"

The three of them laughed gaily, and Caroline's apprehension faded. "I knew I should not be sorry for your company, Fiona. I am all agog to see the interior, every last corner of it!"

Niall Doherty sat at his desk in the school room at Oak View whilst he waited for the nursery maid to claim her charges. It was a suitable desk, if a trifle small, as it served as the unapproachable barrier betwixt him and Lady Bissell's hellions. Masters Charles and Christopher had little respect and nary a thought for Niall's person, his possessions, their books, clothing or the world at large, but somehow Niall had managed to put the fear of God into the lads regarding the desk. Whatever disaster befell the room, Niall was almost certainly safe once he had got himself behind it.

"Sir," eight-year-old Charles whined, "Kit ate my luncheon, and I am that hungry. When shall we get our supper? Miss Deakin should have collected us by now."

Niall agreed, but hadn't the least desire to give Charles the slightest cause to mount an insurrection. "You must wait patiently; she shall arrive when she arrives. Once she has, you are both," he said with a warning eye for Christopher, who never failed to make the most of a failure to be clear, "to proceed with the utmost silence. There are guests in the house and your brother should not like it if you were to make your presence known."

Charles' mouth turned down at the corners, and his eyes narrowed. "I have no wish to be silent. I wish to have dinner with my brother and my mother!"

"Now, Master Charles," Niall cautioned, "I shall not have this. You are perfectly aware that you are only allowed to dine with the family on special occasions."

"Then why is it allowed for you?" Christopher, aged seven, asked in all innocence.

"I am only expected when guests are not invited, or, most especially when your brother is in London and your mother does not wish to dine alone." As little as he had to say to the mistress of the house, any conversation with an adult was a longed-for development.

"Then you are not to dine with Mama tonight!" Charles proclaimed. "My brother has guests, and you shall remain in your room."

Niall hoped he would have no need to employ the switch Miss Deakin had presented to him with a patent air of relief on his first day of service. She had done her best to care for the rapscallions after their governess had quit the premises. Thankfully, they appeared to be settling down under Niall's tutelage. And yet, it seemed that nothing made as much of an impression on the lads as a sharp whack to an open palm.

"I shall feign ignorance of your disrespect," he said in brisk tones. "Meanwhile, you, Master Charles, shall behave as I, Miss Deakin, your mother, and the baron expect."

Niall was met with a pair of belligerent glares, but as the nursery maid chose that moment to arrive, he suffered none of the usual ill effects.

"Mr. Doherty, I regret that I have kept you waiting." She swept into the room and took each boy by the hand. "I was required to assist with some of the dinner preparations. As you may well suppose, the servants are in an uproar."

"I had not thought it possible," Niall said in some surprise. "In truth, I have not been here long enough to witness an event on this scale."

"Well," the very English nursery maid exclaimed, "it is more than a little appalling. I have never seen a more superstitious body of people in all my days. Which reminds me, I am meant to say that Mrs. Walsh has asked for you."

"The cook? Me?" he asked warily as he regarded Charles, who had taken to wriggling in an alarming fashion. "What could she possibly have to say to me?"

"I have a supposition, but it is best left to her," Miss Deakin said with a twitch of her head in the direction of the lads.

16

"I shall go down to her directly. Good evening to you," he said as the nursery maid led the lads from the room. He hadn't the slightest hope that she should have any such thing, but he pushed the thought aside as he went down the passage to the door that separated the family portion of the house from the servants' quarters, clattered down numerous flights of narrow stairs, and into the chaotic kitchen. "Mrs. Walsh," he said upon spying her, "I am told that I am wanted."

"Oh, Mr. Doherty; how good of ye to come!" she cried with a blow of her hands to her apron that sent errant flour billowing into the air. "I am sorry; 'tis all for naught, for ye are now to have the words from her ladyship's own lips. She waits for ye in her chamber."

Niall had questions but the cook turned away to scold the eavesdropping scullery maid. He had no choice but to take himself off and retrace his steps. It wasn't until he once again encountered the baize door that separated one world from the other that his steps slowed. Despite his tendency towards the fanciful, he was not a dishonest man, and was persuaded that the unusual attentions he received from Lady Bissell were of concern. This, however, was the first time he had been expected to enter her boudoir, and his courage nearly failed him.

Taking a deep breath, he pushed open the door and made his way down the hall. As he regarded the doors he passed, he realized he hadn't any idea which belonged to her ladyship. "Pardon me," he asked an approaching maid, "which is Lady Bissell's chamber?"

The maid blushed scarlet and looked away as she pointed to the door one down from where he stood.

Aware that he had made at least one *faux pas*, Niall was too rattled to offer any word of thanks. Instead, he waited until the maid had entered a room farther down the passageway before rapping on the door. He now felt more confounded than before. The conventions of a large, English-run household were not those to which he was accustomed. He found that he unintentionally and rather regularly spoke out of turn and treated the servants too familiarly. He was essentially a man alone; too low to be regarded as the gentleman he indeed was, and too far above any of the servants to converse with them as a peer. And now he rapped at the door of his mistress without the slightest notion of what to expect.

Finally, the door swung away from him. To his immense relief, he was greeted by the downcast eyes of another maid. As he had never before seen this particular girl, he realized that her ladyship's boudoir was where the maid spent the main of her hours. He was not required to explain his presence but was immediately ushered into the room. Niall entered in hopes that he found Lady Bissell appropriately draped.

She was, fortunately, dressed for dinner in the same hue of lavender he had known her to wear since his arrival at Oak View. The tears on her cheeks, however, were an accessory to her ensemble that he had never before seen.

"Mr. Doherty. I fear much has gone wrong. This is my first house party since my husband's death, and I know not how to proceed."

Shocked by her weeping, Niall regarded her closely. He was astonished by her tears almost as much as the youthful appearance her usual haughty expression failed to imply. He

18

had never met the old baron but, based on the age of his oldest son, borne to him by his first wife, Niall had assumed Lady Bissell to be on the windy side of forty. As he watched her, taking in the faded blue eyes and pale yellow hair that unduly aged her, he realized she must be at least a decade younger than he had supposed.

"I daren't consult with Lord Bissell on this matter," she said with a sniff. "He shall only find fault with me for not taking great enough care, and I do so wish to create the impression that all has happened precisely as I planned." She put a handkerchief to her nose and looked up at him expectantly as her eyes filled again with tears.

"I am at your disposal, Lady Bissell, though I hardly know how I can be of any use." He hoped the strain he felt did not show on his face.

"I suppose it is not as bad as all that," she said with a sigh. "I merely need you to make up my numbers at dinner. It seems one of my guests has brought another young lady as companion to his daughter, and I am all uneven."

Niall felt her explanation to be suspiciously simple. "Surely, you should do better to arrange for an extra plate than to risk Lord Bissell's wrath at my unintended presence," he suggested.

"You do not fully understand: the trouble is with the servants. With the addition of Miss Fulton's companion, there shall be thirteen to dinner. It seems that everyone from the butler to the lowliest kitchen maid refuse to lay dinner with such an unlucky number."

The relief Niall felt at her words was almost enough to prompt a smile. "Ah, yes, I perceive your trouble now. We Irish are a superstitious lot. Though, I had supposed you to be Irish, as well, my lady."

She gave him an oblique look. "I am, of course! Irish, that is; not superstitious. However," she explained with a roll of her eyes, "the problem is that I am far too capable a hostess to invite uneven numbers for dinner. It has, quite simply, never occurred."

"I do beg your pardon," he said as he sketched a brief bow. "I ought to have known better. If I do come down to dinner, am I to linger over the port with the men and play cards with the ladies until midnight?"

"No and yes. Leave the men in order to join the ladies. I should think they will find it most diverting. And do put on a more suitable jacket. You look a farmer in that corduroy, and your cravat is askew."

Niall refrained from informing her of the juvenile force that dragged his punctiliously-tied cravat into regular disorder. "I am possessed only of the blue suit I wear when I dine with the family. Will that do?"

"Hmmm." She stood and stalked about him as if he were a side table she was considering for the grand salon. "I do believe you are a size with my late husband. His clothes are yet hanging as they were when he died."

Niall suppressed a shudder; the notion of donning a dead man's clothes was anathema to him.

"Yes," she said firmly. "I believe the black shall do very well. Have Carter fetch it for you."

Niall gave her another bow, this one far deeper than the last, and hastened from the room. As he executed her instructions, he reflected on his good fortune. It had been weeks since he had sat down to dinner with more than the lord and lady of the house. He hoped he remembered how to make polite conversation, but owned that even the chance to listen whilst others conversed was worth any amount of time in a dead man's suit.

Chapter Two

In the years since her father had grown rich, Caroline had become accustomed to the trappings of wealth. Their house was the largest in the village and her gowns were done up in Dublin, created from fabrics smuggled from France. She delighted in making her morning calls in her very own jaunting car which she tooled herself. None of this prepared her in the least for the sumptuous grandeur of Oak View.

The chamber that had been given for her use was so entrancing that, upon her arrival, she nearly flew from one thing to the next. The sheer size of it made a thorough exploration impossible prior to dinner, so she set herself to the task of unpacking her trunk. All of the gowns went into the clothes press, save the azure blue silk. She intended to don it for the evening meal, along with her loveliest evening slippers.

Caroline was startled from her ruminations by a sharp rap at the door. She pulled it open to reveal a woman in a splendid gold gown. The effects of this charming ensemble were destroyed by the addition of a dark cape and black hat with a veil so thick it obscured the wearer's face.

"It is I," Fiona hissed. "Do let me pass!"

"Hurry and come through, then," Caroline said in equally muted tones. "What are you about in that silly outfit?" she asked once Fiona had swept into the room.

"I have come," Fiona replied as she removed her chapeau, "to do for you and for you to do for me."

"But why have you donned a hat? We are about to go down to dinner."

Fiona smoothed the curls ruffled by the hasty removal of her headpiece. "I have no wish to meet anyone until I have had my hair properly done up."

Caroline laughed. "I shall be pleased to help, but first, assist me into my gown."

"Of course!" Fiona dropped the cloak to the floor. "And you must properly tie me up," she said with a twirl that exposed the limp tapes at the back of her gown.

Once they were both properly dressed and coiffed, they stood in the pier glass to survey the results. Fiona's red hair and gold gown were the perfect complement to Caroline's blonde and azure blue.

"I do believe," Caroline said merrily, "that our appearance in no way betrays our lack of a maidservant."

"I agree!" Fiona replied, her eyes twinkling. "Ah! And there is the final dinner gong. Shall we be on our way?"

"We shall!" With a last glance in the mirror, Caroline followed Fiona through the doorway and down the passage to the top of the staircase. As they descended, they joined nearly a dozen ladies and gentlemen. Caroline observed that each was dressed more fashionably than the last.

"I confess, I feel a country mouse amongst all of this finery," she murmured into Fiona's ear.

"I daresay they are all English and aim to make hay whilst the sun shines."

23

"What do you mean by that?" Caroline asked.

"Only that now the war is over, they are making the most of it," Fiona explained. "Indeed, I do believe some of those gowns are rather *de trop* for a country house party."

As Caroline had observed quite a number of wildly plunging *décolletage*, she rather agreed. "There, now, we mustn't let it distress us. We shall hold our heads high and look at the bright side; we need not be in the least concerned that a pea might fall from its fork and lodge itself betwixt our breasts."

Fiona's horrified demeanor was belied by her quickly stifled laughter. "Caro, pray cease or I shall only look even more the fool."

"Not as foolish as you should were there a pea held fast in your bosom," Caroline unwisely said. Try as she might, she failed to suppress the bubble of laughter that rose in her throat. She clapped a hand to her mouth and looked wildly to her friend, who yet struggled with silent laughter.

"Whisht!" Fiona urged as she collected herself. "Lady Bissell awaits us at the bottom of the stairs."

"Of course," Caroline agreed. "And what of the baron? It was not so odd that he did not greet us when we first arrived, but I wonder that he has not taken this opportunity to greet his guests."

Caroline hadn't time to respond before reaching the bottom step. She gave her hostess a warm smile and executed a perfect curtsey.

"*Céad míle fáilte.* A hundred, thousand welcomes, Miss Fulton." Lady Bissell smiled. "And your friend is Miss O'Sullivan, I believe your father said. Now listen; all has been arranged so you mustn't be overwrought on my account."

"Indeed, I shall not." It was the only response to this puzzling speech that came to Caroline's mind. "This is Miss O'Sullivan. The O'Sullivans are prominent among the families of our county."

Lady Bissell smiled faintly and inclined her head. "We shall consider ourselves fortunate that we have not one, but two such lovely Irish ladies to grace our party."

As Fiona curtsied, Lady Bissell waved her hand towards a room across the passage.

Caroline took her friend by the arm and drew her along beside her as she made her way to the drawing room. "She is Irish! I had not thought it."

"Perhaps her son shall prove a better match than you have supposed," Fiona said with a smile of delight.

As they entered the drawing room, Caroline blinked against the brilliance of two enormous chandeliers. The aroma of candle wax permeated the air, but the anticipated sting to her eyes did not occur. It seemed Lady Bissell quailed not at spending good coin on superior candles.

"Let us take up a seat on the sofa," Fiona suggested.

Caroline eagerly led the way, but was forced to come to an abrupt halt upon beholding a man who quite simply took her breath away.

"What is it?" Fiona hissed in Caroline's ear.

She dragged her attention from the man and forced her limbs to take her towards the sofa. "Whatever do you mean?"

"Only that if you continue to come to unexpected halts, I shall most certainly suffer a broken nose and shall be robbed of my chance to find a husband at this house party," Fiona said sweetly under her breath.

"Oh, my dear," Caroline said as she spun about to assess the damage. "Are you injured? Do let me see."

"I am well enough," Fiona said a bit frostily, "no thanks to you. Whatever induced you to do such a thing?"

Caroline held back her reply until they were safely ensconced on the sofa. "Do you see the man standing by the mantelpiece there?"

Fiona opened her fan and peeked over its folds in the direction of the fireplace. "I have never seen such a colossal fireplace," she whispered. "There are no less than three men standing in the vicinity. Of which do you speak?"

"Why, the interesting handsome one."

"Which one? They are all three rather attractive."

"Three?" Caroline cried in disbelief. "I hadn't known you were so generous in your assessment of masculine beauty."

"When had you the opportunity to learn in the backwater in which we live?" Fiona asked with a sigh of mock despair.

Caroline gave a trill of laughter. "Very well, then. He has black curls, dark brooding brows over almost unnaturally light eyes, and is exceptionally well-formed. He is surely the youngest of the lot; I expect he must be the baron, himself."

Fiona gave the men at the mantel another measured glance. "I should be most surprised if he were. The one with such speaking eyes is no more than a boy."

"No, he is older than that, surely." Caroline murmured behind her fan. "However, the other gentlemen in the room all look far too old to be the son of Lady Bissell. The one on the right, in particular, looks old enough even to be her husband."

"I believe we are soon to learn the truth of the matter," Fiona replied.

Caroline looked up far more quickly than was seemly. Indeed, she wished she had not, especially when she saw that it was the oldest gentleman of the three who now approached.

"Pray forgive me if I am too bold," he said in a pure English accent. "But I must beg your pardon. I was meant to stand with Lady Bissell, but I tend to do exactly as I please. Clearly I have erred, since it has prevented us from being properly introduced."

"But, of course, you are pardoned, sir! I am Miss Fulton, and this is Miss O'Sullivan. It seems it is I who must beg your pardon, for I do not believe I know your name."

The man studied her face for a moment before he threw back his head in hearty laughter. "Oh, that is rich, Miss Fulton. But, truly, how were you to know?" He bowed deeply, and there was a twinkle in his eye when he raised his head. "I am Lord Bissell, and this is my house. I am pleased that you have come to my party, Miss Fulton, and that you have brought along your friend, Miss O'Sullivan," he added with a charming look for each of them in turn.

Caroline put her hand to her mouth to cover a gasp. To her chagrin, her gaze flew to the young man at the mantel. He immediately lowered his gaze; it was as if a pair of candles had been snuffed out. There was an air of agitation about him that only served to further rouse her interest. Forcing her attention again to the baron, she made herself smile. "I am pleased to meet you, Lord Bissell. We are delighted to accept your invitation. Oak View is very lovely."

"I am most pleased that you have all come to stay," the baron insisted. "Together, with my other guests, I daresay we shall make a merry party."

"T'ere she is, me girl, me heart!"

Caroline turned towards the familiar sound. "Papa, you rogue! You were very nearly late."

"Ah, but as ye can see, I have arrived in time." Mr. Fulton smiled broadly over his meaty hands as he rubbed them together in anticipation of his dinner. "Lord Bissell, I see t'at ye have met me daughter. She is the apple of me eye, t'ere be no doubting!"

"Indeed," the baron said with an inclination of his head. "She is as charming as you have described. I should like nothing better than to take her into dinner on my arm, but here at Oak View, we might as well be in London."

Caroline was astonished when the baron turned on his heel and walked away with no further explanation. "Are we not fine enough for him?" she asked her father.

"You needn't trouble yerself on t'at score, me darlin'. It is only t'at, as the host, he is required to take in to dinner the lady of highest rank. Lest ye allow the envy to eat ye up, she is already wife to Lord Chorley."

"One wonders what pleasure one might hope to enjoy when expected to behave as if in London," Fiona mused.

"I confess, I had not expected the air to be quite so stiff," Caroline said softly. Nor had she expected the baron to be quite so old, his hair to be quite so thin, nor his teeth to be quite so yellow. How her father expected her to marry such an ancient, she could not reckon.

The young man by the hearth was a much more attractive possibility. He put her in mind of Naoise, the wildly romantic husband of the legendary Deirdre of the Sorrows. Caroline darted a glance his way and nearly came undone when he gazed back at her, frank as any school boy.

"Papa," she said quietly as she turned her back on such impudence. "Who is that, standing by the fire, there?"

"I've naught seen him before," he said with a dismissive wave of his hand. "Ye should only have eyes for the baron, young lady!"

Caroline was rescued from composing a reply by the entrance of Lady Bissell.

"Lord Bissell and I are grateful for the safe and timely arrival of all our guests," she announced. "We shall now go in to dinner, after which there shall be port and cigars whilst we ladies amuse ourselves in the drawing room. Shall we?"

The baron stepped to the front of the room, whilst the other men took the arm of the lady whose place most closely mirrored his own. Eventually, they fell in line, one pair behind the other.

Caroline was gratified when her father guided her, as she hadn't the slightest notion of the names and titles of the other guests. How the young man with the haunting eyes had the presence of mind to take Fiona's arm and guide her to the end of the line was a notion at which to wonder. She did, however, come to a pertinent conclusion: he did not have a title. As such, she would never be allowed to marry him.

Niall had never known such an ache. He was seated next to one of the wittiest, most beautiful women he had ever been so fortunate to meet. However, it was the blue-eyed girl with the golden hair seated across the table from him who had captured his utter absorption. He felt helplessly drawn to her, as if he knew her from some misremembered time and place. Since the moment she entered the drawing room, his heart hadn't ceased its hammering against his ribs.

It was not of the slightest use to remind himself that she was surely meant for Lord Bissell; he felt curiously certain that he would wither and die if Miss Fulton were not forever buckled to his side. The loneliness that had consumed him prior to his first glimpse of her was nothing compared to the desolation he knew whilst she sat a mere few feet away. He felt himself a man dying of thirst, and she the sparkling wet salvation he was unable to grasp. He was reminded of the matchmaker's words and knew he would not rest until he had learned her name.

Forcing his gaze away from her, he drew a deep breath. "It is Miss O'Sullivan, is it not?" he asked of the red-haired lady at his right. He hoped he correctly recalled the name he had overheard. "Yes, and you are?"

"Mr. Doherty. I am pleased that we have met."

"Indeed," she said warmly. "I am delighted to have been invited. I expect it is due only to my friendship with Miss Fulton and her father, Mr. Fulton."

"I see," he said shortly, unwilling to speak idle words whilst yet in want of Miss Fulton's given name. "Have you been long acquainted?"

"Yes, to my good fortune. We first met at finishing school in Dublin. There is not a better soul in all of Ireland."

Niall followed Miss O'Sullivan's fond gaze across the table to take in the sight of her glorious friend. She was in animated conversation with a man to her left, her eyes sparkling and her cheeks flushed a delicious shade of red. As he watched her, he experienced a heady mixture of admiration and resentment. He wanted nothing more than to meet the fellow at dawn unless it was to indulge his desire to fold Miss Fulton in his arms and cover her mouth with his own. So lost was he in his reflections that it took him a moment to realize Miss O'Sullivan still spoke.

"She excels at everything she tries her hand at, but, pray: do not reveal you know as much. I promise it shall only prove to make her self-conscious. Tell me, Mr. Doherty, how have you come to be invited to the baron's party?"

To his surprise, Niall felt a flush rise along his neck and into his cheeks. He considered offering a falsehood in explanation, but knew that if he were to win the admiration of Miss Fulton, there must be no untruths between them. "I am tutor to Lady Bissell's lads." He sat back to watch Miss O'Sullivan's reaction.

"Say you do not," she said, her eyes wide, "set Lord Bissell to the books!"

Laughing, Niall felt instantly at ease. "I am certain we should both be at daggers drawn! No; he is the child of his father's first marriage. It is his young half-brothers, Masters Charles and Christopher, who grace my school room each day."

"Well, that makes matters most clear. Caro felt certain a woman so young could not be mother to Lord Bissell."

Niall quelled the stab of alarm that assailed him. "Did you say Caro?" he asked in hopes he had heard amiss.

"Yes. Miss Fulton is called Caro, or Caroline. Why?" she asked with an arch look.

"Forgive me if I have been too bold. It is not a common name in Donegal, and I do not wish to misunderstand."

31

Miss O'Sullivan smiled. "Yes, I see. A man in your position must be certain to be always correct."

"Of course," he said wryly. "Of what use is a lads' tutor, a mere servant, really, who fails to discern the given name of every lady in his orbit?"

She made no reply, but he thought her eyes gleamed in appreciation before she turned to answer a question posed by the man on her right.

As the person to his left was an unresponsive Mr. Fulton, Niall had none with whom to speak. He reflected on the fact that the chair taken up by her father should have customarily been occupied by Miss Fulton. Such an unusual circumstance could have occurred only by design. And yet, his position afforded him a superior view of her face.

He could not say what it was about her countenance that called to him so. Though her creamy complexion and perfectly formed nose were pleasing, they were hardly uncommon. After further study, he determined that it was the demeanor of her countenance that so drew him in. If she were not already laughing, her features were poised for such, her lips curved in a perpetual smile.

To have such decided feelings for a stranger was disconcerting, to say the least, but the music of her continuous mirth served to soothe his apprehension. Though it was difficult to determine what it was she found so amusing from across a noisy table, he found that his delight in watching her animated face had no end. Hers was a face he could watch with as much pleasure until the end of his days.

Chapter Three

When dinner was at an end, Niall left behind a nearly full plate and the warm promise of port to follow the ladies from the room. He fretted over how he was to explain his presence at such a time to the guests, but Lady Bissell came to his rescue.

"I do pray none of you are made uncomfortable by Mr. Doherty," she said in a voice that brooked no argument. "He is present at my request, as I find him excessively diverting."

Niall bowed just as he ought, despite the discomfort her words produced. He found he did not relish the role of a trained animal.

"As such," Lady Bissell continued, "he shall entertain us with a tale whilst we go about our usual activities. I am persuaded it shall not trouble him in the least if we fail to pay him the strictest heed."

"I am gratified that you should find my stories in the least diverting, and I am pleased to honor your request," he said as he took up the offered chair. To his mingled satisfaction and misgiving, Miss Fulton sat directly across from him. He could not fail to see her unless he made a point of looking away.

"It shall be an Irish story I'll be tellin', though most of ye present be English." His native accent was mild after years of schooling in England, but it was never more prominent than when telling a tale. He knew that a brogue gave his stories more color, and he had yet to hear a complaint. "There was once a beautiful but fearsome queen who ruled the north of Ireland for nigh on sixty years. Her hair was a flame of red, her limbs crawlin' with sinews such as one finds in a tree, and she most often was seen with a squirrel or a stoat on one shoulder. As for the birds, well, they would forever be flyin' about her glorious head.

"One morning, Maeve, as she was known, and her husband, Aillil, were discussing which of the two of them was the most blessed with wealth. For you see, a year and a day ago, which is to say, a very long time, women were allowed to own property, and they ruled in their own right." He was gratified by the murmurs that rose into the air upon this revelation.

"Maeve herself was the ruler of Connacht. Any man she married became the king, but only until she tired of him and chose another. And so it was that Aillil, who had once been the captain of her guard, was in a hazardous position. He never uttered more treacherous words than when he spoke these: 'It is good for a woman to marry a wealthy man.'"

"Indeed, it is!" cried an unknown voice.

Niall was never to know who so heartily agreed, but the room was filled with the sound of hastily squelched laughter.

"Indeed! Maeve took umbrage and asked why he would air such a dangerous notion. His reply only made matters worse, and soon they were entirely caught up in the countin' of their possessions to see who was the richer. Every item was included in their assessment, from their precious jewels to the lowliest pots for the cookin'. When all that the house contained was added to the list, they went on to the cattle, the sheep, and on and on until it was determined, at long last, that Aillil was just one bull richer than his wife.

"'Twas only a bull but before it disdained being owned by a woman and transferred itself to the herd of Aillil, it was Maeve's. Wild with envy, she was, so she sent her servant to inquire of the great cattle lord, Daire mac Fiachna, if she might rent a bull from him to make her number equal. All was well until her servant, drunk on wine and pomposity, revealed to Daire that if he had refused, the bull would have been taken by force. This so angered Daire that he refused to loan the bull. As can well be imagined, this news was not met with joy by Maeve. She gathered her men and her allies round about her and marched out to do battle with Daire mac Fiachna. And so, it began: the great Cattle Raid of Cooley."

The end of the tale was met with an almost complete silence, with the exception of one brave young lady.

"Queen Maeve was an admirable warrior."

Niall was startled to note that it was Miss Fulton who had dared to speak, her cheeks enticingly pink and her eyes glittering with pleasure.

"That she was eventually killed," she continued, "with such a trifle as a piece of hard cheese is a notion at which one can only wonder."

Niall felt a rush of pleasure at her remark but was downcast by that of Lady Bissell's.

"It would seem that your story of Maeve," she said, "was a dash too coarse for the ladies."

He looked about the room and saw that a great number of the women did appear to be shocked. "I beg your pardon," he began, but was interrupted by Miss Fulton.

"Do you think so, Lady Bissell? Perhaps your guests are simply unaccustomed to Queen Maeve. The stories of her are among the best-loved tales in Ireland."

There was another short silence before one of the English ladies looked up from her cards to venture a remark. "She sounds a most remarkable woman, though I should have preferred a story about fairies or brownies or some such."

"Brownies are not the fodder of Irish tales," Niall explained. "Nevertheless, I know more than a few stories of those canny mischief-makers from my travels in Scotland."

"Pray tell us of the brownies," urged another lady, and another, until they were all in agreement.

"I should be delighted," Niall said as he risked a glance at Miss Fulton from beneath his lashes. She was smiling, and leaning forward in her seat with an eagerness that nearly took his breath away. When he had finished the tale, another was requested, and another until his voice grew hoarse. Once the men joined them, Miss Fulton asked for more tales of Maeve, which were met with vast appreciation by all assembled. In short, it was the happiest night of his adult life.

And yet, when the hour grew late and he had returned to his room, he felt his dissatisfaction to be profound. Since he had come to Oak View, he found himself almost entirely confined to the school room and his airless quarters in a house so grand that in the beginning he had often lost his bearings. From the moment lessons began directly after breakfast until the lads were turned over to their nursery maid for their evening meal, Niall often had sole charge of Charles and Christopher. He had only the time between dinner and when he blew out the candle each night to himself.

Even those sacred moments were sacrificed once per fortnight when Miss Deakin had an afternoon and evening off, leaving Niall to sit in the nursery to watch over the lads. He only left the house in company with his charges, save on his own rare days off which he spent walking into town or reading in his room. Dublin was more than a few days journey away. As such, the bridge o'er the River Liffey seemed farther away than ever.

These thoughts consumed him as he removed the former baron's suit of clothes, washed at the basin, and got into bed. He watched as the candle on the nightstand sent light flickering to and fro on the ceiling. For the first time since he had come to Oak View, he was in no hurry to blow it out and escape into sleep. Instead, he linked his fingers behind his head and reflected on Miss Caroline Fulton. She put him in mind of the dance of light and shadow above, the revealed and the unknown, the spark of hope and the darkness of despair.

Forcefully he reminded himself that he was but a penniless tutor, and young ladies like Miss Fulton were meant for a life of luxury such as that afforded at Oak View. He was privy to very little of the gossip that circulated amongst the servants, but he knew that the baron was in search of a wife. Niall also knew that the Irish tenants of Oak View had long ago been run off by Lord Bissell's purely English ancestors, who had no pressing need for their rents or the patience for the lack of them. Generations of lavish living had depleted the family coffers, and the new baron was in search of an heiress to save him from financial ruin. Doubtless Miss Fulton was only too willing to oblige.

No, Miss Fulton was not for the likes of Niall Doherty. He

was naught but a tutor, who needed his sleep if he were to tend to his duties on the morrow. With a sigh, he blew out the candle, but sleep did not find him.

Caroline woke early the next morning with an ache in her stomach that owed nothing to hunger. As she rolled over onto her back, the dread in her center demanded all of her attention. It was an extraordinary sensation, one she could not recall having ever before felt.

And then it came to her: she was expected to marry the baron. It wasn't simply that he was too old and too English; her dread had more to do with a certainty that marrying Lord Bissell would be an error of grave repercussions, not only for her but for others. Why her choice of husband should be of consequence to any but herself was a mystery beyond her power to interpret. The ache in her middle only deepened with the effort.

It had been her intention to lie abed only until a girl entered and took the chill from the room with a suitable fire. However, the maid's query as to whether or not Caroline had anyone to assist her in dressing prompted a desire to burrow even deeper into the downy layers. Once the girl had gone, Caroline rose and readied herself as far as she could without help. Then she threw a cloak over her shoulders to disguise the fact that she had not yet been laced into either her gown or her stays and scurried down the passage to Fiona's room.

"My darling!" Fiona cried upon opening the door. "Come in quickly before you are seen!"

"You needn't create such a pother, Fiona," Caroline whispered without knowing why.

Fiona looked down, suddenly contrite. "I do beg your pardon. It's only that I have come to realize that we are not entirely unexceptionable."

"To whom?" Caroline demanded.

Fiona took her friend by the hands and looked up. "Did you not hear what the young woman in that shocking gown was saying last night?"

"No," Caroline said, perplexed.

"Never mind. Doubtless it will all blow over," Fiona said with an air of frustration. "Come about and allow me to fasten you up," she said, forestalling the posing of further queries.

The discomfort caused by Fiona's actions was merely a pinch compared to Caroline's increasing apprehension. "Will you not tell me what was said?"

"I shall not, so do not ask." Fiona drew the gown up over Caroline's shoulders with a jerk and began to tie the tapes at the back.

"Whatever it is, my dear, it is clear you are troubled. Though, I confess I cannot perceive what anyone might have to say against you." A sudden realization occurred to her. "It quite simply cannot be because we are Irish!"

The tapes tied, Caroline turned to discover that Fiona's face had become crimson.

"It would seem that we Irish are too unrestrained for the English," Fiona confessed.

"'Tis sure that we are," Caroline said with an indulgent smile. "However, that should come as no surprise. The English are far too humdrum. What else?"

Fiona looked down at her hands. "I do not wish to say. It would reflect poorly on your papa."

"Now, you mustn't be bothered about that," Caroline said with a wave of her hand. "You can't have forgotten our little chat about Papa before we set out. He does not come from wealth and is only tolerated by society because, despite his lack of illustrious ancestry, he is quite rich."

"Yes," Fiona said slowly. "That is part of it. If it were only that, I should take no notice. In my mind, the blame belongs to your father alone. However, that woman is determined to drag you into it."

Caroline refused to allow her smile to slip away. "Whatever can you mean, Fiona? Surely we shall not allow the tittle-tattle of others to impinge on our good natures."

Fiona went to the dressing table and fidgeted with the various jars and pots. "Of course, we shall not. In which case, what does it matter what was said?"

"Very well, then," Caroline said kindly. "You know better than I what should be said and what should not. Now, let us finish with our *toilettes* and make our way downstairs for breakfast."

Their reception in the breakfast room was mixed. There were a few guests who presented a friendly face, as well as those who looked as if they had been caught telling tales.

"Good morning," Lord Bissell said, rising to his feet, as did the other gentlemen in the room.

"Good morning to you," Caroline said, even as she noticed how most of the assemblage kept their eyes fastened to their plates. She looked about for the young man with the otherworldly eyes, but he was nowhere to be seen.

"We were wondering when we should see you," Lady Bissell said with a faint smile. "I trust that you slept well. Do take up your plates and help yourselves to whatever you wish at the sideboard."

"Thank you, Lady Bissell," Caroline said, and proceeded to pick up her plate. It lay directly across the table from the young lady who had worn the shocking gown the night prior. Caroline received a withering glance in return for her daring, and it was all she could do to refrain from laughing aloud.

Fiona took up a plate as well, and the two of them went to the sideboard at the far end of the room. The sheer enormity of it afforded them some privacy whilst they filled their plates.

"You can see how ill-disposed that woman is, can you not, Caro?"

"Is it the Chorleys' daughter, Lady Anne, to whom you refer?" Caroline asked. "I believe she need only become better acquainted with us."

"She knows us well enough, Caro, and she does not intend to waste a moment on such wretched subjects unless it is to make of us objects of fun and gossip."

"Well, then," Caroline said with a bright smile, "we needs must improve her opinion of us."

They returned to the table but the moment they sat, Lady Anne took up her plate and rose to find a seat next to Lord Bissell.

Caroline felt as if she had been slapped. She refused, however, to allow anyone to know it. She had no wish to add to what must be a great deal of apprehension on the parts of her host and hostess. "What a lovely view this window affords!" It was the very one previously blocked by Lady Anne. "I believe I shall take my watercolor box out into the garden to paint directly after breakfast. That is unless you have plans for us, Lady Bissell."

"Not at all," their hostess replied with a wave of her bejeweled fingers. "Our guests are at their leisure for most of the day, are they not Lord Bissell." It was not a question. "Please do avail yourselves of all the delights that Oak View has to offer. There shall be time spent together in the evening."

"Splendid!" Caroline turned to Fiona. "Do let's take a stroll to determine the best prospect for a landscape painting."

"I cannot think of a lovelier way to spend the morning," Fiona replied.

"Then, it is settled," Lady Bissell said. "I shall have Mrs. Walsh pack up some food, and you may have your luncheon *al fresco*."

"You are very kind," Fiona replied.

Caroline squeezed her friend's hand under the table. She knew what it cost Fiona to be so polite after Lady Anne's rudeness.

"I am afraid that I have no one to keep me company but my mother and father, and they are most dreadfully dull," Lady Anne said with a pout.

Caroline felt that there was never a more flattering frown, though it was difficult to imagine Lady Anne anything but perfectly lovely. Her hair was a rich, lustrous dark brown, as were her eyes. Her skin was so smooth and creamy that it fairly glowed from her forehead all the way down to the tops of her shoulders. This had been made all too apparent the night previous, so sparsely had the neckline of her evening gown been cut. Caroline suspected it would require more than a sour disposition to render Lady Anne unremarkable.

"We should be happy for you to join us," Caroline offered.

Lady Anne behaved as if she had not heard. Turning away, she laid her hand on Lord Bissell's arm. "I am persuaded it shall rain today, are you not? I should very much enjoy a look at the house. Surely you are not too busy to escort your guest about the premises."

Lord Bissell gave her an apologetic smile. "Plans have been made, already, for a shooting party; men only. They are my guests, too," he said as he nodded at the men seated at the table.

"All save Miss O'Sullivan," Lady Anne said in a whisper meant for all to overhear. "I do believe it boorish of Miss Fulton to have allowed the creature to tether herself to those who have been intentionally invited."

"Lady Anne," Lady Bissell said a bit shrilly, "I should be delighted to escort you about the house. It is truly a beautiful edifice. Now, why don't you go to your chamber and rest before we begin? There promises to be a great deal of walking."

Lady Anne knew when she had been bested. "Thank you, Lady Bissell." She stood and made her way from the room with enviable grace.

Once she had gone, Lady Bissell gave Caroline a conciliatory smile. "Your father sent us word that Miss O'Sullivan was to accompany you to Oak View. His letter arrived only just before you did."

"Oh!" Caroline felt the blood drain from her face. "I believe my father has been rather indecorous. You are very kind to overlook it, Lady Bissell."

She smiled in response, but the atmosphere was strained. She and Fiona were only too glad to escape to their rooms to retrieve everything needed for their outing. By the time they returned to the front hall, Carter, the butler, waited for them with a basket of comestibles.

"Well!" Caroline said as she looked inside the basket. "At least we shall not starve." With a determined smile, she led the way through the door and out into the garden.

Chapter Four

Niall foretold disaster the moment the lads appeared in the front hall, dressed in anticipation of their daily, after-luncheon walk. Somehow young Charles had possessed himself of his butterfly net, an article that had been stowed at the back of a high cabinet in the nursery. To obtain it, he would have been required to engage in a plethora of dangerous antics, the very thought of which brought Niall out into a cold sweat.

"Master Charles, you know very well that you are not allowed to fetch items from that particular cupboard," Niall said sternly.

"Yes, I do," Charles said matter-of-factly. "If I were to ask you to fetch it for me, I should never see it again."

"And there is a perfectly good reason for that," Niall said as pleasantly as he could manage. "If you might be counted on to waft it through the air in pursuit of winged insects rather than drag it through the grass, the water, and wherever else suits your fancy, I would have no need to hide it in the cabinet."

"Why mustn't Charles use it to catch frogs if he wishes?" Christopher asked, his expression quizzical.

Niall lowered himself into a crouch so as to look into Christopher's face. "To begin with, it collects filth in the net.

What moth or butterfly should wish to find itself caught in such a smelly apparatus?"

"I should think the butterflies would enjoy it. I know I would!" Christopher said with an abundance of enthusiasm.

"Perhaps, but your mama does not wish to have such a wet, dirty contraption in the house," Niall explained for what must have been the hundredth time. "If you insist on treating it so distastefully, we shall be forced to leave it on the dung heap before we go inside."

Neither boy verbally acquiesced. Rather, they surged forward with a clatter of boots against the polished marble floor. This prompted the butler to spring forward to open the door before its pristine surface was sullied by a pair of wet noses.

Niall stood with a sigh. "I beg your pardon, Mr. Carter. I hope to have better management of them as the days and weeks go by."

"You can hardly have less," Mr. Carter observed. "But, lads being what they are . . ."

"I suppose you are correct," Niall said with a perfunctory smile. It seemed that he had offered nothing but lifeless grimaces since he had come to Oak View. Dispirited, he followed the lads down the drive and onto the path towards the copse of trees that grew alongside the stream. They would doubtless use the net to catch frogs, as well as snails and fish, and Niall knew he would allow it. Their habitual walk was the most pleasant portion of his day, one he refused spoilt over a matter so paltry.

As Christopher and Charles scampered along the path ahead of him, Niall found himself beginning to relax. He looked up into the brilliant blue sky and noted the softness of the breeze against his face. The water chortled merrily between its banks and the mingled aroma of the flowers alongside the stream was intoxicating.

And then it happened: the cries and the shrieks. Niall broke into a run. "Master Christopher? Master Charles! Are you hurt?" He made his way down the bank to the stream and arrived to behold not his young charges, but Miss O'Sullivan and Miss Fulton, her pink face framed in golden curls under her bonnet. The ladies were disposed on a large rock behind a stand of trees, their bare feet splashing in the water. In point of fact, they were attempting to make one another as wet as possible. If he judged based on how damp were the skirts of their gowns, they were succeeding equally.

Heart hammering as it had the night previous, Niall reversed his direction in hopes he had not been detected. He had just managed to devise the means to a stealthy retreat when he heard Miss Fulton call his name.

"Is that Mr. Doherty?"

"Pray, take no notice of me," he called over his shoulder. "I am looking for the young masters. Perhaps you have seen them?"

"We have seen none but you."

He thought she meant to mock him until he remembered that laughter was ever in her voice. It came to him how blessed any would be to hear such a voice every day, and a genuine smile began to form on his lips. It instantly fled away when his gaze was caught by a slight motion across the stream from where he stood. There huddled Christopher and Charles behind a clump of bushes, barely discernable between the leaves.

47

The air seemed to freeze in Niall's lungs. "Never mind; I do believe I have found them," he said in a tone he knew the lads would fully comprehend. Before he could find a means of crossing the stream without becoming wet, the lads had scrambled away. To his chagrin, they quickly found a fallen log that took them across the water in the opposite direction of Niall, and directly into the waiting arms of the young ladies.

"Oh, what sweet lads!" Miss Fulton cried.

Niall was powerless to avert his gaze any longer. Upon looking, he was powerless to do other than fill his gaze with the object of his admiration. He had yet to behold an unhappy Miss Fulton, but he had never seen her face so effulgent. As the lads buzzed about her, asking questions, inspecting the contents of her basket, and generally doing all in their power to pester and annoy, her face grew incandescent with happiness.

"Masters Christopher and Charles," Niall chastised as he made his towards the homely scene, "these ladies are guests of your brother's. You are not to trouble them." He refrained from mentioning the trouble that would come his way if their mother were to learn of what they had witnessed. He could not help but look at their feet and was relieved to note that the ladies had already donned their stockings and shoes.

"They are no trouble, are they, Fiona?" Miss Fulton queried of her friend. "Perhaps they might stay and share our feast with us," she said, indicating the basket.

Niall knew he should decline, but could not resist what might prove to be his only opportunity to learn more about the fascinating Miss Fulton. "Doubtless the lads should enjoy it every whit. Perhaps we should move up the bank," he suggested as he grasped the basket by the handle and headed for a more even piece of ground.

The ladies followed nearly as quickly as the lads and soon they were seated on a swathe of emerald green grass that had been warmed by the sun. Miss O'Sullivan laid out the comestibles whilst Miss Fulton set aside a parcel Niall had failed to notice previously. It consisted of a paint box, a sketchbook and a folding easel; all tied up with string.

"Do you paint, Miss Fulton?"

She flashed him a brilliant smile. "A little. Miss O'Sullivan and I have chosen this spot for the purpose." She sighed as her eyes swept the horizon. "Even a wretched painter such as I could not fail to get a beautiful canvas out of this."

Miss O'Sullivan rolled her eyes. "It is a façade, Mr. Doherty. She regularly creates beauty from the most loathsome of scenes with those brushes of hers. The one she has begun today is no exception."

"A beautiful painter, an accomplished student, and ever so demure about the lot of it," Niall said in approval.

"Accomplished student!" It was Miss Fulton's turn to roll her eyes. "Someone has been telling tales, to be sure. If I have my own way, she shall rue it before the sun sets," she said with a fond smile for Miss O'Sullivan.

"'Tis no wonder," Niall said as he reached for a particularly plump scone, "that you have chosen this spot. There is a small spring down where the stream becomes a brook. It has long been a place to offer prayers to Brigid, goddess of much, including the handiwork of women."

49

"Do you not mean St. Brigid?" Miss Fulton asked in some surprise.

"Yes. There are some who come to pray to the patron saint, especially for the sake of their lads and lasses. But, before that, it was Brigid of the Tuatha De Danann to whom they prayed."

"Do you mean to say that St. Brigid and another, older Brigid are the same lady?" Miss O'Sullivan asked.

Niall shrugged. "Who's to say? It was all so long ago."

"Well, I refuse to believe it other than a matter of design," Miss Fulton said with contagious enthusiasm. "What could possibly prove to be a better place to offer prayers to St. Brigid than at another Brigid's shrine? But, pray tell, Mr. Doherty, how is it that you know such things?"

Niall paused to check that the boys were still in sight before he replied. "My grandfather was a man of many parts," he began as he linked his hands behind his head and leaned back against a grassy bank. "He was very nearly a bard, was he, so many stories did he know to tell. And tell them he did! Many a night found the Doherty family kneeling at his feet in want of a tale or two. So interested was I in his tales of old Ireland that I read a great deal about such things whilst a student at Cambridge."

"Cambridge!" Miss Fulton exclaimed. "What fortunate children to have such an educated tutor. Surely you were meant for better things."

Niall sat up and rested his arms along his knees as the heat of humiliation crept along his neck. "It's not a story for the telling," he said with a glance towards the children. "However, the story of the spring is a lovely one, if you do not fear it should be a bother to you."

50

"I am persuaded there is nothing you could say that would prove tedious," Miss Fulton said with an ardent air that made the blood sing in his veins.

"Very well," he said with a nod. "The ancients made a habit of making offerings at such shrines: bits of jewelry, helmets, even ornamental shields have been found at these shrines."

Miss Fulton smiled her interest. "Have such things been found here?"

"Not that I'm aware of," Niall replied, "despite the many treasure hunts the lads and I have mounted."

"Let us go hunting now," Miss Fulton suggested. "I should like it above all things!"

"If you do, you needs must count me out," Miss O'Sullivan insisted. "I have had enough sun for one day. What's more, I do not care for such relics."

Niall noted that Miss Fulton looked uncommonly downcast at her friend's pronouncement. "Perhaps we might meet at this time tomorrow?" Niall suggested. "Shall you have more liking for such a venture then?"

"Not for a moment," Miss O'Sullivan said with a smile of apology. "Caro, shall I carry the basket and your sketchbook and colors to the house whilst you and the lads attend to your hunt?"

Miss Fulton's face lit with joy. "Would you?" she cried. "I promise I shall not be long."

"Pray do not hurry on my account. I do believe I am in want of some rest. I daresay no one shall miss you, Caro, before we assemble for dinner. Shall you be joining us again, Mr. Doherty?"

Niall had not given the matter a thought. "I am persuaded Lady Bissell has had time enough to invite another gentleman for dinner. However, I suppose I shall be there if she has not."

"We should be most sorry if she has done," Miss Fulton insisted as Miss O'Sullivan rose to her feet, the parcel of painting supplies in her hands. "Thank you," Miss Fulton said quietly. "I daresay I shall see you before the ringing of the final dinner gong," she said in a mysterious fashion.

"Yes," Miss O'Sullivan replied. "Do come and wake me so that I am not yet asleep when, uh, my girl scratches at the door to help me dress." Her manner was equally obscure.

Niall waited until Miss O'Sullivan had walked too far off to overhear his words before speaking. "She seems a good friend to you."

Miss Fulton seemed to agree. "She is more like a sister. We met at school, but her family soon after moved to my village, and we became fast friends. I shall be quite bereft should marriage carry either of us away from the county."

"Do you not have a sister of your own?" Niall asked as he gathered the lads to his side and led the way to the spring.

"It is only Papa and me," she said cheerfully as she walked by his side. "My mother and brothers were carried off by sickness when I was but a babe. It is true that I have never known anything else, and, naturally, Papa is good to me, but Miss O'Sullivan has been such a boon."

"Yes, I see." Truthfully, he could not claim to see anything but the way the dark red cherries dangling from the brim of her hat danced against the sky-blue of her eyes. To his utmost surprise, he would have rather offered to be her bosom friend, life-long companion, and sole protector. He was besotted, to be sure, but he managed to collect himself. "How did you come to know the baron?"

"I know him not at all. How he came to befriend my father, I cannot say, though I suppose it has something to do with mutton. Papa has made his fortune in sheep, and it is said that the baron intends to set himself up with lambs of his own."

Niall broadened his step to look past the poke of her bonnet, and into her face. "And it is yourself who shall be mistress of it all?" Niall knew it to be a question too bold. He awaited her response with a mixture of unaccountable hope and dread.

"Perhaps." Her smile did not reach her eyes. "He has not asked for my hand, if that is what you wish to know. And if he were to offer, I am not sure that I would accept. However . . ." she sighed, "Papa has his mind made up that I should wed a title."

Niall grunted in sympathy. "This is no world for the unfortunate. Your father is only looking after you." He said the words without a qualm, but they left a bitter taste in his mouth.

She gave him an arch look. "I needn't marry a rich man, if that is what you mean. I am sole heir to my father's estate. His money is disgracefully new, and the house is not entailed. Had I fallen in love with a poor man, I should have been most content."

"But what of him?"

"Papa? He should learn to accept it," she said, naively optimistic.

"No, I refer to your would-be husband. Should he be happy

living in a grand house, with no means of his own, and all of his needs dependent on the wealth of his wife? Any man who could live thus is beneath you. Surely, you deserve better."

"You are too kind, Mr. Doherty," she said, with a coy smile that set his heart to racing. "But I fear I have said far too much. Now, where is this spring?

Niall looked up and saw that, in his distraction, he had missed it. "Come," he called to the lads who had raced ahead. "We have overshot it." Determined not to look a fool, he stalked back through the low-hanging branches that fringed the brook in search of the shrine. "'Tis here!" he called and turned to find that Miss Fulton had followed along behind and already stood at his side.

"What a cunning little thing it is!" she cried as she moved to kneel near the shrine, in utter disregard of her charming sprigged muslin gown. "It seems that someone has carved this little well out of stone."

"And what a task it must have been," Niall said with appreciation. "To be sure, it was carved before the invention of tools such as we have now."

She looked up at him with such trust and confidence that his heart turned over in his chest. "Where shall we look first? In the water? Or perhaps in the dirt up behind the well?"

"First, give me your hand," he said, holding out his own for her to grasp. "You mustn't return to the house covered in dirt. The lads are up to the digging," he said as he indicated a pair of small shovels leaning against the bank.

She did as she was told and he marveled at how small and soft her hand felt in his. As he led her away from the flying mud, the lads fell to work with relish.

"It shall be a shame if, after all, they find nothing," Niall fretted. The thought of a fruitless search had never distressed him as it did now.

"Then we shall merely have to try again," Miss Fulton said sweetly.

To his utter surprise, a lump rose into Niall's throat. It had been long since he had been treated with kind acceptance by anyone other than his Cambridge professor. The elder Mr. Doherty's death on the heels of his spectacular losses at the gaming table had been but one blow to Niall's standing amongst his peers. The fact that he was the son of a gentleman dissolved into nothingness when the title of the grand townhouse in Dublin was turned over to an Englishman. All of Niall's hopes and prospects went with it. He had no home, money, nor status. Most treated him like a piece of furniture; like a never-played pianoforte that was left to decay by installments in a room graced by no one.

He swallowed his melancholy and cleared his throat. "I thank you for your kindness, Miss Fulton, but you are meant to be elsewhere, I am sure."

She shrugged. "It is of no consequence. I am determined to enjoy myself whilst I am at Oak View, not fawn over or seek the approval of the lords and ladies in attendance."

Niall was again surprised. "Do you not wish the life of a gentlewoman?"

She looked at him, incredulous. "Am I not a gentlewoman, regardless of whom I marry?" When he did not respond, she shrugged again. "Perhaps you recall that Papa's money is new. We are the height of society in our little village, but he is most

55

usually considered a mushroom in loftier climes. Such," she said with a wistful smile, "is the society into which my father would have me wed."

"Whatever others might think of your father, surely they cannot hold you to account for his lacks. Who should wish to scorn such a pleasant, talented, educated young lady with a generous dowry?" Niall asked with a sympathetic smile. The answer was none. Miss Fulton was certain to receive an attractive offer of marriage before the fortnight was out. The very thought was akin to a bucket of cold water dashed in his face. Suppressing a sigh, he turned towards the lads. "Have you found anything, you two?"

"I do believe so!" Charles approached with a small object so covered in mud as to be unidentifiable.

"Do hand it over." Niall placed the long object in his hand and rolled it back and forth between his fingers. The grime began to sluff off to reveal a thin stick, or perhaps a bone. "It is most likely the remains of a small animal," he explained as he studied it. What he saw next made his heart pound in his chest. "Wait a moment! See this small hole at the end?" he asked as he held the piece aloft for Miss Fulton to inspect. "It is most certainly a bone, but it has been carved by a human hand. The hole is the eye of what appears to be the elongated head of a bird. I do believe it is meant to be a swan!"

"Yes, I see," Miss Fulton replied, "but, what does it mean? How old do you suppose it is?"

"The people who commonly created such objects," Niall explained, "would have cast it into the water as an offering to the goddess. It is a feature of the old religion, dating back to hundreds of years before the birth of Christ. This is truly a remarkable discovery!"

"We shall be famous!" Christopher cried, the mud squelching beneath his feet as he jumped up and down in excitement.

"Steady on, Master Christopher. 'Tis not the Elgin Marbles." Niall turned it over in his hand to inspect it more fully. "It is, however, quite old. Older even than the enormous oak trees hereabouts."

"Might I see it?" Miss Fulton asked, her hand outstretched.

"Yes, of course." Niall placed the little carving into her palm. "It is yours if you will have it." As the words flew from his mouth, he marveled at his generosity, but he could hardly retract them now.

Miss Fulton flashed him a look of pure delight before she examined the carving. "I do so love relics, and ever since I heard the story of King Lir, I have loved the swan best of all the birds of Ireland."

"Have you?" Niall could not have been more pleased. "Tonight, if Lady Bissell requests a story, I shall give you 'The Children of Lir.'"

"In that case," Miss Fulton said with an arch look, "I shall be certain to ask Lady Bissell for a story from Mr. Doherty."

Niall nodded his approval, as his voice had utterly failed him. Miss Fulton's kindness was only eclipsed by her appreciation for all that he treasured, a realization that was as bitter as it was sweet. How blessed he would be to possess her heart and hand, but it could not be. He was the precise man he had described to Miss Fulton as being so unworthy of her. All that he could do was to give her a story. He decided that it would be the best telling of 'The Children of Lir' that had ever passed his lips.

Chapter Five

Caroline studied the rigid back of Mr. Doherty as they made their way to the house. Something had gone wrong, but she could not say what. He had seemed pleased that she should beseech a story from him. Then, quite suddenly, he had turned on his heel and stalked away. He did not even shorten his stride so that she could walk alongside him. The lads dashed back and forth, but Mr. Doherty paid them little heed and spoke not at all. The thought that she had somehow offended him provoked in her a perplexing sense of doom.

When they gained the house, he finally slowed his pace and turned. "Lads, run round to the kitchen entrance and divest yourselves of that mud before you are seen."

Christopher continued sifting the gravel of the drive whilst Charles gave his tutor a look of pure mutiny. This piece of impertinence was met with astounding indifference from Mr. Doherty, a circumstance that proved to be disconcerting to the lads. Swift obedience soon followed and they disappeared from view.

"Bravo, Mr. Doherty! I have not seen them so eager to comply all afternoon." He turned towards her at the words but failed to meet her gaze. "I do so look forward to my story this evening," she said, in hopes the subject would prompt a lengthier response than it had prior.

59

"I shall be honored." This economical speech was followed by a brief bow, whereupon he once again turned on his heel and stalked off.

"Wait! Mr. Doherty!" Caroline started after him. "I neglected to thank you for my treasure." She followed as quickly as she was able, but he seemed not to hear her and soon they were crossing the front hall in the company of others. He almost immediately disappeared into the depths of the house to attend to the cleaning up of the lads, or so she supposed. There was nothing left for her to do but make her way upstairs.

To her surprise, her feet dragged, and her fingers trailed listlessly along the banister. It was not like her to feel so languid. When it occurred to her to show the carved swan to Fiona, her step grew lighter. Once at her door, however, Caroline remembered that her friend was most likely still sleeping. She turned away to see several of the ladies in the passageway, but they were too consumed with conversing amongst themselves to take notice of her.

"He is indeed remarkable. Those eyes!" the older lady said quietly to the other.

"What you mean to say is that he is attractive," the younger lady whispered. "I positively agree. And his voice; it is so rich and lyrical it makes the hair on my arms stand on end. But you must know, Mama, he hasn't a feather to fly with."

Clearly they spoke of Mr. Doherty. It was iniquitous that a man such as Mr. Doherty should be spoken of in so dismissive a fashion. And yet, she knew it was his very ineligibility that led her to confide in him. It wasn't only that he was not in a position to gossip about her with the other house guests; there was something about him that engendered confidence.

When she reached her chamber, she looked about for a safe place to store her new treasure. The room held such a variety of wooden and ormolu mounted boxes for trinkets, games, gloves, and the like that it proved a time-consuming chore to decide which should have the honor of cradling the carved bone. In the end, she carefully placed it in her reticule. The notion of having it always near her was a pleasant one.

She laid the little purse on the dressing table and threw open the doors to her clothes press. For some reason she refused to identify, what she wore to dinner was suddenly of utmost concern. Though more vivid colors were perfectly unexceptionable at a country house party, she chose an evening gown as white as swan's down. It boasted a deep flounce embroidered with fern fronds, and was bordered on each side with two rows of white satin ribbon: one for each of the four children of the mythical Lir.

The bodice was also done up in a great deal of similar embroidery, which served as an appealing echo to her paisley shawl that had been dyed to match the color of her eyes. Her favorite feature, however, was the little, fluted collar that protruded from the neckline like wings poised for flight.

She was distracted from her thoughts by the sound of neighing horses. Quickly, she went to the window and looked out at the park. Some of the guests, all men, were returning from their shoot. She supposed the ladies were waiting in the parlor, but the thought of joining them until it came time to dress for dinner held little attraction. Suppressing another sigh, she removed her gown and hung it in the clothes press. Arrayed in only her chemise and stays, she laid herself down on the bed and fell into a dreamless sleep.

Some time later, she awoke with a start, certain she heard an errant noise originating from the edge of the park. She sat up and studied the room through deepening shadows. Nothing stirred. Then the uncanny sound came again, quite clearly from the woods behind the park. Wrapping herself in a shawl, she went again to the window.

The sun was beginning to set and the trees that bordered the lawn were black against a crimson sky. There was nothing but darkness, from the top of the enormous ash trees to the fringe of the rain-washed lawn, each blade of grass sparkling in the last rays of day. All was perfectly still from the roof of the stables to that of the gatehouse in the distance. Shivering, she wrapped the shawl tighter about her and drew the curtains.

All at once, she could not quit the room fast enough. She pulled the white gown from the clothes press and stepped into it. Donning a pair of blue velvet slippers, she plucked her hair ornaments, gloves, and reticule from the dressing table, replaced the shawl to cover the open back of her gown, and slipped out through the doorway.

Hoping to move along the passageway undetected during this state of semi-undress, she was pleased to find herself alone. She had only taken a few steps, however, before she heard the strains of music coming from the floor above. It was a tune she did not recognize, sung by a girl or a very young boy. She moved towards the staircase and met the music as it drifted down through the air. When the solitary voice was joined by a much deeper one, she knew it to be the work of Mr. Doherty.

Almost unintentionally, she moved up the staircase so as to better hear the tutor's voice. It spoke of love and loss in both word and inflection, and it stirred her to the soul. Especially touching was the stanza that referred to a journey of thousands of miles in order to return to the object of one's devotion.

The music ceased, and Mr. Doherty began to speak.

"Very well, Master Charles; I shall go to the kitchens and request some warm milk of Mrs. Walsh." His words were immediately followed by the unmistakable sounds of determined footsteps across the floor.

Caroline fairly flew back down the stairs and along the passage to Fiona's chamber door. Trying the latch and finding it unlocked, she let herself in without rapping. Fiona was just stepping into her gown, but it was the wide-eyed look of alarm on her face that prompted a spate of laughter from Caroline.

"What is it?" Fiona asked. "Is the house afire, or do I sport a second head?"

"Neither," Caroline said, still giggling. "But should either occur, I shall be certain to leave you to open your own door."

"As well you should," Fiona said with a mock frown. "In the meantime, your stays shall need tightening, and all the better to show off that splendid gown."

Once they were properly arrayed, they set to work on dressing one another's hair.

"This is far more pleasant than sitting in silence whilst my girl works," Fiona insisted.

"And to think that Bess and I can't refrain from jabbering! But, 'tis true that I would much rather gossip with you." Caroline surveyed her work in the mirror as she pinned up another lock of Fiona's glossy red hair. "What's more, I needn't hide my most private thoughts from you, which brings me to the subject of Mr. Doherty. When did you learn that he is the tutor?"

"At dinner last night." Fiona did not meet Caroline's eyes in the mirror. "He admitted it quite freely. I must say, I was much taken with his candor."

"Why should he not admit to being the lads' tutor?" Caroline asked. "I feel a simpleton for not having realized it myself."

The lock of hair she held slipped through her fingers as Fiona turned to stare at her friend. "How should you have known? He dresses like a gentleman, speaks like a gentleman, and his comportment, when in company, is superior to that of even the baron."

"That may all be true, but that can be said of most tutors, I suspect," Caroline mused. "It is something more than that, I think. He doesn't quite fit in. And it isn't that he was schooled at Cambridge; I should wish my sons tutored by one who attended Trinity College, at the very least. Many younger sons with no inheritance become tutors, do they not?"

Fiona laughed. "There are not many younger sons of that stamp back home with whom to compare, though I suppose you are most likely right. Why do you ask?"

Caroline noted that, as before, Fiona busied herself with something on the dressing table to avoid having her expression read, or so Caroline assumed. "Oh, I don't know. I suppose I like him."

"So do I, but you mustn't allow your feelings to grow into anything more," Fiona said firmly.

"Why not?" Caroline heard the petulance in her voice and

bit her lip in vexation. "Was it not yourself who left us to become better acquainted only this afternoon?"

"Yes. I know how much you like him, and I thought it would be lovely for you to spend an hour or two in his company. However, I have since come to regret it. Mr. Doherty is not what your father wants for you. He has money, and with it intends to buy you a title."

"'Tis true." Caroline sighed heavily and began again to dress Fiona's hair. "Perhaps you should like to marry Mr. Doherty, yourself."

"I?" Fiona asked, her eyes wide in the mirror. "Was it not just yesterday that you called my dowry doleful? True, my father shan't require a title for me. However, he shall expect my suitors to each have, at the very least, a pillow of his own on which to lay his head."

"Whisht, now!" Caroline laughed and gave Fiona's hair a tug. "You'll set me to laughing over much, and I shall be invited to depart for The Hollows on account of my lack of decorum."

Fiona gave a *tsk*. "For that or for inciting unfavorable attentions from the servants?"

Caroline gasped. "What a ruinous untruth, Miss Fiona O'Sullivan!"

"Ruinous, perhaps, but in no way untrue. I have seen how he looks at you, Caroline, and it shall lead to no good."

Caroline placed Fiona's brush on the table and turned away. "How is it, then, that he looks at me?"

"Oh, no, I shall not tell you that," Fiona vowed. "But, mark my words, Caro; if you allow yourself to like the tutor well, you shall eventually be needing to choose between him and your father."

"Do you honestly believe that?" Caroline kept her face turned away from her friend and her voice free of her keenly-felt apprehension.

"Yes, as do you," Fiona insisted.

"I should not like that," Caroline admitted. "I am all that Papa has. And yet, he insists on marrying me to an Englishman. Such a husband shall wish to spend a great deal of time in London. Doubtless most have a country estate in the countryside, as well. How will Papa get along without me?"

"I suppose that is why he has chosen Lord Bissell: he shall very likely leave you to amuse yourself in Ireland, just as his father doubtless left Lady Bissell. At any rate," Fiona said kindly, "you can't fail to take up residence here at Oak View less often than once a year."

"Indeed." Caroline turned and looked over Fiona's shoulder to survey her hair in the mirror. "I do believe there is naught anyone who could better such a brilliant arrangement!"

"Brilliant, indeed!" Fiona stood and pressed Caroline into the seat. "It is now my turn to play maidservant."

"I expect results nothing short of uncommonly fine," Caroline playfully said as she studied her reflection in the mirror. "Tonight, I must look every inch a baroness."

Fiona removed the fastenings from Caroline's hair and began to brush the long, gold locks. "Ah, so you have resigned yourself to the idea of being mistress of Oak View?"

"Not exactly, though I should not like to leave Papa all alone. Oak View is not as near to The Hollows as I should wish, but the distance does allow for regular visits. And should you marry a man and set up housekeeping anywhere between here and there, I ought to be most content."

66

"The only unmarried man in residence seems to be the baron, himself, more's the pity," Fiona mused.

"And Papa!" Caroline said with a laugh. "And, of course, Mr. Doherty," she said more soberly.

Fiona laughed, as well, though her reply was somewhat terse. "Perhaps I ought to like Mr. Doherty more than I have done. If it prevents you from considering him an unexceptionable suitor, perhaps I shall."

Caroline knew that Fiona was merely making fun, but the thought of her married to Mr. Doherty filled Caroline with such disquiet that she said not another word until it was time to go down to dinner.

"Was that the gong?" Fiona asked as she smoothed a long, kid glove up to her elbow.

Caroline picked up the feathered fan created to match her headdress. "I do believe it was."

"Are you quite ready, then, to charm the baron?"

"It is why we are come." Caroline favored her friend with a merry smile in spite of the twinge of dread that had again invaded her stomach. Together they went down the grand staircase, past the first-floor landing with its ornately plastered walls, and to the ground floor.

They entered the drawing room just as they had before, and yet everything was different. Caroline had now met the baron, whereupon her visions of a young and vibrant suitor had been dashed. She had also met Mr. Doherty, a man who seemed to be everything Caroline wished for in a husband that Lord Bissell was not. If only she were allowed to choose her fate, like Queen Maeve of old.

67

At the dinner table, as he had the night before, Caroline's papa took the seat that should have been hers; the one next to Mr. Doherty. Her father could not prevent her from staring at the tutor, however, who spent most of the meal conversing with Fiona. This left Caroline free to make of him a mental study. He might not be a proper suitor, but his would prove a splendid portrait.

She could not help but notice that his face was paler than usual, and the sweep of his sooty lashes darker against his skin. When he looked up from his plate to find her openly staring, his face lit with a brief smile before he turned away. His clear blue-gray eyes looked deeper without the light of the sun, and unduly shadowed. She wondered if perhaps he had not slept well. It was then that she realized the baron was addressing her from his place at the head of the table.

"I do beg your pardon, Lord Bissell. I'm afraid I was woolgathering."

"I merely asked if you had a pleasant day. I believe you were meant to sally forth with your paints sometime after breakfast."

"Yes, indeed, it was a beautiful morning. Oak View is so lovely and holds true to its name. I had no trouble at all in finding half a dozen prospects to paint. The only difficulty we experienced was in deciding on which to settle, is that not so Miss O'Sullivan?"

"Indeed, I was positively charmed," Fiona replied, exuberant. "Perhaps some of the other ladies would enjoy accompanying us when next the gentlemen are otherwise occupied."

"Such audacity!" Lady Anne said with a trill of laughter.

"As if we should allow her to lead us round by the nose, she who has not even been properly invited."

Caroline looked swiftly to Fiona, whose face had turned scarlet. "Papa," she whispered into her father's ear. "How could you have put Miss O'Sullivan in such a delicate position?"

Her father merely grunted in response and swallowed it down with a spoonful of *blancmange a la vanilla*.

"Miss O'Sullivan is very welcome," Lady Bissell firmly said in Fiona's defense. "I should not wish her to feel otherwise."

"I beg your pardon, Lady Bissell," Lady Anne said demurely, her eyes downcast. "If we were to assign blame to the person most answerable, it should most likely fall on Miss Fulton."

It was a comment too unwarranted for a polite response. The room fell into a silence that was broken by Caroline's father, who trumpeted a large "Harrumph!" To her disappointment, he added nothing that should serve to prove his daughter's utter lack of culpability in the matter.

She took in the expressions on the faces that surrounded the table. The baron, Lady Bissell, and their guests were all quite shocked. As for Caroline's end of the table, her father would not meet her eye, and Fiona looked as if she wished to sink under the table. It was the barely perceptible wink from Mr. Doherty that prompted the right words.

"Lady Bissell, I should dearly love to have a story or two from Mr. Doherty directly after dinner. I daresay a repeat of last night's entertainment would be welcome to more than I."

"Yes, I believe yours to be a splendid suggestion," Lady Bissell said kindly. "Mr. Doherty, we should all be delighted if you would once again regale us with your stories."

Caroline felt it wisest to refrain from turning to see the tutor's reaction, but she heard the smile in his rich, deep voice when he replied.

"There is nothing that should please me more."

The reaction of the ladies, however, was plain for her to see. Even those women long-married struggled to hold back expressions of delight. When it came time for the ladies and Mr. Doherty to make their way to the drawing room, Caroline was certain to claim the same seat as the night prior. The view it afforded of his expressive face as it glowed in the light of the fire was superior to any other.

It seemed as if each lady in the room held her breath as he readied himself to begin. When he sat, he did not settle into his chair. Rather he chose to perch near the edge and lean towards his audience. He took a moment to meet the attentive gazes of each of his listeners, Caroline last. She told herself it was only her fancy that made it seem as if his gaze stopped at hers and lingered.

"I should now tell you the story known as 'The Children of Lir.'" He looked into Caroline's eyes, and spoke as if to her alone. Perhaps she had not fancied his favor, after all.

Smiling, she waited in anticipation of what she knew must come next. She could not help but admire his skill as a storyteller. He did so with his voice as well as with every line of his body. The flex of his long fingers, the rise and fall of his thick, black brows, the curve of his mouth . . . all were every bit as mesmerizing as the musical lilt of his voice.

"A year and a day ago lived Lir, one of the tribe of the Tuatha de Danaan, the Shining Ones, who dwelt among the green of Eire before there was Man. Now, this Lir had thought himself to be made King, but to his profound displeasure, the honor went to Bodb. It was not long after that Lir was to know yet more sorrow, for his wife died and he was left alone and childless. To his credit, Bodb felt Lir's melancholy keenly and offered him one of his young foster-daughters to wife. And so it was that Lir took Aobh, the eldest, and they were married forthwith.

"Soon Lir was a husband most content, and in due time, the father of four beautiful children: three sons, and a daughter. Not long after their daughter was born, however, Aobh died, and Lir was alone once more. Again, Bodb offered one of his foster-daughters and Lir soon married Aoife.

"Aoife was not a happy wife, as Lir's children were rivals for his affection. He was fond of his three handsome sons, but even more so of his daughter whose virtues he was continually vaunting about. Finally, Aoife felt she could endure no more. She had her chariot yoked, and she took the four children far from their home so as to be rid of them. However, when she had drawn her sword, she found that she was not one who could do murder. Instead, she drove them out to the Lake of the Oaks and bade the children go into the water to bathe.

"With their backs turned to her, she struck them with a Druid rod and cast them into the shape of swans. As she returned from the water, however, she saw that the young daughter had somehow passed her notice. Waiting on the shore, she had seen and heard all.

"Aoife was struck with equal parts fear and remorse upon seeing the child, who stood with the tears running down her

71

face like two streams down a hill. So, Aoife put a *geis* upon her: the girl was not to speak for seven years. In that time, she must make each of her brothers a skin that was knitted from yarn made of nettles. These new skins would return them to their proper form. However, if she did not complete them in time, her brothers would remain forever swans. If she were to speak even a single word during all of those long, weary years, the spell on her brothers would never be broken.

"The girl returned to the home of her father with her treacherous stepmother. When her father asked what had become of her brothers, his daughter gave no answer. Aoife had words a'plenty, however, and claimed that the girl had done away with her brothers.

"Lir could hardly believe what he had been told, but he dared not go against the word of his wife, who suggested that he lock the girl in her room for seven years. If the brothers had not returned by then, she should be put to death.

"Aoife ensured that the girl had the nettles and all else that was needed in order to make the skins for her brothers, for she had no belief that the girl should complete her task. She did not know that the brothers came to their sister's window each night to beat wildly on the glass with their wings. She wished nothing more than to give them hope, to tell them how she worked so hard to aid them, but she dared not speak. Each day as she worked, and often, into the night, her tears softened the yarn of nettle, making it more pliable to her touch.

"Finally, after seven years minus a day, it was with a heavy heart that Lir arranged for the execution of his daughter. The morning dawned cold and bright, and the people were gathered

72

round to watch. The girl was brought forth, her knitting in her arms as she continued to work frantically on the last of the skins. Just as she was about to be tied to the pillar that would hold her fast against the flames, three swans came into view, sailed over the heads of the onlookers, and flew directly at the king's daughter.

"With a desperate lunge, she threw the skins into the air. Her brothers, the swans, dived under them so that they settled upon their backs. In an instant they became her brothers, and without a moment to lose, the girl spoke the words that would condemn her stepmother."

To Caroline's astonishment, he stopped short of the end. "Are we not to know what happened to Aoife, Mr. Doherty?"

"I believe some of the ladies should have reason to object," he replied, his eyes dancing.

"Certainly you do not think me too faint of heart to learn the truth, Mr. Doherty," Lady Bissell asserted.

"Nay, 'tis the English ladies who have been raised on gentler tales for whom I tremble."

"'Tis a mercy, it is, that Mr. Doherty, at least, has not found me wanting," Fiona said gaily.

Caroline laughed and turned to the tutor. "I shall tell them if you do not."

"Very well," he said. "Aoife was taken and burned at the stake in the daughter's stead. But the saddest of all was the fate of the youngest brother. His sister, who had worked faithfully for seven years, had not the time to finish the last skin. As such, he spent the remainder of his days with a swan's wing rather than an arm."

"What a delightful story!" Lady Chorley breathed. "I am certain I have never heard any of its kind."

"And I have never heard it told so well," Caroline said, smiling her approval. "But, that cannot be all. Do tell us another, Mr. Doherty!"

To her unending delight, he did.

Chapter Six

Niall dreamed of long-necked swans with feathers as white as snow. In the morning, he woke with a story on the tip of his tongue. It was the tale of the most beautiful swan-maiden of all, and was blessed with a joyous conclusion. Perhaps that was why the very thought of it made him wretched. There was little hope of a happy ending for Niall Doherty.

The closest thing to happiness for him was Miss Fulton and, with every beat of his heart, he wished to give her the tale. It would not do, however, to tell it in the evening by the fire, with all the household listening. For some reason he could not explain, it felt too intimate. To share it with the others would be akin to casting pearls before swine. He decided that he must tell her at his first opportunity, in the case there was not another. As he ushered the lads through the door for their walk, he hoped he would be fortunate enough to encounter her whilst they were out.

So lost was he in reflections of Miss Fulton in her swan-like gown that he very nearly missed her. She and Miss O'Sullivan were on the far side of the park, an easel set up between them. They were paying the easel little heed, however, their attentions seemingly consumed with an alley of towering ash trees. Poised, as they were, against the backdrop of green, the ladies made a very pretty picture in their sprigged muslins, bright, wide sashes, and colorful bonnets.

The lads did not ask permission before they darted across the grassy park to speak with the young ladies. As such, Niall had a perfectly acceptable excuse to do the same.

"Miss Fiona! Miss Caro!" the lads called as they ran to join them.

"Why, Masters Charles and Christopher!" Miss Fulton cried in delight as she spun about. The manner in which her gaze rose over the tops of the lads' heads to meet Niall's made his heart thud in his chest. "Miss O'Sullivan, it is Mr. Doherty," she announced.

"Indeed, it is," Miss O'Sullivan said quietly.

Niall thought her lovely, but Miss Fulton eclipsed her in every way. From the jaunty angle of her pretty hat to the graceful turn of her foot, she was the picture of feminine perfection. "We are just out for our walk," he explained. "I am pleased that my charges have this opportunity to study your work, Miss Fulton. Your execution is brilliant, and I admire that you have chosen to paint such an ordinary scene. One grows weary of ruins amongst the wilds."

"I am pleased that you should think so," she replied, her eyes twinkling, "as there is a paucity of ruins to paint at Oak View."

He knew that, behind her blithe smile, she was laughing at him. To his surprise, it injured him not in the least. In fact, he found he rather liked it. "I confess I am curious as to why there is not a single ash tree on this canvas, there being such noble examples so close to hand."

Miss Fulton's gaze followed the lads as they ran back and forth between the trees. "I should like very much to paint them. However, that is not why we are inspecting them so closely today." She pointed to a window at the third level of the house. "My room is just there, from whence I have heard strange sounds. They seem to be coming from these trees, but Miss O'Sullivan and I have found nothing unwarranted."

Niall paid little heed to her words. His thoughts were nearly all consumed with the knowledge that she slept each night in a bed directly below his. He nodded, and frowned in concern whilst he formulated his reply, but could think of nothing but a recumbent Miss Fulton, her golden tresses spread along her pillow, her lashes pressed against the sweet curve of her cheek. He forced himself to open his mouth. "Aaaah . . . Of what nature were these noises?"

"I can see that you believe it all the work of my imagination, Mr. Doherty. However, I am persuaded it is not so. I have been woken from a deep sleep by loud reverberations of the sort that can't be made by the wind blowing through branches."

"Should it make you feel more at ease if I were to take a look?" His path to the alley of trees would, of necessity, bring him close enough to Miss Fulton to brush his hand against hers as he passed. He waited not for her acquiescence, and surged ahead. When the moment arrived for him to reach out to her as he longed, however, he could not bring himself to do so. The brief contact would easily have been dismissed as a matter of chance, but he admired her too much to compromise her in any way.

Leaving temptation behind, he quickened his pace and,

once under the trees, made a show of looking about in every direction. He gave a trunk or two a sharp rap with his oak-carved shillelagh as he gazed up into the leafy canopies, but found nothing amiss. "All appears as it should. You indicated that you were awakened by the sounds. Do they happen during the night, then?"

"No, not then." Miss Fulton appeared to feel a bit uneasy. "It was near to dusk. I had lain down to rest yesterday afternoon. And then I heard it again this morning before going down for breakfast."

"I see." He gazed intently at the line of trees as he worked on a possible means of keeping Miss Fulton longer by his side. He had a story to tell. He noted that the lads were remarkably content, larking about nearby, and Miss O'Sullivan was not in the least discouraging of his attentions. And still, he could think of no feasible way to suggest they take themselves off so he could tell Miss Fulton the story. Turning to the painting, he studied it at length. "So, you are wishful of painting the ash trees onto your canvas?"

"Yes, but not this one. This is a different landscape altogether," she corrected. Despite his error, her pleasure at his interest was evident. "If you look just here," she said, pointing to a spot along a grassy knoll, "you can see where the brook shall go. We have been to the shrine this morning already. We have only stopped here on our way back to the house on account of the noises I have been hearing."

"But of course," Niall said as he inwardly winced; the painting was clearly of the area around the brook. "Pray, forgive me if I seem indifferent. It is only that a story has been turning itself about in my head all the day long, and it insists on having its say."

Miss Fulton smiled with delight. "We should enjoy it very much, shouldn't we, Miss O'Sullivan?" she ventured.

Miss O'Sullivan's only response was a slight smile.

"Well, I shall not rest until I have heard it," Miss Fulton insisted. "Only first, I believe we must do something about the lads."

"I should think not," Niall said, his heart pounding with hope and apprehension. "'Tis not a story too wild for the ears of children."

"Of course," Miss Fulton replied, "but I believe it must wait until Master Charles is safe. Do you not see how poor Master Christopher has torn his breeches in his attempts to climb up and rescue his brother?"

Niall did not spare a moment to respond. Rather, he tightened his grip on his shillelagh and sprinted for the tree from which Charles dangled like a monkey at the zoo. He was safe at the moment, but should he let go with either his ankles or his hands, the sudden shift in weight would pull him to the ground fifteen feet below. That was assuming that the narrow branch should prove sufficient to hold the boy's weight for any length of time.

Hefting himself up into the crotch of the tree, Niall measured the distance between the lad and the end of his oaken cudgel. "It's quite all right, Master Charles," Niall calmly said as he picked his way up to a higher branch. "We shall have you down in no time." When he decided that he was close enough, Niall braced his feet along the branch, clung to the other with his left hand, and held out the shillelagh with his right.

79

"Now, Charles, very carefully let go of the branch with your hand and catch hold of my cudgel."

Bravely, the boy did as he was told.

"Very good, laddie. Now, as I pull the stick towards me, you must let go of the branch. When you are close enough, I shall catch you." Charles managed a slight nod, such that Niall realized the poor lad was perfectly aware of his danger. Niall took a deep breath and slowly drew the shillelagh through his hands, ignoring the cries of distress from below. They were especially loud at the very instant when Charles was forced to let go of the branch. For a moment, he hung from his ankles around the branch on one end, and from the cudgel he grasped with both hands on the other. Then he was in Niall's arms.

He felt the boy shudder as together they sank into the crotch of the tree. "'Tis all right now, you are safe," Niall said as he patted Charles on the back. He managed to press his face into Niall's cravat before the tears began to fall. "You needn't fear; he is unharmed," he called down to the cluster of white faces below. When the cries of relief rose into the air, Charles lifted his head and wiped his tears.

"What do you say? Should we get away from here?" Niall gently asked. "If you'll just put your arms around my neck, you shall have a ride as I climb down. Will that be all right?"

Charles nodded, his lips swollen and his eyes wet.

"How can we help, Mr. Doherty?" Miss Fulton asked.

"Perhaps Master Christopher will stand at the bottom and advise me as to where to place my feet as I descend. I shan't be able to see well enough around this big, brave fellow," Niall said with a smile for Charles.

He laughed with delight at having been so described as his brother eagerly took up his place at the base of the tree.

"Very good! Now, down we shall go. Hold on tight, Charles, but not so that I can't draw breath."

Charles giggled his relief. "You only wish to spare damage to your cravat, Mr. Doherty!"

"I assure you, Master Charles, I have not given my cravat a thought. Now, here we go!"

Christopher very capably guided Niall down the tree whilst the ladies stood and clapped each time he found solid footing. When they reached the ground, Miss O'Sullivan took the boy into her arms, and Miss Fulton handed Niall the oak cudgel that he had tossed aside once he had a firm hold on Charles.

"Here, now," she said as she put her pretty, white hands to his neck cloth and smoothed it out. "There, that is better. You must excel at tying your own; prior to this moment, I have never seen you anything but perfectly elegant," she said brightly.

"I applaud your good taste," he said as if he were a man who never endured a woefully tied cravat. He felt himself a fraud; for that and for his conviction that he and Miss Fulton belonged together. He knew very well they did not; he was not an acceptable suitor, nor had he met her on the bridge o'er the River Liffey. "Miss O'Sullivan seems to have the lads in hand, but I had best get them back to the house. What his mother would say were she to see Master Christopher's breeches, I shudder to contemplate."

"Well," Miss Fulton said with a mischievous smile, "yours are somewhat worse for wear, as well."

He looked down at his knees and saw that it was so. "I

suppose we had all best enter through the kitchen and throw ourselves on the mercy of Mrs. Walsh. She is the cook here and knows as well as I how imperative it is that we keep this day's work from reaching Lady Bissell's ears." He called to the boys, who had run off, and turned back to find Miss Fulton smiling at him.

"I am feeling faint," she said, though he very much doubted she spoke the truth. "Will you take my arm as far as the house? I shall request that Carter arrange for the collection of the easel, and Miss O'Sullivan shall easily manage the lads."

Now that Niall was faced with the possibility of touching Miss Fulton, of having her close at his side, he knew it to be unwise. Nevertheless, he held out his arm. She was so beautiful, her hair falling in golden tendrils all about her porcelain-smooth face, that he could not deny her.

She put her hand through his arm and, as they walked towards the house, leaned on him enough to persuade him of her genuine distress. "Thank you, Mr. Doherty. I doubted not that you would reach him in time, but my heart was nearly in my mouth, so frightened was I when you carried him down on your back."

"He was quite safe by then, I assure you."

She paused before replying. "I have climbed any number of trees when a girl and I can imagine the difficulties of descending blind. It was for you both that I trembled."

Niall dared not believe the message implied by her words; that she cared for him, even if only a little. "You are very kind, Miss Fulton. I was remiss in my duty towards the lads. I ought to have been paying them better heed. If I had, you would have nothing for which to be afraid. Please forgive me."

"Never say so! You were only doing as I wished. But let us speak of pleasanter things. Was it you I heard singing with one of the lads last evening before dinner?"

"You heard us?" Niall asked in some surprise.

She smiled and nodded. "From the bottom of the stairs."

"Ah, I see. Master Christopher has a natural talent for it. Perhaps I had best confine his lessons to the hours of the day when the guests are downstairs or out of the house."

"He is not the only one in the household who can sing, Mr. Doherty." She turned to look up into his face, her own shining.

"I remember now; Miss O'Sullivan claims you sing like a lark."

"I'm afraid that Fiona exaggerates from time to time. However, it was to you I referred. You have a marvelous voice, and I would very much like to sing with you."

"I should be delighted, but I don't know that it is possible," Niall said doubtfully in spite of the way his heart lifted at her words. "You seem to forget that I am not a guest here. I don't know if I will be invited to join the ladies in the drawing room again. What's more, I daren't leave those mischief-makers," he said with a tilt of his head in the direction of the lads, "to their own devices whilst I spend time in the music room."

"Yes, I see," Miss Fulton mused. "I realize that you know that I am here to prove myself worthy to be mistress of Oak View."

Niall felt as if she had taken his heart between her fine, white hands and squeezed it. "I have," he said shortly. "There are worse fates."

"I only speak of it," she said brightly, "because it has created

83

in Lady Bissell a desire to please me. I am persuaded that were I to suggest that you and I sing for her guests, she would be most happy to comply."

"Yes, I believe you are correct about that." If given the chance, he would certainly choose to please Miss Fulton by any means in his power.

"Then, it is settled! I shall make the request when next I see her."

"I wish you success in the endeavor," he said with sincerity. When she did not immediately reply, he fell to calculating the minutes he had remaining before he was again banished to a world of small boys and their lessons. When she finally spoke, it was of matters he had not the heart to discuss.

"Mr. Doherty, let us have an understanding. We both know my father will wed me to a title. It is not what I wish," she said, looking up at him, her eyes soft but forthright.

He looked away; the tinge of sadness in her eyes was too much for him to bear. "And what is it we are meant to understand, you and I?" *You and I.* Three impossible words but they tasted sweet.

"Only that there need be no pretense between us. Should Lord Bissell make an offer of marriage, I shall live at Oak View. You, as the lads' tutor, shall also live here. Why should we not enjoy one another's company as devoted friends?"

Niall looked down into her face, one bright with happiness and glowing with trust, and knew a fresh agony. To live at Oak View with Miss Fulton as another man's wife; to be required to be in her company, all the while his heart longing for her to be his, was a turn of events not to be contemplated. "Friends?" he echoed. "The two of us?" he asked as he continued to turn the notion over in his mind. To live in the same house, to see her face each day, to breathe the same air as she whom he adored . . . it was too much to endure.

"Yes. Friends. You and I," she said ardently. "I shall need one, should I live here. The baron often travels to London. I imagine that, as his baroness, I shall be with him more often than not," she said matter-of-factly, "but I should like to remain here sometimes, as well. Papa shall not do well if he is too much on his own."

"Yes, I see," he murmured. Sadly, he saw only too well. "If it must be said, I should be honored to stand your friend, Miss Fulton. You needn't have asked."

"Well, now that you have agreed, we may comfortably spend time in one another's company. It is relieving, is it not?"

"Yes, I suppose that it is," he said with an inclination of the head. He had never before lied so capably. "What, then, shall we sing?"

She looked at him in surprise. "Sing? Oh, yes, of course. If you and your charges were to meet Miss O'Sullivan and me in the music room directly after breakfast tomorrow morning, she shall amuse them whilst we debate over music."

Possibilities flooded Niall's mind; not only of songs to sing, but moments spent together, a relationship forged, one that was far from what he dared hope for, but one that had the potential to blossom into something more. He knew it to be a dangerous notion, as well as one he was powerless to resist. "Perhaps it is best if we were to select a song we both know well."

"I agree! The song I overheard you sing was lovely, but entirely new to me. I should prefer an Irish song."

"Yes," Niall said with a wide smile. "We shall give those Englishmen something to make them wish they had been born amongst the chosen."

She laughed, a delightful sound that left him longing to pull her close. "I shall arrange it before the night is done. Here we are," she said with a sigh, "safely arrived at the house." She withdrew her arm. "Thank you for your assistance."

"Good day, Miss Fulton. I look forward to tomorrow morning." How he would endure until the moment arrived, he could not say.

"As do I." Smiling, she put her arm through Miss O'Sullivan's as she drew alongside her.

"Good day, Miss Fiona. Good day, Miss Caroline," the lads chanted.

Once the ladies had disappeared into the house, Niall took each boy by the hand and led them round to the back of the house. "If your mother were to see you now, she would most certainly faint!"

Niall's thoughts did not dwell on Lady Bissell, however, but on Lady Anne. She seemed determined to be mistress of Oak View. If she succeeded, Miss Fulton would not become the wife of the baron. That left Niall with enough of a possibility to sustain his hope. The mysterious matchmaker had predicted he would be happy with whomever he chose. It was foolish; it was mad; it was impossible, but he would have no one if he could not have Miss Caroline Fulton.

Chapter Seven

Caroline, feeling rather splendid in her cerulean blue gown, entered the drawing room and looked about for Mr. Doherty. "He has always been present upon our arrival for dinner," she said in low tones to Fiona.

"Do you not recall what he said?" Fiona gently chided. "When we saw him last, he did not know that he would be invited to dinner."

"But he must be here!"

"Why? So that you might further seduce him, only to dash all of his hopes when your betrothal to Lord Bissell is announced?" Fiona bantered.

"My marriage to the baron is hardly *la fait accompli*," Caroline pointed out.

"Not if Lady Anne has anything to say to it," Fiona said darkly.

Caroline followed her gaze across the room, to behold Lady Anne clinging to the baron's arm. She was once again dressed in a far too revealing gown, and her hair was a stunning concoction of shining mahogany tresses. "She is quite skillful with that fan," Caroline whispered, "but it is the expert wielding of her lashes that does her so much credit."

"Caro!" Fiona put her fingers to her lips. "Why must you

be so amusing? Though it is highly unlikely that I shall make a match at this house party, I do not wish to be known as the young lady who laughs at spurious moments."

"You are quite right, Fiona!" Caroline said with a sage wag of her head. "There is nothing whatsoever amusing about Lady Anne."

"Do not say you are envious of her!" Fiona said in some surprise. "I believed you to be unattached to Lord Bissell."

"Indeed. When have I had the opportunity to become the least attached to him? However," Caroline said with a cheer she did not feel, "Papa is determined to be the father of a titled daughter. As you have pointed out, it is certain I would spend a good deal of my time in Ireland should I marry Lord Bissell, rather than a purely English lord."

With a sigh, Fiona put her arm around Caroline's waist and drew her into a less populated corner of the room. "I should not like to be accused of pleading both sides of this argument, but I do not wish to see you sacrificed for your papa. Perhaps you would be happier in England. I know how much you have longed to have a life of your own, one away from him."

"Oak View is away," Caroline said decidedly. "It makes for a journey that is too long to undertake on a regular basis, but close enough that I may invite him as often as I wish. And, should he become very lonely, he may pay me a visit whenever *he* wishes."

"That is very sensible of you, Caro. I would more readily applaud your conclusions, however, if I believed your desire to remain at Oak View had not one thing to do with a certain tutor."

Caroline could not resist the impulse to glance at the door in search of Mr. Doherty. It was incredibly gauche, as well as the tenth time she had done so since she entered the room. "You needn't be apprehensive on that score; he and I have discussed our feelings and have agreed that there could never be more between us than friendship."

"There is already more between you than mere friendship," Fiona quietly scoffed. "Have you thought how it shall torment him should you both live at Oak View?"

"Fiona, you speak as if he were in love with me," Caroline said in genuine astonishment. "We have but known one another for all of two days."

"It is far too short a time for you to have become thoroughly attached to him," Fiona agreed. "However, it required but a moment for him to love fall in love with you."

Caroline felt her cheeks redden with chagrin. "I suppose I have treated him with more warmth than was wise. I did not fully consider. But what am I to say to him? I have only just this afternoon suggested we spend time together as companions."

Fiona rolled her eyes. "Oh, Caro! You must do your best to avoid him. Give him the cut direct, if need be."

"Yes," Caroline said as she bit her lip and looked down at the floor. "But first, we must sing our song together."

"What song? No, do not tell me," Fiona said, gazing at the doorway. "I am persuaded your scheme shall come to naught, for look who has just now entered the room."

Caroline's heart leaped in gladness, but it was not Mr. Doherty who had newly arrived. "Well! It seems Lady Bissell has invited another gentleman to the party, after all." She felt curiously deflated.

"Yes," Fiona said with a brightened air. "I doubt not that he is unwed, for a wife would again make for one too many ladies."

"I suppose he shall be placed at the end of the table, just as Mr. Doherty was," Caroline mused.

"Where is the fault in that?" Fiona asked.

"There isn't one. I am persuaded the two of you shall be happily engaged in conversation all the night long," Caroline said happily. "Now, I have something I wish to say to Lady Bissell." She walked briskly away before Fiona could quiz her as to her intentions.

Lady Bissell had been making her way towards the front of the room when Caroline encountered her. "Good evening," she said with a sincere smile. "I wonder if I might have the music room to myself tomorrow after breakfast."

"But of course you may, Miss Fulton! The house is entirely at your disposal," Lady Bissell insisted.

"Thank you! I am wishful of performing a duet one evening, and we shall require a great deal of practice."

"I very much look forward to it, as shall Lord Bissell. With whom do you intend to sing?" Lady Bissell asked.

Caroline composed her brightest smile and forged ahead. "Mr. Doherty. I chanced to overhear him singing with your darling lads the other afternoon, and I am persuaded his voice is entirely suited to mine."

"Oh," Lady Bissell said as her smile faded. "What shall become of my sons whilst the two of you are working in the music room?"

"As it turns out, they are quite enamored of Miss

O'Sullivan. She enjoys them very much, indeed, and shall easily keep them amused." Lady Bissell made no reply, so Caroline continued. "It shall be the five of us together in the music room. I expect it shall be quite educational. Master Christopher, I am told, sings like an angel. Perhaps he should enjoy singing along with the pianoforte, as well." Caroline took in Lady Bissell's expression, one of mingled astonishment and doubt, and changed tack. "I ought to become better acquainted with your sons, as well. They are the sweetest lads. We have seen them just this afternoon, as well as yesterday, when they were out for their walk."

Lady Bissell's features settled into resignation. "Is that so? Well, I thank you for your kind words. I am glad to know they have behaved themselves in your presence. They have sadly missed their father, but I do believe they are beginning to recover."

"Then all the more reason to afford them this little treat. Might I depend on you to inform Mr. Doherty of your decision? I am afraid I have no means by which to communicate with him before the appointed time."

"Yes, of course. I am persuaded Charles and Christopher shall enjoy it. However, I fear I cannot allow it to become a regular practice," she said, her smile kind but firm.

"Thank you, Lady Bissell. I should very much like to sing an Irish song. I fear it might offend your guests, however, so I shall be guided by you in that."

"Of course you shall not offend them." Lady Bissell's smile grew broader. "This is Ireland, after all. Now, I really must attend to Mr. Wilkinson, who has only just joined us."

Caroline bobbed a curtsy and watched as Lady Bissell greeted the newly-arrived Mr. Wilkinson. He was quite tall, dressed to perfection, and possessed of a remarkable head of pale hair. She felt that Fiona would doubtless find much to admire in him.

All through dinner, as Caroline had surmised, Mr. Wilkinson and Fiona conversed with none but each other. Caroline supposed that Lady Bissell had written to him the moment she learned of Fiona's attendance. Mr. Wilkinson had certainly been eager to comply; he must have packed up and set out immediately upon receiving his invitation in order to have arrived so quickly.

She was delighted for Fiona, but it was not a pleasant meal for Caroline. Nor did she enjoy a restful night's sleep. The sounds from the ash trees were not to blame, however. The occupant of the room above was quite restless and rose to his or her feet a number of times during the night to pace the floor, or so she assumed. Come the dawn, it seemed to her that the sun rose far too early and was too insistent, as well.

With a sigh, she rose and washed at the basin. As her mind cleared, she recalled her appointment to meet Mr. Doherty in the music room after breakfast. Her mood suddenly lighter, she took more interest in her attire. The jonquil morning gown and Pomona green sash she chose reflected her improved disposition.

She was just about to quit the room when she heard an odd sound against the window. Her heart seized in alarm in fear that the noises from the trees had somehow migrated to her window. Her hands shook with trepidation as she crossed the room and pulled back the curtains.

To her vast relief, the tapping against the glass was made by the wax seal of a letter suspended by a string. It bore her name, a fact she found utterly fascinating. Quickly, she opened the window, slipped the parchment from its fastening, and spread the page wide.

Masters Charles and Christopher very much look forward to their engagement in the music room. We shall meet you at ten of the clock this morning. Mr. D

Caroline nearly crowed with delight, but quickly restrained herself. How Mr. Doherty had arranged to lower the letter to her, she could not guess. However, she was glad of it, for his cleverness, as well as for the information the letter imparted.

In hopes that it would save her from an angry scold, Caroline informed Fiona of the assignation with Mr. Doherty whilst at the sideboard dishing up breakfast. "So you see, it has all been arranged and there is naught to do about it. Lady Bissell has approved the entire undertaking and is very much looking forward to it."

Fiona closed her eyes and drew a deep breath. "I have just counted numbers all the way to ten before I felt it safe to speak. As yet I have conquered the temptations to pull out your hair and screech insults at you," she hissed as she scraped potatoes from the bowl onto her plate. "And, the most tempting of all, to run from the house shouting 'fire'!"

Caroline stared at her friend in bewilderment. "My dearest Fiona, it cannot be as bad as all that. The lads shall be enchanting and you shall doubtless enchant *them*. Mr. Doherty and I shall have the opportunity to select a song and sing it through once or twice. Tonight, or perhaps the night after this, the baron's guests shall be entertained by a lovely Irish melody. Perhaps the baron will be enchanted, as well. That would please you, would it not? When it is all over, I shall speak to Mr. Doherty no more."

"I do not think it wise." Fiona offered a tremulous smile. "However, I think it best if we further speak of it in private."

They returned to the table, but Caroline found her appetite had fled. She had taken only a few bites when Fiona suggested they excuse themselves. As such, they arrived at the music room well before the appointed time.

"Fiona, before you speak," Caroline said, once the door at closed behind them, "I wish to beg your pardon for treating your words so lightly. I simply did not have the heart to break off our engagement this morning. I prefer to explain my actions to Mr. Doherty, face to face, rather than behave as if we had never spoken of our friendship."

"You are my dearest friend," Fiona said as she took Caroline's hand and drew her down to sit beside her on the brocade sofa. "If I were to choose a husband for you, it would be Mr. Doherty. He is intelligent, he is kind; he is Irish. What's more, you like him and shall grow to like him better if you do not take care. That, however, is your own affair. What I cannot abide is sitting idly by whilst you break his heart."

Caroline felt overcome with regret. "I have no wish to injure Mr. Doherty. Do you truly believe he cares so much?"

"You know that I do."

"Very well, then." Caroline twisted her hands together in her lap. "After our hour here in the music room, I shall make it most clear that there shall be no more."

"But what is the point of an hour now if you are not to sing together for the baron's guests?" Fiona sputtered.

"I thoroughly agree!" Caroline said decisively. "So, I shall tell him there shall be no more time spent together after we have sung tonight. I do feel much more at ease with that decision."

"Caroline Fulton!" Fiona warned.

"I can hardly insist he leave the moment he arrives, especially with the lads by his side," Caroline hastened to explain. "After he has bothered to come, we dare not disappoint those lads. What should Lady Bissell say to that? And once we have rehearsed, it seems that we ought to carry through to the end. Lady Bissell shall be expecting us to sing for her guests. It is only right that we should."

Fiona sighed. "I fear you are correct. But you must promise me, after you have sung for the guests, you will either give up Mr. Doherty, or the baron. It must be one or the other."

"How am I to give up the baron? I wish you would tell me, Fiona. If he were to offer for me, Papa would accept him. If I dared to refuse the baron to his face, Papa would find me someone else to wed, most likely outside of Ireland."

"You say that your heart is not yet involved when it comes to Mr. Doherty," Fiona said softly. "Is it not better to risk any further injury to yourself, as well as to him?"

Caroline felt her eyes fill with tears. "You anticipated that matters would come to a choice between him and my father. It seems it has already. If I refuse the baron, I shall spare Mr. Doherty injury, but Papa shall be sorely disappointed, even angry. If I choose to marry the baron, I shall make Papa happy but I shall injure Mr. Doherty."

"It does not have to injure Mr. Doherty, Caro, if you have a care. Discontinue all connections with him; his heart shall repair all the sooner. If you become betrothed to Lord Bissell, you shall then go to The Hollows to prepare for the wedding, as well as to Dublin for shopping expeditions. Once you are married and return to Oak View, Mr. Doherty shall have had the chance to grow accustomed to the idea, or, barring that, to have found employment elsewhere."

"Yes, I perfectly comprehend you." Caroline drew a deep breath. "But we are agreed that we must go through with the singing, is that not so?"

"I cannot like it, but I do not see how you might avoid it," Fiona whispered. "Mr. Doherty even now walks through the door."

Caroline could not deny the flutter of her heart when she looked up and saw him standing there; the hand of a restive little boy in each of his, his black curls tumbled along his brow and his large, blue-gray eyes alight.

"Master Charles, Master Christopher," Caroline said with gladness, "how good of you to come. Miss O'Sullivan should very much like to be shown about the room. I suppose you two know more about it than any one of us."

"I know all there is to know about this place," Charles said proudly, perhaps as an antidote to his sniveling the day prior.

"I am persuaded that is the case. Do tell Miss O'Sullivan all about it first, and when Mr. Doherty and I have finished, you may show us about. And then perhaps Master Christopher should like to sing for us."

Both lads found favor with this plan, and soon they and

Fiona were occupied on the far side of the room from the pianoforte.

"You are very good with them," Mr. Doherty observed. "We must begin immediately, however. You have seen for yourself how quickly circumstances change when those two are about."

Caroline laughed merrily. "Never say so! They are merely being the lads that they are. But, do let us select a song," she added as they moved to the rosewood Canterbury that overflowed with sheet music. "I have not had a moment to see for myself, though I would be very surprised if we hadn't a choice of any number of pieces by Thomas Moore."

"We must be particular when it comes to Moore," Mr. Doherty advised. "Many of his songs are laments having to do with the English oppression of the Irish. I daresay those would not be well received by the baron's guests."

Caroline felt her eyes grow wide. "I had not considered. Well, then, it shall have to be," she mused as she shuffled through the music, "this one!"

Mr. Doherty took the sheet of music from her hand and smiled. "'Believe Me If All Those Endearing Young Charms.' Yes, 'tis a lovely one, no? But who is to play for us?"

"Oh!" Caroline felt her fame burn with chagrin. "I had not thought of it. Do you not play?"

He shook his head. "I fear not well enough to do you credit."

"Well, when the time comes we shall simply have to ask one of the guests to play for us. I am persuaded someone shall. In the meantime, we shall do without," Caroline said as she sat at the pianoforte. "Perhaps you might give us the proper note before we begin."

Mr. Doherty sat on a stool next to hers and put his finger to the sheet of music, his shoulder brushing against hers. "That is where we ought to start, unless that is too high for you."

"No, not at all," she said a little breathlessly. Surely she had brushed against a man before; though, she owned, not one so young and handsome. "Now that we have our note, might it be best if we move to the window? The quality of the light is far superior."

"Certainly," he said as he stood.

She was pleased when he held out his hand to assist her in rising, but was astonished that the touch of his bare fingers on her own renewed the breathlessness she had been at pains to avoid. "Well, then!" she said, removing her hand from his as they took their places by the window. "Let us take a few deep breaths and begin."

By the second note of the song, Caroline knew their voices were indeed an excellent match. As the perfectly harmonized notes soared into the air, her entire being filled with joy. When they drew near to the end of the lyrics, she found herself mourning the fact that Mr. Moore hadn't written several more verses to this particular song.

"Is that the end already?" Mr. Doherty said, as if he had divined her thoughts. "It is far too beautiful to be over so soon."

"I was more than a little astonished myself," Caroline agreed. "Let us sing it through again."

"I fail to comprehend," Fiona offered from her place on the sofa, "how your performance could possibly be improved upon."

"You are very kind, Miss O'Sullivan. I agree that Miss Fulton has no need of further practice, but I thought my voice rather rough in a place or two."

"Indeed, no!" Caroline glanced into Mr. Doherty's beautiful, fey eyes and renewed her encouragements. "I heard no lacks whatsoever."

"I thank you. Nevertheless, I wish to sing it at least once more prior to singing it for the baron's guests." He gazed at her intently for a moment before he turned away to address the lads. "But first, Master Charles must give us a lesson on the music room and Master Christopher shall have the opportunity to sing as well."

Charles immediately left Fiona's side. "Miss Fulton, do come see the antique instruments that are kept in the far cabinet."

"And then," Christopher piped up from his place on the brocade sofa next to Fiona, "I shall sing my song."

Caroline enjoyed the ensuing tour of the music room, and Christopher's performance was charming in spite of Mr. Doherty's rudimentary skills at the pianoforte. To her delight, Christopher sang the very song she had overheard the other day.

"Bravo," she said with a sound clap of her hands. "I am so pleased to have learned all of the words. Who has written them and what is it called?" she asked with a look for Mr. Doherty.

"'My Love is Like a Red, Red Rose' by Robert Burns," he said with a faint smile. "I heard many of his tunes performed whilst I was in Scotland. There is one that I thought lovelier than this by far, however." He went to the music cabinet and rustled through the sheets. "Ah, here it is: 'Ae Fond Kiss and Then We Sever.'"

"Sever?" Caroline asked with a tiny shudder. "It sounds rather violent."

"Ah, 'tis nothing to the violence of his love. Here, I shall play as best I can so as to give you the tune." He sat again at the pianoforte and placed his fingers on the keys.

"I suppose I have been given no choice," she said for the benefit of a disapproving Fiona. Taking her seat next to Mr. Doherty, she joined him again in song. This time the brush of his shoulder against hers was not in the least distracting. Rather, it seemed a fitting intimacy alongside such tender lyrics. It was not a difficult song, but her voice wavered, particularly when the words spoke so keenly of her particular predicament: *Had we never loved sae kindly, Had we never loved sae blindly, Never met—or never parted, We had ne'er been broken-hearted.*

When his fingers paused on the keys, her gaze was caught in his before she could think to turn away. Naught was spoken, yet so much revealed in the depths of his startling blue-gray eyes that her cheeks grew hot and her breath shortened. She knew that he longed to kiss her. As she listened to the tempo of her pounding heart, she realized that she longed for it, too.

When a gentle cough sounded from the direction of the sofa, Caroline forced herself to think. "Oh, what a lovely tune!" she said with a bright smile designed to hide her discomposure. "Now, I do believe our time is up, Mr. Doherty. I should tell you that a Mr. Wilkinson has arrived to take your place at table." She stood and looked down at her skirt, brushing away imaginary wrinkles in the folds of her gown. "I shall not fail to insist that a message be sent as to when Lady Bissell expects you to appear tonight. I so much look forward to our song."

There was a short silence before Fiona spoke in reply. "Do give Mr. Doherty your attention, Caro."

Widening her smile, she looked at him to find that he gazed up at her with an expression of mild distress. "What is it?" she asked in alarm.

"Oh, 'tis nothing. Only, the young masters are growing restless, and, as you have said, our time is up. I should prefer to delay our performance until tomorrow night. I shall feel more at ease after we have gone through it again. Tomorrow morning perhaps?"

The twinkle in Mr. Doherty's eye was unmistakable, but Caroline dared not acknowledge it without making it known to Fiona. "I am sorry," she said around a difficult-to-subdue grin. "I did not think. Of course we should wait until we have a better command of the song. I shall speak to Lady Bissell when next we meet and let her know that we shall require the music room again tomorrow morning."

"Very good," he said as he stood and gave her a bow. Before he raised his head, however, he lifted his gaze to her; both of his eyes twinkling now, as something of mischief playing about his lips. By the time he had straightened to his full height, he looked his usual self.

"Masters Charles and Christopher, we must return to the schoolroom. Mathematics and science await."

"I do not wish to study mathematics," Master Christopher whined.

"Come now, lads," Mr. Doherty said briskly. "You shall give the ladies a disgust of your manners. Whatever shall they think of you?"

"You should not think less of me," Christopher said plaintively, his gaze turned up into Fiona's face, "if I never learned mathematics, would you?"

"I could not say," Fiona said uncertainly.

"Come along," Mr. Doherty said, his hand outstretched. "Perhaps we shall have our walk now and return to mathematics after luncheon."

"Oh, yes!" Christopher cried. "Let's do! And Miss Fiona shall join us, shall she not?"

Fiona's expression flickered between regret and delight until, finally, she turned to Caroline. "I confess, I believe I should enjoy it. Shall it suit you, Caro?"

"Ah, 'tis flattered by the young rogue, you are, Miss O'Sullivan," Mr. Doherty suggested. "We would never disdain your company, or that of yours, Miss Fulton," he added with a slight bow in Caroline's direction, "but you mustn't be giving in to his demands."

"Yes, Miss O'Sullivan," Caroline said, perfectly aware that her voice shook with suppressed laughter. "You mustn't spoil the dear creature."

By this time the brothers both gazed up at the adults in mute appeal, whilst Mr. Doherty looked equal parts vexed and resigned.

"Let us walk with you as far as the front garden," Caroline suggested, in hopes it would satisfy all assembled. "If we were to stay out longer, Miss O'Sullivan and I must first go to our rooms to fetch our gloves and bonnets." She didn't wait for an answer and, putting her arms on the shoulders of the boys, she ushered them through the door of the music room.

Chapter Eight

Niall pondered his good fortune as he followed the lads and Miss O'Sullivan from the room, with Miss Fulton at his side. A few more moments with her, even as far as the garden, were most welcome. In light of the arrival of Mr. Wilkinson, Niall wondered how he would arrange to meet her once they had sung for the baron's guests.

"There you are, my darlings!" Lady Bissell cried as she hastened forth from the other end of the passage. "Come, I must give you each a kiss before you return to your lessons."

"But we are not returning to the school room," Charles said, his expression solemn.

"Oh my, I do hope there has been no tragedy," Lady Bissell soothed. "Have you a pet to bury or some such?"

"We have merely decided to exchange our afternoon walk for an earlier one," Niall explained. "They had a delightful time showing the ladies about the music room and are not quite ready to be shut up for the morning."

"We had thought today was a holiday," Christopher said with an overblown sigh.

"What he meant to say," Charles corrected, his nose in the air, "is that we believed we were to join the house party."

"My poor lads," Lady Bissell cried as she gathered them to

103

her side. With a penetrating look for Niall, she added, "I suppose your brother would not object if you were to have a holiday. Perhaps we might even arrange some activities with the ladies and gentlemen if they are agreeable."

"We are more than agreeable," Miss O'Sullivan offered.

"It all sounds quite promising," Miss Fulton said, a portent of laughter in her voice. "Might we be of some use?"

"Why, yes," Lady Bissell said gratefully. "Perhaps you might take the lads to the stables and inquire as to what can be brought out for a race; a pair of ponies or perhaps traps."

"What about jaunting cars?" Miss Fulton suggested. "I should think it quite amusing to watch an Englishman attempt to tool one."

"Just the thing!" Lady Bissell said, her eyes wide with anticipation. "You all go along, and I shall encourage the other guests to join us in the drive."

She hurried away whilst the lads each took Fiona by the hand and drew her on ahead. This left Niall free to escort Miss Fulton again on his arm as they made their way out of the house and on towards the stables.

She seemed content to be at his side, gazing up at the blue sky before turning to smile at him. "Of what I am about to accuse you does not reflect well on Miss O'Sullivan," Miss Fulton warned, her serious demeanor clearly feigned.

"Does it not? Perhaps you ought to remain silent," he said as he attempted to suppress a smile and failed.

"Nor on you," she said, a smile breaking out on her face, as well.

"In that case," he replied, "I am persuaded you should keep your own counsel."

"Indeed, I shall not," she said with a laugh. "However, I shall give you the opportunity to defend yourself if you swear never to divulge to Miss O'Sullivan that you have bribed those boys to gush over her."

"I most vehemently deny such palaver." He spoke sternly, but suspected his broadening smile belied his tone.

"There is naught you can say to prove your innocence," Caroline teased. "You need only but observe."

They watched as the boys tugged Fiona farther and farther ahead until, finally, there was no hope that Miss Fulton remained deceived.

"If you needs must have the truth," Niall confessed, "they required little encouragement."

"I shall interpret that to mean that it was offered," she replied, her eyes sparkling with mirth.

"I hope they are no bother to her."

"She seems to genuinely adore them," Miss Fulton replied.

"*Those* miscreants?" Niall asked in surprise.

"If you had ever met any of her nieces and nephews, you would then have met a miscreant or two," Miss Fulton said lightly. "Besides which, I am persuaded that Masters Charles and Christopher have developed a *tendre* for her."

"She is certainly worthy of genuine affection," he said, perhaps too warmly. He found, however, that he rather enjoyed the notion of a jealous Miss Fulton. "That red hair shines like none I've ever seen, and those eyes! Well, who would have thought that all the green of every field in Ireland could be contained in a single pair?"

"Oh, I thoroughly agree," Miss Fulton said ardently. "I

greatly fear that she shall any moment succumb to the charms of Mr. Wilkinson of London and Wiltshire. I suppose I shall never lay eyes on her again."

"What charms are these?" he asked indifferently, despite the spark of apprehension her words induced.

"Oh, where to begin," she mused as she put a well-shaped finger to her well-shaped chin. "He is tall, very tall, indeed. And his clothes are exquisite, such as I have never before seen. Most compelling about him is his hair, which is thick and very pale."

"Ah, then he is elderly," Niall concluded in secret relief.

"Not at all. 'Tis why it is so compelling, I suppose."

Niall told himself that it was pointless to be envious of the untitled Mr. Wilkinson. "Sure, it is the baron who is growing old, is it not?"

Miss Fulton flashed him an uncertain look. "If I did not know better, I would be tempted to believe you wish to discourage me from an attachment to the baron."

"Is that not what you are plotting, then?"

Miss Fulton sighed. "'Tis a plot, to be sure, though not of my making. And yet, if I am to stay close to my father, I must go along with it. Which brings to mind something I must say to you," she added in a voice that trembled ever so slightly.

"If it is of a private nature, then we had best come to a halt; I see Miss O'Sullivan and the lads just ahead."

In unison, they stopped and turned towards one another. She even allowed him to take her hands in his.

"Mr. Doherty, after we have sung our song," she began, but was interrupted by the cries of the lads.

"Miss Caro!" they called in unison as they ran back the way they had come, Miss O'Sullivan following at a more sedate pace.

Quickly, Niall let go her hands as they turned to face the coming fracas.

"We have found another treasure!" Charles said excitedly as he arrived at their side, gasping for air.

"Do let us see it," Niall said, holding out his hand.

"I wish to give it to Miss Caro," Charles explained.

"Very well then," Niall said, pleased.

"Yes, indeed," Miss Fulton said as she took something from between Charles' fingers to inspect it. "It looks to be a stone of some kind."

"We think it must be a pearl! Christopher shouted.

"Surely, not!" Miss O'Sullivan gasped as she joined the group.

"'Tis round and it appears to be white under all this mud," Caroline remarked with wonder.

"May I?" Niall once again held out his hand, and Miss Fulton dropped the treasure into his palm.

"Is it a pearl, Mr. Doherty?" Charles implored.

"I am not thoroughly convinced," Niall said as he held it up to the light. "We shall have a better look at it under your microscope once we return to the school room."

"Very well," Charles said as Niall pocketed the small, round object. Christopher looked as if he might object, but Niall gave him a warning look, one that produced the desired effect.

"Very good, lads," Niall praised them. "Now, I must go to the stables. Why don't you all go on ahead to the paddock and see which of the horses is running about."

Charles and Christopher dashed off, and Miss O'Sullivan

followed, calling to them to slow down. Miss Fulton moved away at a more gradual pace, as if she were reluctant to leave his side.

"Would you like to come with me?" he asked as he took her hand. It felt soft and small and all the sweeter when she did not draw it from his grasp. "You may be first to choose a jaunting car."

"Yes, indeed," she said, "I should like it above all things."

Surprised that she had agreed, he searched her face. To his chagrin, his gaze fell at once to her bow-shaped mouth. Consumed with the longing to take her lips with his until her luminescent smile should become his own, he forced himself to think of other things.

"Lord Bissell is a great one for the jaunting cars," he said as he led her into the stables.

"Perhaps it is best if I did not have first choice of the cars," Miss Fulton suggested as they made their way to where the cars reposed. "Shan't Lord Bissell wish to?"

"I should be most surprised if he set himself to race against the ladies." The very notion brought out another broad smile onto Niall's face.

"Oh dear! Did it hurt?" she asked, her expression compassionate.

"Was something meant to hurt?" he asked, bewildered.

"That smile. Because I am persuaded," she explained, her eyes twinkling, "that I heard the corners of your mouth split."

Niall could not help himself; he threw back his head and laughed. "Am I so very morose?" he asked.

"I'm afraid the answer is yes, since the moment we met." She stepped up to the nearest jaunting car and regarded it closely. "I wonder what has happened to provoke in you such sorrow." The nonchalance of her manner was belied by the warmth in her voice.

He watched her run her hand over the blue-painted footboard as he considered his reply. It was impossible, however, to conjure a satisfactory answer in light of such delicious distractions. The manner in which she stepped forward and back again to regard the red-spoked wheels was as graceful as any dance; the line from her brow to the tip of her nose flowed like music. The sweep of her lashes as she lifted her gaze to look at him was artistry of a different sort, whilst the compassion in her eyes spoke of virtues more eloquent than beauty.

"Won't you tell me?" she asked, her blue eyes moist and her brows drawn together.

He opened his mouth to speak when he was startled by a violent sneeze issuing forth from one of the horse stalls. "McCauley, is that you?" Niall called into the gloom of the stable.

"Aye," the groom replied as he stepped out from behind a stall and moved towards them. "What ye be needin'?"

"Her ladyship would have her guests race in the jaunting cars. Take this one here," Niall said, indicating the one Miss Fulton had admired, "and pair it with the fastest horse in the stable."

"T'at would be the master's stallion," McCauley said doubtfully. "I don't t'ink he should be likin' t'at."

"Yes, of course, he is a hunter," Niall said for Miss Fulton's benefit. "The brute is unaccustomed to anything but a rider." He returned his attention to the groom. "The horse that copes

109

best with wheels, then," Niall amended. "Once you have done so bring it out into the yard, then return to hitch up the other."

"Very good, sir," McCauley said a bit scornfully.

Miss Fulton said nothing until they had exited the stables. "What a rude man. He ought to have shown more respect."

"It is good of you to say so, Miss Fulton, but as I have explained, I am without status in this household."

"But you are a gentleman," she said in disbelief.

He led her to a bench under a sprawling oak and bade her sit. "A gentleman, indeed, but one who must sustain himself through work."

"Yes, I comprehend you," she said as she sat. "However, there is no call to treat you like a servant." The outrage on her face warmed him to the core.

"That is what I am. It is the same with all tutors, regardless of the family from whence they come. The eldest inherits all whilst the younger brothers choose a career in the military or the church."

"I assume you had no taste for either," she said, looking up at him with wide eyes.

"Not exactly." He was suddenly so very tired. "May I sit?"

"Yes, but only if you swear to tell me all," she said as she made room for him beside her on the bench. "I should dearly love to know how many brothers you have and whether or not you have sisters."

Drawing a deep breath, he focused on the distant curl of smoke from the gatehouse chimney. "I am the eldest of three, no brothers."

"The eldest?" she asked in disbelief. "Then how is it that you are here?"

He turned to look at her and smiled. The sight of her never failed to lighten his melancholy. "Through the good offices of a generous man who refused to allow tragedy to limit my potential."

"He seems the sort of man I should like to know." Her voice was soft, but her eyes skeptical. "If he were so generous, surely you would be better placed than this."

"He was my professor at university, not a man of unlimited means. I was at Cambridge when my father's money ran out. Professor Luce ensured I had what I needed in order to complete my schooling. He also provided valuable recommendations for a number of positions I have filled since then."

"I see." She leaned forward and placed her hand on the seat of the bench alongside his. "But I believe there is more to your story, is there not?"

"There is." He stared down at their hands, side by side. If he were to merely wiggle his little finger, he could not fail to come in contact with hers. "My father lost everything with a single turn of a card: the money, the house, the carriages, and cattle . . . even the furniture. Then he died."

Miss Fulton gasped. "Not . . . ?"

"Self-murder? No, it was an apoplexy brought on by his losses and my mother's grief. After the funeral, she and the lasses went north to live with my aunt, and I returned to university."

They sat in silence for a few moments, the silence

111

companionable. He looked down again at her lily-white hand. "How foolish of me! I have kept you in the sun without your gloves."

She gasped. "I had not intended to wander from the house before returning to my chamber. I certainly had not planned on taking the reins."

"Shall I go back to the house and arrange for someone to fetch a pair for you?" he offered.

"You are kind, but I think it best if I were to retrieve my gloves myself. I shall first collect Miss O'Sullivan. Shall we meet you here when we return?"

"Not here," he said, rising to his feet. "I suspect that by then the cars shall be out on the drive. However," he said as he assisted her to stand, "I shall hold back the one with the red wheels for you."

She gave him a dimpled smile and, lifting her skirts, made haste for the paddock where Miss O'Sullivan yet entertained the lads.

He turned to watch her go and was about to call Charles and Christopher to his side when something caught his attention from the corner of his eye. He turned towards the opposite end of the stables, to find that a woman had emerged and was quickly walking in his direction. What an unaccompanied, richly-dressed woman was doing in the stables he could not guess; then he noted her black hair and dusky complexion. Quickly, he turned to ascertain that the lads were in company with the ladies. To his relief, each looked in the opposite direction of the mysterious matchmaker.

She was tastefully dressed in a green gown with a fashionably high waist, an exquisite paisley shawl, and a straw bonnet over a lace cap. As she drew near, he could see that, in the full light of day, she looked neither young nor old. He sketched her a bow and quietly, in the case he was overheard, posed the question that had troubled him since he had first met Miss Caroline Fulton. "Have you come to tell me you were wrong?"

"Wrong?" She tilted her head and regarded him through her astounding almond-shaped eyes. "I am not wrong, Mr. Doherty."

"You must be. Her name does not start with an "L"; neither her last nor her Christian name."

"Her?" the matchmaker asked with a gentle smile.

"Miss Caroline Fulton, the young lady whom I most ardently admire."

The matchmaker regarded him for a moment before she spoke. "Why are you here, Mr. Doherty? Did I not say that you would meet her on the metal bridge that spans the River Liffey?"

"Yes," he admitted, "but I have no purpose in going or means to be conveyed there."

The matchmaker clasped her hands in front of her. "Meet her on the River Liffey or do not; it is your choice."

"Yes," he said with a heavy sigh, "you have said as much. You also said that I should prove happy with whomever I choose," he challenged.

"And so you shall. Trust yourself, Niall Doherty, son of the long-ago Niall Noígíallach, King of Connacht. Trust in your perception, in your gift of sight. You will not choose wrong."

"I have already chosen," Niall began in frustration, but the matchmaker had turned away and was walking back the way she had come. "How are you here?" he called to her, the others who might overhear all but forgotten.

She paused and turned. "I go where I will. I go where I must." Smiling, she resumed her journey back to from wherever she had come.

"Tutor!"

Startled, Niall whirled about to find McCauley pulling the horse and jaunting car in his wake.

"Here's yer car. I'll be back with the other when I'm done."

"Very good, McCauley," Niall said as he took the horse's lead from the groom. "Bring it to the drive at the front of the house when you have finished."

With a lift of his brow and a roll of his eyes, the groom turned on his heel and stalked away.

The lead in his hand, Niall collapsed on the bench and listened to the thudding of his heart. He had thought never to see Miss Pearl again. He looked towards the far end of the stables, but she was nowhere to be seen. He looked over his shoulder towards the paddock, but she was not there either. Neither was Miss Fulton nor Miss O'Sullivan. The lads, however, were. He called to them, and they were soon at his side, pestering him for a ride in the jaunting car and refusing to be denied. "Very well, then; Master Charles, you take this side, and I shall help you, Master Christopher, to sit on the other."

Once the boys were properly settled, Niall made his way to the driver's seat, picked up the whip, and gave it a flick. The car pitched forward, the gravel grinding under the wheels, and they were off.

"Let's go very fast!" Charles cried.

"We mustn't be tiring out the horse before the racing," Niall replied.

"Why are the stables so far from the house?" Christopher grumbled. "I am that hungry and I want candy."

"The horses are kept far away so that we needn't endure flies in our food and unpleasant smells filling the house."

"I should like to have flies in my food," Christopher insisted.

"Yes, I suppose you would," Niall replied. "Your mama, however, would not. Ah, here we are." Niall tugged on the reins, and the horse came to a gentle stop outside the kitchen door. "Find Mrs. Walsh and request from her the candy. Once she has given it to you, return directly here. I am expected out front."

"Yes sir!" the lads called as they jumped down and disappeared through the doorway.

Niall's thoughts immediately returned to the words of the matchmaker. None of what she had said made sense in the least. She said he was to trust himself; that he would be happy with whomever he chose. His heart had chosen for him, but Miss Fulton was not free to choose him. Her disinclination to go against her father's wishes was only one obstruction in his path. On what would they live if her father did not approve her choice?

His thoughts were disrupted when the lads reappeared, their hands full of sugared almonds. As they drove on and neared the house, Niall caught sight of the baron's guests as they milled about on the gravel drive. He looked for Miss Fulton and, once he had found her, wondered how he could have

115

missed her. She looked eminently appealing in a jaunty military-style hat and a matching pelisse in deep green. Her hands were protected from the sun by York tan gloves that echoed the jonquil of her gown, and she carried a smart, silver-mounted whip.

As he pulled on the reins, their gazes met and she gave him a brilliant smile. He wanted nothing more than to dash to her side and present his Maeve, warrior queen, with her noble chariot. He, however, was no Aillil; not king or even captain. To behave too familiarly should only prove to bring censure on her head. It was with a stinging disappointment that he lowered his eyes and decorously descended the jaunting car.

Once he had lifted the lads to the ground, he cleared the seats and foot board of their crumbs and whatever had made its way from their pockets and the bottoms of their shoes. Then he waited, his eyes fixed on an imaginary object above the heads of the guests. When Miss Fulton stepped up to him, he bowed and offered her the reins.

"Thank you, Mr. Doherty," she said playfully, as if laughing at him for his servility.

They were joined by Lady Bissell. "Miss Fulton, you shall be among the first to race. Mr. Doherty, where is the other car?"

"I gave instructions for it to be brought round," he replied, turning towards the direction of the stables. "I should have thought it arrived by now."

"Very well," Lady Bissell said. "Who shall drive it when it comes?" She looked around at each face. None seemed willing.

"Shouldn't Lord Bissell drive the other?" Lady Anne asked, with a coy glance for their host.

"I shouldn't think so," Lord Bissell replied. "When the ladies have had their turn, the men shall race against one another."

Lady Anne turned to him with alacrity. "That shall be most stimulating. We shall then have one male winner and one female. Would it not be diverting for the two of them to race one another?"

Niall waited for the baron's reply with interest.

"I shall consider it if it pleases you, Lady Anne."

"I have no doubt that you shall be the victor," she replied with a flutter of her lashes, "but which female shall drive against you?"

Niall felt a flicker of apprehension. There was something about Lady Anne's manner that did not sit easy.

"I don't pretend to know who shall win," a man, most certainly the newly-arrived Mr. Wilkinson, remarked. "However, I should give any amount of money for the opportunity to drive a jaunting car. I have heard tales," he said with a shake of his head. "They are not for the inexperienced."

"And I suppose you are not among such?" Lady Anne said with an arch smile.

"I am," he said with a brief bow. "However, it is my intention to alter my status."

"I shall like to see you going about it, Mr. Wilkinson," Lady Anne remarked.

"Lady Anne," the baron said, his manner sullen. "I would be honored to race against you."

"I?" she said with a hand to her throat. "I should only make a muddle of the entire affair. I ride capably; I have even been

117

known to tool a phaeton upon occasion, but this is something entirely different."

"If you would prefer, Lady Anne," Miss Fulton ventured, "I would be happy to instruct you."

"It will not be necessary," Lady Anne riposted. "I am persuaded it is a course a true lady should not pursue."

Chapter Nine

Lady Anne's remark was so cutting that Caroline knew not where to look. She stole a glance at Mr. Doherty from the corner of her eye. Though he gave no sign of it, she knew he was angry; the very air around him seemed alive with indignation.

Lord Bissell was the first to breach the silence. "Here is the other car now," he said with hearty enthusiasm, striding forth to meet it.

"Miss O'Sullivan," Caroline said loud enough for all to hear. "I challenge you to a race. What say you?"

"Nothing could prevent me," Fiona replied, her eyes flashing like a pair of emeralds in the sun.

"Very well, then. Mr. Doherty, will you assist me?" Caroline asked.

He sketched a bow and took her hand to support her as she stepped up to the driver's seat. Once she had settled herself, she looked down to find him gazing up at her with a gleam of approval in his eyes. "Thank you, Mr. Doherty," she said. "As you can see, I am quite secure."

Rather than move away, he stepped up onto the car and leaned over her to test the reins. He smelled deliciously of soap and corduroy warmed by the sun. "Pardon me," he said. Then, in a voice meant for her ears alone, added: "I had feared she meant you some harm. However, I had not thought she would risk such a conspicuous attack."

"Thank you," Caroline whispered in return, her lips close to his ear, "but you needn't fear that my sensibilities have been injured. 'Tis a pity, though; I should have enjoyed a race against her."

She was delighted when her remark earned her a sunny smile, one he took care to hide from the others. She owned that his was an expressive face, but when he smiled it was if the sun had broken through a sky of gray.

"I wish you good luck," he said as he returned the reins to her keeping.

By the time he found his footing on the ground, Lord Bissell had drawn the other car forward so that it stood aligned with Caroline's. He then assisted Fiona as Mr. Doherty had Caroline, who could not resist a glance in the direction of Lady Anne. She leaned heavily on the arm of Mr. Wilkinson, consternation evident on his face as well as in the manner in which he waved his handkerchief to and fro in her aid.

Caroline thought Lady Anne rather brilliant; a fainting spell was an excellent means by which to deflect censure. Caroline turned to share a smile with Fiona, whose attempts to refrain from dissolving into laughter appeared futile.

"Ladies and gentlemen," Lord Bissell called with a wave of his arm. "I bring to your attention the Irish jaunting car. As you see, it is open like the English pony-drawn trap, but the passengers sit facing the road rather than the driver. Furthermore, it is not pulled by a pony, but by a spirited horse.

The wheels are similar to that of the Phaeton. The tooling of it requires a specific hand on the reins; not too rough, not too gentle. I suspect this pair of Irish ladies shan't have the least trouble," he said with a bow in their direction. "The first one through the gate at the end of the drive is the winner!"

Caroline stole another glance at Lady Anne, who now stood without aid, her expression crestfallen. Mr. Wilkinson, who had moved away from her, seemed to be anticipating the race with glee. He also had his eyes fixed on Fiona with an admiration that tore at Caroline's heart. As she looked away, she exchanged a last glance with Mr. Doherty, who still stood with his hand on the horse's flank.

Then Lord Bissell was waving his arms and shouting. Fiona's car lurched forward, prompting Mr. Doherty to dash out of the way of Caroline's start. Already behind, she gave a flick of her whip, and they were off.

"Huzzah, me girl," Caroline's father bellowed. "Swift as the wind, ye are!"

The wind snatched his words away as she attempted to make up lost time. Urging her horse into greater speed, she assessed that she had little time to gain the advantage before the gatehouse was obtained. Casting her gaze at what was meant to be the finish line, she realized that the gate was shut.

Her alarm eased when the gatekeeper ran out through the doorway of the gatehouse and began to fumble with the latch. She knew that she ought to slow down to ensure that the gate was fully open before she barreled through. It was then she noticed how very narrow was the area spanned by the gate. They could not hope to race side-by-side under the arch of the gatehouse without either crashing into each other or the gatehouse. The only solution was for her or Fiona to pull far enough ahead of the other so that they went through the arch one by one.

She had only a moment to determine which course would be hers, to slow down or to go even faster. If she chose to go faster and she ran into trouble, the choice would no longer be hers. Even if she pulled back on the reins, the horse would never be able to stop in time. She checked and saw that the horses were neck and neck. Her ears burst with the sound of their hoofs against the road. The dust as it rose in the air partially clouded her view of the gate, but she knew it could not yet be fully opened.

"Throw it wide!" she cried as she leaned forward in her seat and gave the horse a crack of her whip. Leaving the gate to its keeper, she concentrated on pulling far enough ahead that the cars did not catch together at the wheels. Fiona gave no indication that she was aware of the possible danger; their mutual safety appeared to be the sole province of Caroline. Once her horse's nose cleared the gate, she nearly cheered aloud. Then, to her horror, she realized the person in the most immediate danger was the gatekeeper. He would be required to run like the wind to avoid being struck by the jaunting car as it went past.

Just as she was about to submit to the urge to pull back on the reins, the way cleared, and she was through the gate. The thunderous echo of the car as it passed under the stone archway of the gatehouse assailed her ears, and then, to her relief, she was through to the other side, and all was well. By the time she had brought her car round again, Fiona was through, as well, and slowing her horse to a trot. Their eyes met, and together they burst into laughter.

"I don't know why it all seems so amusing," Caroline called out as Fiona lined her car up with the other. "What a fine thing that we are both such capable drivers."

"I agree," Fiona said as she wiped the tears from her face. "And yet, I find that I am about to have a fit of the vapors."

This observation set them to laughing again so that, for a few moments, speech was rendered impossible.

"Oh, my," Caroline said, tears of hysteria flowing down her face. "We must restrain ourselves! If we don't drive the cars back to the house, they shall be riding out to rescue us."

"Yes." Fiona took a few deep breaths. "I believe you are correct. Until we are seen, they shall be anxious for our welfare."

It was a sobering thought, one that had the desired dampening effect. This time, Caroline held back to allow Fiona to drive through the gatehouse ahead of her. As she followed her friend, Caroline noted that her horse was not in the least winded, and evidently anticipating another race. She should have taken into account the horse's experience and superior instincts from the beginning. The danger had, in fact, been minimal, though her tumult of emotions felt entirely genuine.

As they drew near to the guests clustered at the other end of the drive, cheers filled the air, but she had no thought but to assess the reaction of Mr. Doherty. She quickly discovered him standing nearer to the house than the others. He smiled, but she thought he looked paler than usual. By the time she had drawn to a halt, he was well-placed to assist her in stepping down from the car.

She expected him to leap onto the car to assist her in descending, and was surprised when he merely held out his arms to her. Without a thought for her safety, she jumped; he caught her skillfully at the waist. As he lowered her to the ground, she noted the apprehension in his face. He had been afraid for her! She smiled her gratitude as her feet touched the gravel of the drive, but immediately lost her balance.

Taking her by the elbow, he steadied her. "Forgive me," he murmured, "I forgot myself. It's the lads who are always wanting to jump."

"There is nothing to forgive," she said with another smile.

"Ah, me girl, what a hand at the toolin' ye are!" her father cried as he approached. "I t'ought surely you would never make it," he said as he pulled her close and wrapped his arms around her.

It was not the embrace for which she longed. He held her so tightly that she could barely draw breath, a mercy when one considered the stink of alcohol on his breath. As the fetor rose from his clothing, it was obvious that he had feared for her life, as well.

"I am quite all right, Papa, as you can see," she said with a hand at his chest. She pushed herself from the circle of his arms and looked about. "Who shall race next?"

"After that feat, who should dare?" Lord Bissell cried, evidence of his admiration in every word.

"I dare!" Lady Anne cried as she hurried to the jaunting car Fiona had only just vacated through the offices of Mr. Wilkinson.

"Would you be kind enough to hand me up?" she asked him, her smile sweet.

"But, of course," he said in some surprise. He lost no time, however, in handing her up to the seat. He also stood beside the vehicle until she was settled in the case she lost her balance and fell.

Once seated, she bent down to favor him with a beaming smile. "You are a true gentleman." She took the reins in her hands and asked in a loud, clear voice, "Who shall race against me?" She punctuated her challenge with a flick of the reins, which sent the horse into sudden motion. As the car moved forward with a lurch, Mr. Wilkinson gave a cry and fell to the ground. There was a collective gasp as the others surged to his side so quickly that Caroline could not see him through the crowd. Lord Chorley, who had been near so as to smile his pleasure in his daughter, was first to Mr. Wilkinson's side.

"The wheel has run over his foot!" he cried. "That blasted beast had no call to take off like that!"

"Carter," Lady Bissell said to the butler, who had been standing by in the case he was needed, "arrange for someone to fetch the physician."

"I shall go this instant!" Mr. Doherty insisted. "It shall be faster to take the jaunting car than to run to the stables and have a horse saddled," he suggested.

"Yes, you are quite right," Lady Bissell said. "Now, go!"

Caroline watched with mingled admiration and misgiving as Mr. Doherty leapt up onto the seat and drove off at a spanking pace. Mr. Wilkinson, his face blanched with pain, was supported on either side by Lord Chorley and Lord Bissell. Mr. Knight assisted Lady Anne in descending her jaunting car, whilst the other guests made way for the wounded and his escort. Just as they reached the front steps, a cloud burst overhead and poured rain down upon the proceedings.

Caroline looked to Fiona and saw the anxiety on her face. "My dear," she said as she went to her friend's side, "let us get out of this rain."

"I agree, but I am concerned for the lads," she replied. "Where can they be?"

Caroline looked about and saw no sign of them. "They must have already returned to the house. I am certain their mother would not have forgotten them."

"Yes, you are right," Fiona said, though she still looked overwrought.

"It is Mr. Wilkinson, for whom you are most concerned, is it not?"

Fiona nodded as Caroline gathered her to her side and drew her towards the house. They were the last of all assembled to step inside, and were met by an array of wet hats and gloves that had been abandoned by their owners. Carter indicated that they should divest themselves of their wet things, whilst a footman scuttled back and forth with as much as he could carry into the antechamber to dry by the fire.

Most of the guests had made their way into the drawing room, whilst the three men made their labored way up the stairs to Mr. Wilkinson's room. Caroline watched as they finally disappeared into the passage above. She did not lack compassion for poor Mr. Wilkinson, yet it was the way in which Fiona responded to the stoic manner that most dampened her spirits. He had surely risen in her esteem from her initial opinion of interesting to wildly romantic. Should she offer to sit by his bed and nurse him, Caroline feared she could expect to learn he had offered marriage in a matter of days.

She sighed and turned to her friend. "Let us go upstairs and change into dry clothing."

"Yes," Fiona said weakly. "I do believe this has all been too much."

"I think perhaps you ought to rest. We shall go directly to your room," Caroline insisted as they slowly mounted the steps, "and get you into bed. Then I shall find someone to bring you some warm milk."

Fiona nodded, and when the time came for Caroline to peel off her friend's wet half-boots and pelisse, she resisted not at all. "If we had a maidservant, she would carry these off to dry somewhere," Fiona mused.

"Yes, but it is Mr. Doherty for whom I am apprehensive," Caroline said before she had considered the wisdom of airing her thoughts. "He is most certainly wet through and through by now. Who does for him in these circumstances? Is he to put his clothing in front of a little fire up in his tiny room in the attics?" Caroline wondered.

"It is doubtful that he has a valet, but I am persuaded they shall take care of him in the servants' quarters, aren't you?" Fiona replied. "It is Mr. Wilkinson for whom we should be concerned."

"But of course, you are right. Thanks to Mr. Doherty, Mr. Wilkinson shall be cared for, whilst his rescuer needs must return to his little room at the top of the house."

"How very snappish of you!" Fiona said with a frown. "Truly, Caroline, you fret for nothing. A tutor does not live in the servants' quarters. His room ought to be near to the children as is that of a nursery maid."

Caroline forced herself to smile. "I pray that you are correct. You are right to scold me; I have been too anxious on his behalf. It is only that he was raised a gentleman of means. He was never meant to live such a life of deprivation."

"That is unfortunate, indeed. How is it, then, that he is here?" Fiona asked weakly.

"His family suffered a tragedy, and he was forced to earn his keep." Caroline offered her friend a sad smile as she folded down her blankets. "But he is lonely, Fiona, so very lonely."

"Surely he has the lads to speak to, as well as the other servants," Fiona murmured as she lay down and allowed the blankets to be pulled up under her chin. "You rather make it sound as if he were all alone."

"You have taken my meaning very well," Caroline said, sitting on the bed at Fiona's side. "Speaking only to children all day should grow tiresome, surely. He does dine with the family on occasion, but, as a servant, he may never be first to speak. As such, he is not allowed to choose the topic of conversation. All that he says is wholly determined by the remarks that go before. And as for the other servants, he is so far above them that they have nothing to say to one another. Quite naturally he does not spend his free time below stairs. It is an untenable situation. How he endures it, I do not know."

"I should think he would be relieved to allow his tongue to rest after a day of teaching," Fiona observed sleepily. "Either way, you mustn't go into a decline because of it."

"'Tis true," Caroline asserted as she rose to her feet. "I shall leave you. Come to my room when you have rested," she added with a fond smile.

Fiona, her eyes closed, nodded her approval against the pillow. "What will you do now?" she murmured.

"I believe I ought to see if there is anything I can do to help Lady Bissell."

When Fiona did not respond, Caroline went quietly from the room. Just as she shut the door behind her, Lady Bissell appeared on the landing at the top of the staircase. "I was just about to go in search of you," Caroline said as she hurried down the passage. "How might I be of use?"

"And here I was," Lady Bissell replied, "in search of you or Miss O'Sullivan. With Mr. Doherty not yet returned, there is no one to mind the children. Miss Deakin is with them now, but it is her afternoon off, and she insists on going into town. I wonder if you would be willing to stay with Charles and Christopher until Mr. Doherty returns? I shall have luncheon for the three of you sent up."

"I should be delighted," Caroline said. "I believe the school room is one flight above this, is that right?"

"It is. The door shall be open. I daresay you shall have no trouble in locating it," Lady Bissell said over her shoulder as she hurried back the way she had come.

Caroline followed in her wake as far as the landing, whereupon she went up the stairs from which she first heard Mr. Doherty sing. The open door was immediately visible, and she had no trouble in finding where it was she was meant to go. Pausing on the threshold, she surveyed the scene.

Charles sat at his desk, both a pencil and a pocket knife in his hand, one of which he employed to carve figures into the desktop. Christopher slumped in his chair, his foot swinging so that his heel pounded against the leg of his chair. He had wound his parchment into a ball with which he was playing catch. The nursery maid was seated at the desk in the front of the room. In one hand she held aloft a book that screened her view of the lads; in the other, a beastly-looking switch.

"Miss Deakin," Caroline said. "May I enter?"

The nursery maid lowered her book and offered Caroline a tight smile. "But of course. I have been waiting for your arrival. It is imperative that I keep my appointment in the village."

"Then you shall," Caroline said with genuine warmth. "I cannot think of a better way to spend my afternoon than with these dear lads."

Miss Deakin plucked a quizzing glass from the desk. Slowly, she raised it to her eyes to stare at Caroline. "You are an unusual creature, are you not, Miss Fulton?"

"I hope I am unexceptionable, even if not precisely like everyone else," Caroline replied.

Abruptly, Miss Deakin lowered the glass and rose briskly to her feet, switch in hand. "I recommend you stay behind the desk at all times." She did not favor the lads with even a look as she walked towards the door where Caroline stood. "You shall need this," she said as she handed the switch to Caroline.

"No, I do not believe that I shall," Caroline replied.

Miss Deakin's shock was evident in her eyes. "Very well; if you say so." She brushed past Caroline and into the passage.

"Is she gone?" Charles asked in hushed tones.

"She is," Caroline replied with a smirk.

The lads jumped to their feet and ran to her side.

"Well, then!" she said as she took each by the hand. "What a delightful room! You must explain everything to me."

The lads both began to chatter at once so that Caroline could not make out but one word in ten. "Lads, lads," she said, laughing, "one at a time!"

"I shall go first because I am the eldest," Charles said.

"But I have something that I must say to Miss Caro this very moment," Christopher insisted.

"Very well, Christopher, you shall have your say first," Caroline decided.

"I need the chamber pot!"

Caroline cherished a lively desire to laugh, but the expression of alarm on Charles' face put an end to her amusement.

"I shall take him to the nursery. It is just through here," Charles said as he quickly ushered his brother into the next room.

Weak with gratitude, Caroline crossed over to the window to inspect the view. She was not surprised to discover that it framed the same grassy park with its edging of ash trees as did her own. Recalling the note Mr. Doherty had lowered that morning, she opened the window and peered down to see if she could determine whether or not her room was just below where she stood. She was leaning nearly halfway out of the window when she heard a horrific screech. Whether the noise came from man or beast, she could not guess, but it was coming from somewhere beyond the ash trees, as had the others, of that she was certain.

"Miss Caro!"

She whirled about, her heart still pounding. "What is it? What is wrong?"

"Nothing. We have returned; that is all."

"Were you shouting for me?" Caroline asked. "Are you hurt?"

"No," Charles said, puzzled.

"Never mind," she assured them despite her continuing dread. "Please sit at your desks for a moment whilst I catch my breath." She went immediately to sit in the chair behind the large desk at the front of the room, and closed her eyes. So as to still the thundering of her heart, she took some deep breaths. When she again opened her eyes, the lads were standing, one on either side of her, peering into her face. Christopher, who regarded her through the quizzing glass, seemed particularly absorbed in his scrutiny.

"Oh!" she said in amusement. "What is this?"

"Christopher wants to know why it is you are so pretty," Charles offered. "I am older and do not require a glass in order to know the answer."

"I see," Caroline said gravely, despite her pressing desire to laugh aloud. "As it is not likely that we shall get through any lessons today, let us think of something else."

Christopher lowered the quizzing glass. "What kind of something?"

"Well," she drawled as she stood and returned to the window. "It seems that the rain has ceased. Perhaps we ought to go for a walk after we have eaten luncheon. You haven't had your usual ramble yet today."

This suggestion was enthusiastically approved, and once

they consumed their luncheon, the three of them found themselves out on the gravel drive.

"Let us pay a call on the gatekeeper," Caroline suggested. "He did capital work today with that gate. There was a moment when I greatly feared he would be struck by the jaunting car, but he got himself out of the way just in time."

Christopher nodded sagely. "Mr. Doherty was sick with fear for him," he revealed as they walked along the drive.

"It wasn't for John Gatekeeper that Mr. Doherty feared, you gudgeon," Charles said.

"But 'twas," Christopher insisted. "All of the ladies and gentlemen were shouting at the gatekeeper to go faster, faster, faster; Mama, too! They were smiling and excited. But Mr. Doherty was too frightened to speak."

"He did speak, Chris, you simply did notice," Charles corrected. "He marched right up to Arthur and shouted at him for not informing the gatekeeper of the race."

"Did he now?" Caroline asked, surprised. "And what did Lord Bissell say to that?"

"He said that Mr. Doherty should remember his place," Charles said with a frown. "I have never seen him so angry."

"Who was angry?" Caroline asked, her heart twisting with anguish. "Your brother or Mr. Doherty?"

"Mr. Doherty. He wished to knock my brother down; I know it!" Charles said vehemently. "I am pleased that he did not; I should not wish Mr. Doherty to leave us."

"Then it is right that we are even now on our way to beg pardon of John Gatekeeper for our negligence," Caroline pointed out. "I am at fault as much as your brother for setting out without ensuring that it was safe."

133

"I am glad that you and Miss Fiona did not get hurt," Christopher said, taking her hand. "So was Mr. Doherty."

Caroline smiled at the thought his words conjured. "And how is it you know that?" she asked in bantering tones. "Or shall Master Charles correct you in this, as well?"

"No, he is quite right," Charles asserted. "After Mr. Doherty begged Arthur's pardon, he insisted that we return to the house. He left us in the front hall, and we peeked through the window as he paced back and forth on the portico. He was that agitated."

"We could not see the gatehouse from the window," Christopher said sadly, "so we do not know who won the race. Was it you, Miss Caro? Mr. Doherty seemed so happy when you got back, that it must have been you."

"He didn't give a farthing for who won, you dimwit!" Charles said with a roll of his eyes. "He was simply glad that she was safe, that is all."

"I am persuaded that he was happy to see both me and Miss O'Sullivan safe," Caroline insisted.

"Naturally he had no wish to see either of you hurt," Charles said.

"But you especially," Christopher added.

Caroline felt herself blush as she contemplated their words. She felt full to bursting with happiness, and there was a fluttering in her stomach. "Thank you, both," she said with kindness, "but I should not wish you to say anything that Mr. Doherty would not have me know."

The lads both hung their heads and were silent until they reached the door to the gatehouse. Charles took it upon himself to rap upon the door, and it was opened by the man who kept the gate.

"Why, Master Charles!" he said. "Master Christopher, too. It is good of you to come to call," he said with a smile for Caroline.

"Hello. I am Miss Fulton," she said. "I am afraid I must beg your pardon. I had not realized you had not been told to open the gate before I started out. Naturally, the driver of the other car followed my lead. I should never forgive myself if you had been hurt."

The gatekeeper grunted, his faded brown eyes alive with understanding. "'Tis me business to open the gate. I am only happy t'at none were hurt."

"Thank you." She favored him with a warm smile. "I am so grateful for the same."

"Is t'here anyt'ing else I can do for ye?" the gatekeeper asked.

"There is," Caroline revealed. "Master Charles and Christopher, do run along back to the house. I shall be with you directly."

Charles immediately did as he was told, whilst Christopher dragged his feet and investigated several matters of interest to him along the verge of the drive.

"Go on now." Caroline remained silent until certain the children had gone too far to overhear her words. "Less than an hour past," she said to the gatekeeper, "I heard a disturbance in the woods that edge the park. Did you hear it as well?"

The gatekeeper regarded her from the corner of his red-rimmed eyes as he stroked his beard. "From the woods, ye say?"

"Yes. Less than an hour past," Caroline repeated. "Please do me the courtesy of speaking the truth; you must have heard it."

"I might have. I be a bit hard o'hearing . . ." the gatekeeper began.

"A gatekeeper who is hard of hearing is soon required to find a new place to live," Caroline insisted.

The gatekeeper nodded in agreement. "If I am caught in a bit o'deception, it is only t'at me wife has been feeble as of late."

"Then you are indeed hard of hearing but do not wish it known," Caroline suggested.

"Not a-tall!" the gatekeeper said, his eyes round with alarm. "I heard t'ose cars the moment t'eir wheels began to turn. I should have had t'at gate open all the sooner but I was upstairs tending to me wife; it takes a while to get me old bones down the steps."

"I'm so very sorry," Caroline said. "But what of the sounds from the woods?"

The gatekeeper's eyes filled with tears. "'Twas the banshee, 'twas."

Caroline's chest constricted with apprehension. "A banshee," she breathed. "Yes, that must be what I heard."

"T'en t'ere is no hope for me poor wife," the gatekeeper said, choking on sobs.

"But it was not o'er your house that she was heard," Caroline insisted. "Whomever it is the banshee wails for, he or she must surely lie beneath the roof of the main house."

The gatekeeper seemed to crumple, and he put a trembling hand on her arm. "T'would be wrong for me to hope t'at ye are right. Now," he said, straightening to his full height, "I must return to me wife."

Caroline lingered until he had shut the door behind him before setting out after the lads. With every step she took, she fretted. *For whom did the banshee wail?*

Chapter Ten

Niall took the back stairs to the school room two at a time. The physician had proved difficult to locate, and Niall had been absent from his duties for too long. Pausing at the baize door, he considered his appearance. The rainfall had been brief but heavy, and he was wet to the skin. He slipped through the doorway, then through that of his room, and changed into dry clothes.

Quickly, he found a towel and dried his hair, which defied his attempts to brush it into a semblance of order. His cravat left much to be desired, but he dared not keep Miss Deakin waiting a moment longer. She would be anxious enough about her curtailed day off as it was.

Studying his appearance in the glass, he deemed himself presentable, then made his way down the passage to the school room door. He had conjured words of abject apology, but the moment he reached the threshold, they fled. He stared into the room, taken aback by the scene that unfolded before his eyes.

Charles and Christopher busily copied sentences from the blackboard, written in a fine but unknown hand. More surprising was their apparent willingness; they seemed happily engaged. The room itself was far tidier than he had yet seen it; the blackboard bore no unsightly white smudges and the books were nearly all perfectly perpendicular on their shelves and ordered by height. Most astonishing of all was the sight of Miss Fulton absorbed in the continued tidying of the bookcase.

As he watched her, he was shaken by the sudden violence of his emotions. He was wholly unprepared for the furor of intense desires that assailed him. He craved the right to keep her always at his side, always under his protection, always where he might merely look up, and she would be within his sight.

An image rose into his mind, one in which he walked through the door of the dispossessed Dublin townhouse. Miss Fulton stood before him, smiling at his return. He strode to her side, took her in his arms, and tenderly kissed her. She sweetly acquiesced, his attentions entirely welcome. As the vision faded, he noted how the whole of it felt far more real, more reasonable than what currently lay before him.

"Miss Fulton," he said uncertainly.

She whirled about, her expression one of vivid consternation. "Mr. Doherty!" she said in some surprise as her face relaxed into a smile. "Do come in. The lads have so much to show you."

They proved her statement correct, jumping up from their chairs to present him with their parchments filled with carefully inscribed words.

"And, we have studied our geography," Charles asserted, "and learned a phrase or two in French, as well."

"Indeed," Niall said, tousling the lad's hair. "We must contrive a means to thank Miss Fulton for her generosity."

"It is I who should thank them. They have been so very pleasant."

She smiled with such warmth that Niall fancied it was for him alone. It, together with the memory of her slight waist between his hands and the awareness in her eyes as he lifted her from the jaunting car, was nearly enough to undo him. He dropped into the nearest chair before the trembling of his limbs threatened to land him on the floor.

"You must be utterly spent!" Miss Fulton proclaimed.

"It has been rather a long day." He resisted the impulse to run a hand through his disordered hair. "The physician was not immediately available, and I was required to drive from one place to the next until he was found."

She moved to sit in the chair closest at hand. It was Christopher's, and diminutive in size. He regretted it not, as it afforded him a splendid view of the top of her head, adorned with dozens of golden curls.

"It is that odd to see you here," he said in a low voice.

"It does not feel in the least odd to me," she said happily. "The lads have been a delight."

"If only you were at hand every day. I daresay they have learned more in the few hours you oversaw the school room than in a week under my direction."

"Not at all," she denied archly. "I should never be able to teach them a single word of Latin, and I have an especial horror of mathematics. I do so love history, but only the pleasant aspects, so I am not of much use in that regard, either."

So absorbed was he in this unintentional revelation of her intelligence that he did not at first realize Lady Bissell stood in the doorway.

Niall rose hastily to his feet as Christopher cried, "Mama!" He held his work aloft. "See what I have done today!"

"Yes, indeed," Lady Bissell said, genuinely pleased. She then turned her attention to Niall. "Mr. Doherty, I must thank you for fetching the physician. Mr. Wilkinson is doing as well as expected. Miss Fulton, I must thank you, as well, for looking after the lads. It seems it was a successful afternoon."

"They were as good as gold," Miss Fulton replied.

"I do hope that is the truth. I should not like it if they were to give you any trouble," Lady Bissell said with a look for each of her sons. "Now, Mr. Doherty, as Mr. Wilkinson has been advised to refrain from walking even a very slight distance, I shall need you to make up my numbers again at dinner."

"Yes, of course," Niall replied.

"Oh!" Miss Fulton said, "In that case, I shall be needed to remain with the boys until the nursery maid arrives. She signified that she should not return until it is quite late."

Lady Bissell heaved a sigh. "I had quite forgotten that it was Miss Deakin's afternoon off. You are very generous, Miss Fulton, but if you do not appear at dinner, that shall put my numbers back at thirteen, and that I cannot have."

"Might I make a suggestion, my lady?" Niall asked. "If both Miss Fulton and I were to take our dinners on a tray, your number would be an even twelve."

Lady Bissell cocked her head and narrowed her eyes. "I suppose that should prove unexceptionable, if Miss Fulton is willing."

"Indeed, I am," Miss Fulton said graciously. "My only concern is for my father. I should not like him to be anxious on my behalf. Perhaps if you were to speak to him?"

"Shall I claim for you a slight indisposition?" Lady Bissell asked, her eyes twinkling.

"That should do very nicely," Miss Fulton replied. "Since Mr. Doherty and I shall not have a chance to sing tonight, I wonder if we might use the music room to practice again in the morning."

"Yes, but only if the lads remain in the school room with Miss Deakin," Lady Bissell replied decisively. "Today's departure from routine was quite enough."

"Thank you, Lady Bissell." Miss Fulton bobbed a curtsey. "Now, I shall just go and speak with Miss O'Sullivan before retiring to my room to read. Good evening, Mr. Doherty. Good evening, Lady Bissell." She flashed a look of uncertainty at Niall over her shoulder as she went through the doorway.

Lady Bissell kissed each of her children and took her leave, as well. "Good evening, Mr. Doherty." She shut the door behind her with such finality that it served to make Niall feel all the more isolated.

"Why has Miss Fulton gone away?" Christopher asked.

"I had thought she would have dinner with us in the nursery," Charles said.

Niall felt not one whit less bewildered. "That was certainly my intention when I suggested we each take dinner on a tray," Niall explained. "Perhaps she did not understand. Suppose we issue her a proper invitation?"

"Do you mean that we should write one for her?"

"Precisely my meaning," Niall said. He procured a piece of fresh parchment and put it on Charles' desk. "Now, what do you think we should write?"

"That she must come back," Christopher suggested. "But we must say please."

"Very good, Master Christopher. Now, Master Charles, mayhap you have an idea as to how to improve on his composition somewhat."

"I believe so," Charles said. "What if I were to write: 'Dear Miss Fulton, please join us in the nursery for dinner tonight'?"

"Excellent. Do write that, exactly."

Niall watched with mounting impatience as Charles wrote out each word with agonizing care. There was no time to lose as, once it was written, dried, sanded and sealed, Niall must still lower it on a string to Miss Fulton's window and pray that she discovered it before too much time had passed.

"Shall I pull the bell for Carter to deliver it?" Charles asked when he was satisfied with his work.

"I believe it would be best if I rang him from my room," Niall advised, taking the parchment to his own desk. "Now, whilst I am absent," he said as he quickly sanded the letter, "the two of you must make a most solemn vow to behave."

"Of course we shall, Mr. Doherty," Charles insisted. "We are not always naughty."

"Indeed, you are not," Niall said with a sense of wonder at its truthfulness. "I believe we have Miss Fulton to thank for this discovery." He held the wax stick to melt over a candle flame.

"She will come, will she not?" Christopher begged.

"We shall hope so," Niall said absently. He dripped just enough wax onto the folded parchment to ensure its closure, and rushed from the room to his own. Retrieving the string that still hung from his window, he secured the letter and lowered it down. Before he closed the window, he waited for the sound of the wax seal as it tapped against the glass of the pane below.

143

Satisfied that Miss Fulton would be alerted, he waited for a sign that she had read his message.

However, after a few minutes, Niall determined that he could wait no longer. Tying his end of the string to the window latch, he reluctantly returned to the schoolroom. To his relief, nothing of note occurred whilst he was away. He read to the lads until the dinner trays appeared.

The three of them were desultorily stirring their respective bowls of soup when Miss Fulton appeared in the doorway, bearing her tray. "Might I join you?"

Niall jumped to his feet, as did Charles, who crowed his delight.

"Have you had our letter, Miss Caro?" Christopher asked more sedately.

"Indeed, I have, and I thank you," she replied.

"Allow me to take that for you," Niall suggested as he relieved Miss Fulton of her burden. "Master Charles and Christopher, take up the other trays and follow me." He turned to her as they made their way into the next room. "They most usually eat in the nursery, but we thought it best to wait for you in the school room since that door is nearly always open. We did not wish to appear inhospitable."

Miss Fulton nodded her approval. "Shall there be a place at the table for each of us?"

"You shall have my chair, Miss Caro," Charles insisted.

"No, indeed. I could not take your place. I do not know that I am so very hungry, anyway. You take your dinner far earlier than I do most nights."

"I am that hungry and all of the time," Master Christopher said fiercely.

Niall and Miss Fulton shared a smile of amusement over the tray of food.

"Perhaps Miss Fulton, who insists she is not hungry, shall allow you to consume her dinner in her place," Niall said in jest.

"You, sir," Miss Fulton said with a playful smile, "are impudent."

In the end, each enjoyed a full plate. It was a merry meal, one which alternately filled Niall with happiness and highlighted the loneliness of his position. When they had finished, he rang for someone to take away the trays. He then banished Miss Fulton to the school room whilst the lads readied themselves for bed. Once they had climbed under the blankets, Niall went in search of their dinner guest.

She again stood at the bookcase, perhaps in admiration of her work, when he entered. "You must be tired."

Her answering smile of gladness as she turned to him nearly took his breath away. "Not at all. I have been thinking how I might while away the hours until I fall asleep. Though, there are not many books here that I have not already read; how very disappointing."

He went to examine the culprits, most of them his personal property, as a pretext to stand by her side. "I am astonished to know that you have read so widely." He ran his fingers across the spines until he found the book he sought, pulling it out for her approval.

"Shakespeare's Macbeth; I have read that, as well," Miss Fulton said.

"I saw it performed when I was in Scotland this winter past. What do you make of Banquo's words?"

Her expression was indecipherable. "'And oftentimes,'" she softly quoted, "'to win us to our harm, the instruments of darkness tell us truths, win us with honest trifles, to betray us in deepest consequence.'"

Her perception astounded him. "Yes," he said, laughing his pleasure. "Exactly the words I had in mind. Will you assist me to settle the lads?" he asked, holding his arm out to her. "Once they are asleep, perhaps you might tell me what you believe Banquo meant by such words."

She placed one hand on his arm and with the other slid the volume of Shakespeare from his grasp. "My evening has been rescued," she said, her expression one of utter contentment.

His chest swelled with happiness; to have pleased her was the happiest of consequences. "If they quickly fall asleep, there might be time for the story I have been meaning to tell you, as well," he suggested.

Her answering smile, as they walked into the nursery, was full of promise. Releasing his arm, she went directly to sit on Christopher's bed.

Niall decided that Charles would take offense at such infantile treatment and perched on the chair beside his bed. "Who is ready to sleep?" he asked.

"Not I," Charles said with an unnerving promptness. "If I do, I shall wake in the morning to find Miss Caro gone."

"I shall not be far, little one," Miss Fulton replied. "I shall only be in my own chamber, on the floor just below this."

Niall's gaze flew to hers. She said nothing as to whether or not she suspected the truth regarding the placement of his bed just above hers, but the glint in her eye made him uneasy.

"The schoolroom is far nicer with Miss Caro in it," Christopher artlessly revealed.

Niall held her gaze in his own as he replied. "Indeed, it is. I wonder why that is so."

She blushed and looked away. However, despite her efforts, she could not hide her smile.

"It is because she made everything so tidy," Charles stated. "Also, she has pretty eyes and pretty hair, and I like her gown."

"And she is always smiling," Christopher added. "Smiles are lovely, are they not, Mr. Doherty?"

Niall could not restrain a grin in response. "Indeed, they are, especially on Miss Fulton. Now, is it a story you'll be having tonight?"

"I don't think so," Charles said slowly. "I should prefer a song; a duet by you and Miss Fulton."

"Yes!" Christopher eagerly endorsed his brother's suggestion. "Sing songs. Pretty ones."

"Are you of a mind, then, to sing with me, Miss Fulton?" he asked.

"If it pleases the lads, then I shall sing for them, yes."

They sang first the tune they had practiced that morning in the music room. For the rest, Miss Fulton knew every tune Niall suggested, perhaps even every Irish ditty ever composed. It only required five for Christopher to nod off and one more to sink Charles into a deep slumber.

"How strange," Miss Fulton murmured, "to see them here asleep and all the while a party is going on downstairs. I should be not at all surprised if they still sit at table as we speak."

Niall grunted. "And the lads, they are up with the sun."

"How weary you must be. I ought to go to my own chamber so that you may retire for the night." She began to rise from her seat, but he put his hand on her arm to prevent her.

"'Twould be too cruel!" he insisted in low tones, so as not to wake the lads. "You have promised to remain a while," he reminded her.

"Very well. Tell me, though, what you would be doing now if I had gone."

Niall relaxed again into his chair. "I frequently spend this time preparing lessons for the next day, or in reading. If it is my afternoon off, I am usually still in the village at this hour when the weather is fine."

"Do you have friends you call upon there?" she asked.

"I have not been here long enough to have made any. I confess that I am usually too worn out to be much company to anyone. Gratefully, Miss Deakin has charge of the lads until time for lessons. However, my chamber is not far from theirs, and they can be quite exuberant," he said with a shake of his head.

"Ah! That brings to mind a question I have for you," she said in triumph. "Is it from the school room or the nursery that you lower your notes to me?"

Niall's lungs seemed to freeze. For some reason he did not care to examine, he did not wish her to know that he slept in such proximity to her. "It has proved to be a convenient means of communicating, has it not?"

"Indeed. I had never given much thought to the plight of a tutor or nursery maid until I came to Oak View. There seems to be none with whom to speak of your thoughts and feelings. A man such as you, one filled with a wealth of knowledge, must find it insufferable."

Niall could not contain his awe of her continual perception. "It is as if you have read my very thoughts. This is my third post as tutor; it only grows more challenging. But let us speak of other things. Tell me your interpretation of the words of Banquo."

"Very well; we know he is speaking to Macbeth." The bed squeaked as she rose to take up a chair out of the summer twilight streaming through the window. "I believe that he is offering him a warning. Banquo seems conversant with the sort of betrayal that comes of half-truths spoken by those who wish to deceive us, or worse, intend us harm."

"I concur," he mused. Unbidden, the matchmaker entered his thoughts. He could not help but wonder if her words were half-truths, and if she intended evil by them. Forcing her from his mind, he turned his thoughts to the present. "I am ashamed to admit that I think of her as such, but I fear Lady Anne is just such a deceiver."

"Perhaps she is, but I shall not allow her to wound me," Miss Fulton said in spritely tones. "I am afraid, however, of something else. I did not wish to speak of it when the children were awake."

Her face, aglow in the light of the fire, was stirred by emotion. He could have happily watched it forever. "Tell me."

"It is regarding the sounds coming from the woods. I heard something again this afternoon when I was in the school room. I was alone; Master Charles had taken his brother to . . . Well, let us say," she said, adorably flustered, "that he was in need of

149

privacy. When they returned, they gave no indication that they had heard a thing." She drew a deep breath, and her hands trembled in her lap. "It was different this time, more of a screech or a wail than the thumping I heard before. Afterwards, we went for a walk and spoke with the gatekeeper. He heard it, as well. Mr. Doherty," she said slowly as an eerie silence settled over the room. "He said it was the banshee."

Niall was taken aback. "A banshee? Do they not usually do their work at night?" He was soon to regret his words, as she looked immediately to the ceiling through which a banshee on the roof would be most easily heard. "There is no need to be frightened. When a banshee takes to wailing, everyone is sure to be hearing it."

"Then you believe in banshees?" she asked in disbelief. "Old, supernatural crones who wail to warn of an impending death in the house?"

"Ah, well, I wouldn't claim to believe in them. Only, if there were one, she would have made herself better heard, you see."

Miss Fulton bit her lip and nodded, her eyes wide. "Perhaps you might give me your story now."

"I should like that very much." In truth, he would have been more pleased to take her face in his hands, stare into her unfathomable eyes, and kiss her perfect pink lips. "This story is one that I have not been able to put out of my mind since I told 'The Children of Lir.' It is called 'The Swan Bride.' As you may well know, the swan has long been favored amongst the peoples of Ireland. It is said that the white swans of the wilderness were the children of the Tuatha de Danaan, also known as the sidhe.

Swans are associated with purity, love, music, and the soul, as well as with deities of the sun and healing waters. When the time comes to travel to the Otherworld, it is the swan that aids us in the journey."

"Let us not speak of the Otherworld just now," she said with a shiver. "'Tis 'The Swan Bride,' is it? I do not recall having heard such a story."

"Then I shall take e'en more delight in the tellin' of it," Niall said. "A year and a day ago, there was a king of Ireland who, in his old age, lost his wife. He had naught left but his son called Eoin. As the king was not long for this world, he told Eoin that he must find a bride. However, she must be the right woman, the very one for him. 'Twas important in those days, you see, that a man find the very one who was made for him; to marry her, and no other. The only person who could tell them the truth of such matters was a druid. So, the king had the druid brought to him and the question was put: 'Who should be the bride of my son?'" It was only as Niall was saying the words that he wondered if such information might prove more accurate from a druid than a wandering matchmaker.

"The druid claimed that only the youngest daughter of the White-Bearded Scolog could be the wife of Eoin. The druid, however, did not know how to find this Scolog. So, Eoin took his leave and traveled to the home of his foster-mother. 'Twas she who told him of her three brothers who all lived on the same road he must take to find his bride. However, they lived far and away out of Ireland, and were all three murderous giants. 'But I have the remedy for that,' she said and went into the kitchen, returning with three cakes made of flour. 'When my youngest brother comes at ye, ye must touch him on the breast with a cake and then he will be delighted to welcome ye. He will tell ye how to get to the next brother's house, and he the next. Each must be touched on the breast with a cake, or they shall kill ye. It is the last who will tell ye how to find Scolog and his daughter.'

"So, Eoin took the cakes and traveled long and far. When he came to the castle of the first giant, a woman greeted him at the door. When Eoin explained why he had come, the woman sat him down to wait. The giant could be heard returning home long before he came through the door. He had a live boar under one arm and with the other he wielded a thorny club. He was that angry and threw down the boar whilst he charged at Eoin. But Eoin was quick, and touching the giant with the cake, found, to his amazement, that it did all that was required. Immediately the giant welcomed Eoin, fed him a splendid meal, and put him to bed on a mattress of feathers. In the morning, Eoin was fed just as splendidly and sent on his way to the second brother.

"This visit went much like the first except that the second brother gave to Eoin a Curragh in which to sail to the home of the third brother. This last giant lived in a luxurious castle high on a promontory overlooking the sea. After feasting, this giant asked Eoin why he had come, and the lad told his story from beginning to end. 'Ah,' said the giant, 'I shall tell ye what ye must do.'" As Niall told the tale, he was surprised at how much emotion it stirred in him. He felt an affinity for Eoin despite the fact that he was far more obedient than Niall.

"The giant said that the next day, at noon, Eoin would

come to a lake. He was instructed to hide and wait. 'Twelve swans will land in the rushes,' the giant said, 'and remove their orange crests. When they do, the feathers will fall from them, and they will turn into the most beautiful women you have ever seen. Once they have gone into the lake to bathe, you must take their crests.' The giant went on to instruct him thusly: that he should return all of the crests but one, that of the youngest. To her he should say that he cannot return it until she carries him over the sea to her father's castle on the Isle of Enchantment. 'She will say that she has not the power,' the giant warned, 'but if ye refuse to return the crest, she will be forced to agree.'

"All happened as the giant said and soon Eoin was being carried on the swan-maiden's back over the water to Scolog's castle. She warned him that every suitor who came to the door was killed immediately and that there was only one way to avoid such a fate. 'Stand with your head under the lintel, your right foot inside the threshold, and your left foot outside. If you vary from this in any way, he will cut off your head.'

"Eoin did just as he was told. He was taken to a stable and given a paltry dinner and a poor bed. As he wondered how he was to make a meal of what he was given, the youngest daughter of Scolog appeared. She magically provided him with a delicious meal and a luxurious bed upon which to sleep, and told him that in the morning, he was to turn the bed over whereupon it would shrivel into a little stick which he was then to throw into the fire. He did as he was told and was glad of it, as her father sought him out first thing in the morning.

"'This is your task,' said Scolog. 'On my property is a lake. You are to drain it by digging through a neck of land two miles

153

wide, and here is the spade to do it. You must be done by evening, or I shall take the head off ye.' Eoin was taken to the lake, and he began to dig. For every sod he dug out, seven grew back. In despair, he threw the spade, sat down on the ground, and began to cry.

"That is when the daughter appeared to him with a bundle and a cloth in her hands. 'Why are ye crying?' asked she. 'My head shall be off come sunset,' Eoin said. She shook her head and opened the bundle, whereupon there appeared a fortifyin' breakfast for him. Whilst he ate, she dug up some sod, threw it away and lo, every piece of sod jumped up and followed the first. Soon the land was gone, and the lake drained dry.

"At the end of the day, the girl provided Eoin with a lavish dinner and went away before her father came. He was unhappy to see that Eoin had accomplished the task, and he went away wondering how he could best him the next day. This time, Eoin was required to cut down a huge tree, make enough barrels out of it to cover the field in which the tree stood, and fill them all with water before the sun set.

"Eoin went to work. The first blow of the ax bounced off the tree and hit him in the head, leaving a great gash. He struck it a second and a third time so that he finally fell to the ground, the blood and the life pouring out of the three gashes in his head. To his great relief, the daughter appeared. She laid out his breakfast as before and whilst he ate, she cut a chip out of the tree with an ax. The chip turned into a barrel and other chips followed until the field was full of barrels. She then produced a wooden dipper and a pail and set the king's son to work filling them up.

"As he worked, she told him of what he must do next. 'My father will invite you to sleep in the castle tonight, but you must refuse. Tell him that you are happy to lodge where you have for the last two nights." With that, she disappeared. All happened as she said and Scolog again went away annoyed. Eoin went to his lodgings, and the swan-girl appeared once again with his bed and supper.

"The next day the task he was set was to build a castle out of stone he chipped from a quarry. He was to fill it, also, with priceless furnishings, servants, and luxuries of every kind. Once Scolog departed, his daughter appeared and gave Eoin his breakfast. Then she made one chip with the chisel, and the most grandiose castle built itself, complete with all that her father required. When all was complete save one spot by the hearth, she handed Eoin the trowel and told him that he must do the last bit himself. 'When my father comes, he will invite you again to stay in the castle. This time, ye must agree. After dinner, he shall throw red wheat onto the table, and three pigeons will come and eat it. My father will ask you to choose which of his three daughters ye wish to marry, and ye must choose me. I shall be the one with the black speck on my wing.'

"When the time came, Eoin saw the black speck and made his choice. Immediately, the three pigeons jumped from the table and turned into three beautiful women. A priest and a clerk were called, and Eoin was married to Scolog's youngest daughter that very night. When the festivities were over, Eoin wished to return to his own kingdom, but his bride warned him that it would not be so very easy.

"'My father will agree to let us go, but he will follow and try to kill you. Before we leave, he will offer us a horse and shall take you to a field to choose. There will be many beautiful horses, but you must choose the old, gray nag because she is my mother, enchanted by my father.' So, Eoin was taken to choose, just as she said. When the choice was made, and Eoin was mounted on the horse, the girl turned into a swan and bore the nag with her husband into the air over the mountains and out to sea.

"When Scolog saw that Eoin had escaped him, he turned himself into large balls of red fire and went off after them. He found them on an island where they had stopped to rest from their journey for the night. When the daughter saw him comin', she turned the nag into a boat, Eoin into a ragged fisherman, and herself into a fishin' rod.

"As such, Scolog did not recognize them and went all round the earth in search of them until he ended up back at his own castle. He started out again and this time, he caught up to them on a different island. The daughter made a spinnin' wheel of her mother, an old hag of her husband, and bundle of flax of herself. Scolog asked if they had seen a couple on a gray mare and Eoin, as the old woman, replied that they had been seen fifty miles north.

"Scolog went all round the world again, and when he caught up with them, he saw them in their natural form as they landed safely on the shores of Ireland. Scolog cursed angrily, but he had no power in Ireland and was forced to watch the three of them borne away in a chariot drawn by four white horses. When Eoin brought his wife and her mother home to his father's castle, the king wept tears of joy. And then he laughed when he realized that he now had, in his old age, a wife of his very own.

"And that, my dear Miss Fulton," Niall said, gazing into her lovely face, "is the story of The Swan Bride."

Chapter Eleven

Mr. Doherty sat back in his chair as the spell the story wove dissolved into the air.

Caroline heaved a sigh of pleasure. "That was a most captivating tale. Why is it, I wonder, that the women of Irish mythology are all so gifted and strong?"

"Do you?" He searched her face. "I have yet to meet one who was otherwise."

Blushing, she looked away; she knew his words for the compliment he intended. "You are speaking of Miss O'Sullivan. Lady Bissell, as well."

He said nothing in reply as he leaned forward and possessed himself of Caroline's hand. "Tell me, Miss Fulton. Once you are the baron's wife, do you see yourself sitting here, with me in the nursery, listening to stories as you are tonight?"

"That would most likely be impossible," she said, tears starting in her eyes.

"And what of singing by the pianoforte after dinner?" He stroked the back of her hand with this thumb.

She shook her head. "I don't know." It was the truth; she could think of little but the tingling of her skin beneath his.

He brushed his finger along her cheek, and held it up against the light of the fire. Caroline turned away from the sight; she already knew that his finger shone with her tears.

"I cannot stay," she said, rising to her feet. "I must go."

He rose as well. "Wait," he said, refusing to release her hand. "I will light a candle in the case the fire in your room has been allowed to die down."

"Thank you, but there is no need." She hurried to the door, but he followed.

"Miss Fulton, please, I must beg of you a boon."

She turned to look at him over her shoulder. The pain in his eyes prompted in her an emotion far deeper than compassion or even pity; she felt faint with the weight of his woe. "Very well," she whispered, so he would not hear the tears in her voice.

"I must ask you to meet me; at the brook, early; before breakfast. I shall not beguile from you too much of your time; the lads shall be looking for me directly after breakfast."

She could do no such thing, and yet she felt her head bob up and down in agreement. Quickly, before she did aught else she might regret, she opened the door and fled down the passage. She descended the stairs as quietly as she was able, and felt herself safe once she turned into the passageway that led to her room. Leaning against the wall, she waited until her heart regained its former pace and her breathing quieted. To her relief, the wall sconces had been lit since she had gone to the school room and she was soon safe in her own chamber.

The fire had indeed been stoked whilst she was out, and it burned merrily in the grate. There was nothing left for her to do but burst into tears and throw herself onto the bed. It lurched noisily against the wall, but she knew the other guests would still be in the drawing room and would not be disturbed by her actions. This left her free to cry until she was so spent she could not muster the strength to rise.

Miserable, she lay still until her head cleared and she could decide what was to be done. She did not wish to marry the baron, of that she was certain. Nor did she wish to hurt her papa. To alienate her dearest friend was a thought most untenable; the danger of adding one whit to Mr. Doherty's sorrow unbearable.

And what of her own sorrow if she were parted from him? She had never met anyone she liked as well as Mr. Doherty. He was everything she could wish for in a husband. She attempted to picture herself as she boarded her father's carriage bound for The Hollows and could not. The very notion filled her with desolation. Too weary to stay awake long enough for Fiona to come and help her undress, Caroline decided to sleep in her gown. It would be more convenient should she slip out early to meet Mr. Doherty, anyhow.

It was as she waited for sleep to claim her that she heard it: the wail from the direction of the ash trees. Her heart immediately began to hammer, and she lay in fear for what seemed like an eternity. Once she calmed a little, she heard what seemed to her a soft echo of the previous wail. Listening carefully, refusing even to breathe, she thought she could make out a low moaning that went on and on. It seemed somehow less frightening than the screeching, and she was soon overcome by fatigue.

She woke with the sun, knowing she could not prevent herself from meeting with Mr. Doherty. He deserved the opportunity to speak with her, and with what privacy they could arrange. As she bundled her hair into a bandeau, she found that her fears had somehow vanished. Nothing had been resolved but, somehow, the doubts she had entertained in regard to her father's and Fiona's disapproval had melted away.

The house was very quiet as she slipped down the stairs to the first floor, and down again to the front hall. The footmen had not yet taken up their posts by the door, and she was able to quit the house entirely unseen. The gravel in the drive seemed intolerably loud beneath her feet, and she was glad to make her way onto the grass. As she moved towards the stream, she spared a glance to her left. The row of ash trees that edged the park were still in shadow, whilst the stream on her right sparkled in the rays of the rising sun.

She endeavored to prepare for whatever it was Mr. Doherty wished to discuss, but her thoughts were continually drawn away by the beauty of the day. The lawn she walked upon felt spongy, and the breeze blew soft against her face. The effect of the sun on her skin tantalized nearly as much as the trilling of the birds. Though she had expected to feel utterly spent, she felt every bit as vibrant as the water that chortled along the stream.

When the stream became a brook, she moved down the side of the bank to the water's edge. Though he hadn't mentioned precisely where he would wait for her, she knew she would find him at the spring. Picking her way carefully among the rocks, she looked up and there he was. The sight transfixed her, just as it had the night she had first seen him.

He stood with his head bowed, his far hand braced against a tree. His other hung at his side, his long fingers turning over and over an object that flashed in the sun.

She knew she ought not to spy on him, nor did she wish to

deprive him of his privacy by revealing her presence. Unsure of which course to take, she continued to watch as he stared into the water. Suddenly, the tension in his shoulders eased, and he began to speak, too softly for her to discern the words. Then he drew back his hand and tossed the object into the deepest part of the water, just below the well of the shrine.

He peered again into the water and, seemingly satisfied, leaned back against the tree, his gaze trained on the ground. Just as she was about to go to him, he lifted his gaze and saw her. He became utterly still, as if to draw a single breath might frighten her away, his eyes brilliant under black brows. She realized that he had believed she would not come; that he read some significance into the fact that she was there.

Suddenly she was overwhelmed with doubts and fears. She had come to Oak View to please her father and, if possible, the baron as well. She had promised her dearest friend that she would not entertain the attentions of the tutor. How could she please them and herself as well? As she and Mr. Doherty gazed at one another, the questions were replaced with one consummate truth: there was nothing she wanted more than to ease the loneliness of the man who stood in wait of her.

She took a step forward, and he sprang to life. Splashing through the water to meet her, he took her hand and led her to the spring. She leaned on his arm in order to gain her footing along the side of the shrine until, together, they stood at the water's edge and looked about.

"I heard it," he said quietly. "The wailing, after you had gone. Does it frighten you?"

"Not now," she said, looking up into his face. "Not when I am with you."

He frowned as if her words pained him. "There is something else. Yesterday, when I was in the village, there was talk of a highway robbery. It is said that it happened the night prior."

"How dreadful! Was anyone hurt?" she asked in alarm.

"Shots were fired, but I do not believe anyone was injured."

"Then I am glad, but," she said, pausing to consider her words, "this is why you wished to meet?"

"I hesitated to speak of it before you retired for the night. The wailing that so frightens you was enough, or so I thought. Have I done wrong?"

"No, you were right to delay; I was frightened enough as 'twas. Only, I wonder that you did not simply tell me of it later today when we are in the music room."

He nodded. "Perhaps I was too anxious on your behalf. Truly, I only wished to warn you as soon as possible. I beg you not to go into the village alone," he said fervently. "Take an escort, such as your father or one of the baron's other guests; one in possession of a firearm."

"Very well, I shall do as you ask," she said, crestfallen. "Is there anything else you wished to say?"

He gave her a terse smile, and she knew he meant to deny the necessity for any further confidence. Then his face fell, and he sagged away from her to lean his shoulder against the tree. He said nothing at first as he reached up to pluck a leaf from the branch above his head. Shredding it between his fingers until only the stem remained, he tossed it into the water beneath the well of the shrine. Together they watched as it was carried away by the current.

"I suppose you witnessed my offering to St. Brigid," he said with a pointed gaze at the shrine. "It was the last possession I had of my father's; the only one not claimed by the debtors."

"How precious it must have been to you! I myself wear my mother's ring every day of my life, though I cannot recall ever having met her." She held out her hand to display the ring with its row of blue-gray rhinestones.

"It is lovely. So was my pocket watch," he said wryly. "It was cased in gold and rather valuable."

She strained to catch a glimpse of it shining in the water, but could not. "You must have sunk it very deep."

"It is best. Should the brook run dry, the offering will be exposed. If so, the gift I seek will be taken from me or never given in the first place. It is what the old ones believed," he said with a shrug.

"You must have requested something singularly remarkable to have taken such care," she prompted, her heart pounding in anticipation of his reply.

He opened his mouth then pressed his lips together. "I have not the right," he said, shaking his head. "And yet, I find that I cannot hold back the words." He turned to face her, leaning his back against the tree. "There is a notion buried deep within my heart that says you are meant to be mine. I cannot argue with it; I cannot silence it; it insists that you, like Eoin's swan bride, were made for *me* and no other."

Her heart soared; she had hoped for these words! "Mr. Doherty," she began, but paused in confusion. What exactly was she to say? He had not asked for her hand. She stared into his eyes, willing him to divine her desire. When he did not, she took a step closer and leaned her cheek against his chest. She felt how his heart beat beneath her ear; how his breath caught in his lungs at her touch. Breathlessly, she waited for him to wrap his arms around her and crush her against him.

Instead, he put his hands on her shoulders and gently moved her away. "Have a care. You do not know what it is you do."

"Do I not?" she asked hotly, stumbling a bit as she regained her footing. "Do you suppose my feelings vary so widely from your own?"

"I cannot say. I have not dared to hope." He reached out to caress her face, his hand trembling.

Covering it with her own, she pressed her cheek into his palm. She saw how his gaze vacillated from her eyes to her lips and back again with such affection that her knees weakened, and her stomach fluttered.

"My dear Miss Fulton," he murmured, "I have been so alone."

"You are alone no longer," she said breathlessly, yearning for him to comprehend the state of her heart.

He raised his other arm and took her face in his hands, then suddenly dropped both to his side. "The gift of your affection," he said as he took her fingers and drew them to his lips, "shall keep me company long after you have gone." The kiss he seared into her skin spoke of a tenderness unknown by mere affection.

She looked away, her eyes filling with hot tears. "How I long to have been born in an opposing world," she murmured, her gaze fixed on the mighty Ben Bulben in the distance. "One

165

in which I might, with ease, behave like Maeve of old and choose my fate. Or even better, the swan bride who not only chose but who gave of her talents so as to determine her path. I should remain silent for seven years as did the daughter of Lir, and happily so if it won me a husband I could truly love."

"How do you not perceive the truth?" he said, briefly taking her chin in his fingers and drawing her round to face him. "You are every one of them. You are strong and self-possessed like Queen Maeve. Your talents, beauty, and intelligence have worked magic on my heart. My fate was nearly as lonely as that of a child of Lir until you arrived to rescue me from my solitude."

She swallowed the lump that rose in her throat. "I am glad of it," she said, smiling so as to prevent herself from bursting into tears. "I suppose that we now must look about us for a chariot to appear and carry us off to our castle."

He gave a shaky laugh. "'Tis true, 'twould require magic such as that."

"Or perhaps such as *that*," she indicated, tilting her head in the direction of the shrine.

He smiled as he gazed intently into her eyes. "One can hope. Now," he said with a sigh. "I must return to the school room, and you are surely expected somewhere, as well. It is best if we are not seen together; perhaps you should go first," he suggested. "I shall follow when it is safe. As I shall be using the servants' staircase, we shall not be in danger of meeting on the landing."

She nodded again, her gaze full of him; the light in his eyes, the curve of his smile, committing them to memory as if she were never to see him again. Then she turned and fled as swiftly as she dared. She picked her way along the side of the stream and marched up the bank. As she crossed the lawn back to the house, she was relieved to find that all was still quiet; no one stirred. Only the footmen, who had taken up their posts by the door, saw her as she passed through the doorway and up the staircase.

Praying that it was too early to encounter anyone else, she quickly continued on her way. She was nearly to her chamber when farther down the hall a door opened, and Fiona stepped out into the passage.

"Caro!" she said. "I have waited for you, but you have not come. I thought I would go to you."

"I am sorry. I . . . I am late," Caroline said weakly.

"Oh, no, Caro, this will never do!"

She fought to prevent her alarm from showing on her face. "Won't it?"

"Not the jonquil gown again! What about the dull red jacquard? It is my favorite of your day dresses," Fiona said as she took Caroline by the arm and drew her into her chamber.

"Thank you," Caroline replied with as much equanimity as she could muster. "I wonder that I did not think of it myself."

There was a rustling of skirts as Fiona sorted through the gowns in Caroline's clothes press. "Here 'tis," Fiona said, pulling it out for Caroline's approval. "I believe it is finest paired with your blue sash, but you must decide for yourself."

"The blue, then," Caroline agreed. "What say you to this bandeau in my hair?"

"It's lovely, but not with this gown," Fiona said doubtfully.

"If it is not rude of me to ask, why did you not come down to dinner?"

"Oh!" Caroline said, unprepared for such a question. "That is indeed a tale. Do turn about and allow me to tie your tapes whilst I tell you." Fiona obeyed, and Caroline set to work. "When I left you after the jaunting car race, I encountered Lady Bissell in the passage. She was desirous of someone to sit in the school room with her sons, as Mr. Doherty had not yet returned with the physician. Quite naturally, I was pleased to do so. When she came to see the boys some time later, she asked Mr. Doherty to come down to dinner, as Mr. Wilkinson is too lame and she did not wish to cope with uneven numbers."

"Poor Mr. Wilkinson!" Fiona said fervently. "I am surprised that you were alone, however, with Mr. Doherty in the school room," she said with such a contrasting lack of concern, Caroline could only wonder.

"We were not alone," she said as she submitted to having the tapes of her jonquil gown untied. "There were the lads, and it was only for a few moments before Lady Bissell arrived."

"Then why did Mr. Doherty not come to dinner?"

"It was the nursery maid's afternoon off," Caroline replied as she stepped out of her gown. "It fell to Mr. Doherty to sit with the lads until she returned, which, I have been told, is sometimes rather late. I suggested that it was I who should stay with them, but, as he pointed out, even if I did, there would still be uneven numbers at dinner." Caroline was aware that she was babbling, but she hadn't the least desire to share the complete account with Fiona. She would not approve.

"I comprehend that uneven numbers are far from

desirable," Fiona asserted. "However, under the circumstances, everyone would doubtless understand."

"Lady Bissell's guests would, of course. However, the number, in this case, would have been thirteen," Caroline said meaningfully.

"Oh! Yes, I see," Fiona agreed. "So, the both of you remained in your rooms so as to prevent bad luck."

"Precisely!" Caroline said. "Now, do help me into the red gown, please."

Fiona did as she was asked. "Why did you not come to my room to tell me?"

"I did, directly after I left the school room, but you were not there."

"No, I wasn't," Fiona replied, her face aglow. "I have been so wishing to tell you all about my evening."

"What is it? Has Mr. Wilkinson proposed?" Caroline jested.

"You make sport of me, Miss Fulton!" Fiona insisted. "However, if you must know!"

"Indeed, I must!" Caroline cried in earnest.

"In that case, I shall tell you. When I awoke, I went in search of you. As you were absent from *your* room, I went downstairs and came upon Lady Bissell. She was vastly relieved! It seems that Mr. Wilkinson was in need of a nurse of sorts, and there were none she could spare from the staff. A maid or kitchen girl had taken ill, and Lady Bissell was driven to distraction by her attempts to ensure that everything was in readiness for dinner."

"So, you spent the afternoon with Mr. Wilkinson," Caroline suggested, a sinking feeling in the pit of her stomach.

"Yes, and he was very good-natured for a man with a broken foot. He is an Englishman, of course, but ever so pleasant and kind. I hope to sit with him again today if I am allowed."

"That puts me in mind of something," Caroline said in tones of fabricated impartiality. "I am to meet Mr. Doherty in the music room again after breakfast, do you not recall? However, Lady Bissell has insisted that the lads not attend. Perhaps you would enjoy giving them a lesson in French or history whilst we practice?"

"What of the nursery maid?" Fiona asked.

"I do not know," Caroline mused. "I suppose if Lady Bissell wishes to request it of Miss Deakin, it is entirely her own affair. Perhaps we ought to ask her when we see her."

"I do not mind it, truly I do not," Fiona replied. "It is only that I am not certain it is wise to allow you and Mr. Doherty to remain in a room together, unchaperoned. I shall be most glad once this song has been sung and you shall behave as if he does not exist, as promised."

Caroline felt as if she might sink under the weight of her guilt. "Indeed, but we have agreed that it is best to go through with it so as to avoid unpleasantness. And what of you and Mr. Wilkinson alone in his room?"

"That is an entirely different affair," Fiona pointed out. "He is an invalid and needs someone to tend to him."

"I do not see how my situation differs so widely from yours," Caroline asserted. "All shall be aware of exactly where Mr. Doherty and I shall be, and with Lady Bissell's blessing."

Fiona said nothing, but she did not hesitate to register her frustration as she tied up Caroline's gown with more than required force.

Finally, when they were gowned and coiffed, they descended to the breakfast room. They were rather late, and only the baron and Lady Bissell remained.

"Ah, I have been waiting for your arrival," Lord Bissell said. "I have taken Lady Anne's complaints to heart and intend to spend time with my lady guests today. What say you to a jaunt into the village?"

"Do say you will go," Lady Bissell urged. "We intend to hold a ball before the week is out and I am persuaded you ladies shall require a frippery or two."

"Shall we, Caro?" Fiona asked. "If there is a lending library, perhaps I might look for a book for Mr. Wilkinson."

"Of course," Caroline said. "We should both be delighted to accompany you, Lord Bissell. However, I have a prior engagement directly following breakfast. I shall be through in an hour or so. Might we meet in the front hall at half-past eleven?"

"Splendid," the baron said. "We shall take luncheon at the tavern, shall we not?"

"That would be lovely," Caroline agreed. "In that case, we shall have only a light breakfast."

She and Fiona went to the sideboard to discover that only cold toasted bread and smoked salmon remained.

"I perceive that going forward," Caroline whispered for Fiona's ears alone, "we must be down to breakfast all the sooner."

"Indeed, yes," Fiona agreed.

They returned to the table and took up their seats. "Lady Bissell," Caroline ventured, "shall Miss Deakin entertain Masters Charles and Christopher whilst Mr. Doherty and I have our song practice?"

"I am afraid not," Lady Bissell said with a distracted air. "I have pressed her into service in the kitchen. One of the girls is sick, and between that and Mr. Wilkinson's injury, I am woefully short of help. Would you be willing to sit in the school room for an hour, Miss O'Sullivan?" she asked.

"I should be delighted," Fiona replied.

"Thank you. Now," Lady Bissell said as she rose to her feet, "I must see to a great number of things today. I shall see the two of you when you return from your shopping expedition."

As Lady Bissell left the room, Caroline returned her attention to the baron. "You have said, my lord, that there is to be a ball. How lovely. Shall the neighbors be invited or shall we remain your sole guests?"

"I believe she," he replied, looking in the direction of the departed Lady Bissell, "has already invited more guests than the ballroom can hold. We shall contrive, however," he added with a practiced grin.

"I for one am very much looking forward to it," Caroline attested. "I cannot think, however, of a single thing that I shall need in the village. Nor can you, is that not right, Miss O'Sullivan? Perhaps we ought to stay behind," Caroline suggested, the highway robbery foremost in her thoughts.

"No, indeed, Miss Fulton!" the baron exclaimed. "I regret that we have not had an opportunity to become acquainted."

"The house party is to last a fortnight, is it not? There seems to be time and enough," Caroline said with a diffident smile.

"Be that as it may," the baron asserted, "I should like to have you by my side today. I was most impressed with your skills with a whip. I have never seen a young lady tool a car or cart or carriage of any sort as you did yesterday. I find it quite fascinating. I find *you* quite fascinating, and should like to learn more about you." He said this as if Fiona did not sit between him and Caroline.

"In that case, my lord, I should be pleased to come along to the village." Briefly, she wondered what she must say to undo the damage of such a lie. "Am I correct in assuming your invitation extends to Miss O'Sullivan, as well?"

"I would be a brute to deny her a visit to the lending library, would I not?" He rose to his feet. "I shall count on the both of you to meet me in the front hall no later than half past eleven."

"We shall be there," Fiona said, rather breathlessly.

Once the baron had fully exited the room, Caroline turned to her friend. "What is it about the notion of time spent with the baron that you find so thrilling?" she teased.

"You are funning me, I know, but 'tis not the baron I have in mind. I am glad that I shall be able to choose a book for Mr. Wilkinson. It shall assist me in seeing him through some painful hours. The physician left laudanum, of course, but the dosage does not equal the pain. I only wish to distract poor Mr. Wilkinson."

"You are very kind," Caroline soothed. "Well, then, since the balance of the day is all but arranged, I shall repair to the music room to await Mr. Doherty."

"And I shall go directly to the school room. I believe it is just the floor above ours?"

"The door shall be open; it always is," Caroline said happily.

173

However, once she found herself alone in the music room, she began to feel some misgiving. She was behaving just as Fiona had warned her against; entertaining the attentions of Mr. Doherty, a man she would never be allowed to marry and who was far too dear to treat so callously. She could not think how to break it off with him, nor did she wish to. She wanted to spend every moment in his company, to get lost in his tales, to study his speaking hands and eyes; to stand with his strong arms around her, his warm lips pressed against hers.

She was startled from her reverie by the sound of his voice murmuring from the other side of the door. Her heart began to pound; the rattle of the knob as it turned was as welcome as music. The door began to creak inward, but still he spoke with someone in the passage. Just when she thought she would expire of anticipation, the door swung wide, and Mr. Doherty stood on the threshold.

"Good morning, Miss Fulton," he said with a light bow. "May I come in?"

"You are expected," she said tremulously. She could not say when she was ever so happy to see anyone, and yet she felt as if she might break down in tears with the slightest provocation.

He stepped into the room and shut the door behind him. "I should not like to disturb anyone with my caterwauling." He looked round the room as if to ensure that they were alone.

Caroline laughed. "Caterwauling? You jest, surely!"

"Indeed, I do not!" he said in spirited tones that failed to coincide with the intensity of his expression.

In her estimation, his eyes should have been dancing and his mouth curved into one of his rare smiles. Instead, he looked at her with an eloquent bemusement that revealed his emotions: incredulity that she should care for him mingled with certainty that it would never lead to their mutual happiness.

"Shall we sit at the pianoforte?" he asked, indicating the instrument with a sweep of his hand.

"Of course." She rose from the sofa and took up her seat. He sat beside her just as he had the morning prior. Someone had been in the room since, and she found it necessary to shuffle the music until she found the right piece. "Ah, here it is. Shall we begin?"

"Perhaps we had best stand at the window," he suggested. "Yesterday you proclaimed the light to be better there."

"Did I? Well," she said, somewhat flustered, "there seems enough light today, does there not?"

"Indeed, there does," he said as he lifted his arm to shift the music a trifle closer to him.

"I rather thought it perfectly placed where it was," Caroline said, risking a glance into his face.

"Very well, then," he said, lifting his arm again to restore the music to its former location.

Caroline minded not in the least as each movement of his arm caused his shoulder to brush against hers, just as it had the day before. It was hardly an embrace, but it was enough for the moment. "I suppose we ought to sing. If we do not, passersby might wonder what prevents us. Perhaps they might even enter the room to see for themselves." She felt herself blush at the possibilities her words implied.

"If someone does enter, there shall be nothing untoward to be seen," he replied as he once again moved the music.

"Mr. Doherty," she said with a laugh. "I begin to think you require spectacles. Do you truly require the music to be so far to your side?"

"No, I do not," he murmured as he gazed into her eyes. "However, every time I move it, your face turns the most delightful shade of pink.

Chapter Twelve

Miss Fulton's eyes grew wide in mock indignation. "I perceive that I am merely a figure of fun to you."

"That is a lie, Miss Fulton," Niall replied, playfully, "and a cruel one, to be sure. But, please do continue speaking," he added, lowering his voice. "As long as we are heard to banter no one shall think ill of us."

"What is the use of being alone," she said with an enchanting pout, "if we cannot indulge our wishes?"

"And what are your wishes, Miss Fulton?" he asked in airy tones that repudiated the manner in which he brought her fingers to his lips.

"I do not think it wise to say," she said in a trembling voice. "Perhaps it is better if we talk of other things. Let us begin with whom it was you were speaking to in the passage just before you entered."

"'Twas only Carter." With a sigh, he returned her hand to the keys of the pianoforte. "'Tis not often he sees me downstairs without the lads, and he wished to know of what I was in need. I informed him of our musical alliance and, I must say, he was not precisely pleased. No doubt he has his heart set on you becoming the next baroness at Oak View."

"Indeed, he has not!" Miss Fulton exclaimed. She paused

and favored him with a dimpled smile. "I do think it best if we should be heard to sing, if even only a little. I have no wish for Lady Bissell to put her head into the room and see you casting such amorous glances in my direction," she added with a laugh.

"I have done no such thing," he said with a sheepish grin. "As for Lady Bissell, she should not be in the least happy were she to witness such a scene. Carter is not the only resident of Oak View who would choose you over Lady Anne."

"Do you truly think so?" she asked too happily for his comfort. "I had not realized you thought of Lady Anne as a threat to my future here," she added with a saucy smile.

"Had you not?" he echoed, his feelings wounded. He wondered if she had thought of his future at Oak View. "Tell me, what am I to do should you become mistress here? Am I to carry on as if I did not feel what I feel?" he asked with a hand over his heart. "Should I pretend I do not know your feelings for me, as well? What of the baron, your husband? Would he have me here if he knew?"

Her face fell. "Please, Mr. Doherty," she begged. "What if you were overheard?"

"Pray, forgive me," he said with a sigh. "It is wrong for me to burden you with my troubles."

She put her hand on his arm and gazed at him, her eyes blue as a summer sky. "To whom else may you speak of them? And yet, I do not know what you shall do. I do not know what I shall do. I am only thinking as far ahead as tonight, when we shall sing together for the baron's guests."

He possessed himself again of her hand. "And I can do naught else but look past tonight and beyond. When I close my

178

eyes, you inhabit my dreams, my home, my world. Always, you appear perfectly at ease. It is as if you belonged there. And yet, how can that be when I see you in a home that has been lost these six years past and more?"

"Do you doubt, Mr. Doherty?" she asked in a manner more candid than he had ever known her to adopt. "You have made your request and your sacrifice. There is nothing remaining but for you to speak with my father."

"Your father; now that is a task more daunting than to clear two miles of land in a single day."

"But why?" she asked in genuine bemusement.

He could not help but smile at her innocence. "The king's son had the aid of magic to build his castle, but Mr. Fulton's pride can be moved by no one but himself."

"Yes, I see," she said sadly. "But suppose there was a miracle, and he did not insist I marry a title; did not forbid me to wed the one I wished?"

There were never sweeter words, but he dared not allow himself to fall under their spell. "Should I be the one," Niall replied, "I should be the happiest of men. And yet," he said earnestly, "'twould not be right."

"But it is right for Lord Bissell to possess my dowry to spend as he pleases?" she retorted.

"If you should marry the baron, you would have his title and this house in exchange for your dowry," he patiently explained. "Not to mention the London townhouse, the horses and carriages, a sponsored *entre* into London society, and who can say what else?"

"And if I were to marry someone else," she said with a

delectable attempt at opacity, "I should exchange my money for happiness."

Again, he denied himself the bliss such words induced. "I am correct in this, I know that I am," he insisted, "yet somehow you make it sound as if I am in the wrong. What strange magic is this?" he asked with a windy sigh.

"Ah, Mr. Doherty," she said, turning her attention to the keyboard. "A magician must be allowed her secrets." Smiling, she stole a glance at him from the corner of her eye. "Now, if you are ready to permit it, let us sing."

As they sang, Niall attempted to recall when he had last felt so happy. Surely it was on account of his newfound knowledge: that to love and to be loved in return was the greatest of joys. Miss Fulton, as she sat beside him at the pianoforte, appeared to be every bit as content. They sang and smiled and sang some more until Niall became comfortable enough to play a few simple songs. She played some as well; silly tunes that had him thumping his feet in time to the music. He could not remember laughing so often in the whole of his life.

His state of pure contentment began to decay when there came a sharp rap at the music room door. Niall hadn't time to react before it was opened and the baron stood in the doorway. "Miss Fulton, did we not agree that we should meet at half past? It is now a quarter past noon."

"Oh!" she gasped, her face drained white. "I had not realized it to be so late." She turned stricken eyes to Niall. "I am to go shopping in the village with Lord Bissell. Miss O'Sullivan is to come along, as well. Only," she added as she rose and went to the baron's side, "I needs must go fetch my things."

"Of course," Lord Bissell said with a bow and a censorious look for Niall, who had also risen and sketched a bow. "I trust you are providing my brothers with an adequate education, Mr. Doherty."

Niall knew a twinge of uneasiness. He had forgotten all about his students, their half-brother, and all that did not involve Miss Fulton. "I shall go up immediately and send Miss O'Sullivan down to you," he said, executing another bow.

"See that you do," the baron said shortly and was gone.

Humiliated, Niall pounded up the back staircase, the full weight of his situation a burden past bearing. He was a man who was neither this nor that, neither here or there, one continually forced to navigate two very different worlds. Though he did not truly belong to either, he was expected to know them both to perfection.

His step lightened as Miss Fulton returned to his thoughts. Now that she was to go into the village, her safety was the main source of his apprehension. He had not known the baron long enough to determine what he might do if presented with the muzzle of a gun and ordered to turn over his valuables. Nor did Niall know if he was capable of adequately protecting the most valuable Miss Fulton and her friend. At the very least, he was determined to ensure the baron had a pistol secreted in the carriage.

He reached the school room and dashed through the doorway. "Miss O'Sullivan, I must beg your pardon for being so late. Miss Fulton has just gone to her room and shall meet you in the front hall. Lord Bissell already waits."

Miss O'Sullivan swept past him without a word, leaving

Niall free to formulate a plan. He turned to the lads. "Shall we have an early walk today?"

Charles and Christopher instantly clattered to their feet and skipped into the passage, Niall directly behind them. He did nothing to discourage their enthusiasm, and raced along behind them. They were required to descend three staircases and did so in record time, noisily arriving in the front hall just as Lady Anne approached the baron.

"Why, Lord Bissell, it appears that you are going out," she observed in some surprise.

Though Lady Anne did not seem the least concerned about being overheard, Niall thought it best if the lads did not take in the exchange. Quickly, he took each by the shoulder and steered them away from what should doubtless prove to be a private conversation.

"Indeed," the baron replied to Lady Anne in more subdued tones. "Miss Fulton and Miss O'Sullivan were wishful of going on a shopping expedition to the village."

"Surely you meant to invite me along, as well," she asked, affronted.

"I had not thought you comfortable in the presence of two such Irish ladies, as you have mentioned on more than one occasion."

"Not I!" Lady Anne replied, eyes wide with astonishment. "Perhaps you are confusing the comments of Lady Kent, or perhaps Mrs. Knight, with mine."

"Very well, if you should like to join us, there is room in the carriage."

"That should indeed suit me. I shall first require my hat and gloves," she said, turning to the stairs.

Once she had reached the landing, Niall felt it safe to allow the lads to approach their brother. He released their squirming bodies from his grasp, and they ran to their brother's side.

"Arthur!" Master Christopher cried. "Might I go to the village as well? I have not been in ever so long!"

"Nor I," Charles asserted.

"Lads, it is time for our walk," Niall interceded. "Perhaps, if the baron does not mind, you might go out and have a look at the horses whilst he waits for the ladies."

This proved too much of a lure for Charles. "Are the ladies to go, as well?" he asked. "Is Miss Caro one of the ladies? Is Miss Fiona? I should very much like to ride in the carriage with them."

Lord Bissell said nothing that should prove to disappoint his young brothers. Rather, he shook their hands, tousled their hair, and appealed mutely to Niall over their heads.

Niall was only too happy to oblige. "Come along, lads, and let us see the horses. Then we shall go on our walk," he insisted as he herded them past the baron and out of the door. Once they were on the drive, the horse-mad lads lost no time in amusing themselves in patting the horses and chatting with the coachman who sat up on the box.

"McCauley, you have heard the rumors of the highwaymen, have you not?" Niall asked the driver.

"I t'ought it just talk," McCauley said with a shrug.

"Perhaps it is," Niall mused. "The young masters wish to join the outing, and I fear for their safety in the case the rumors are true. Is a gun kept in the carriage for just such circumstances?"

"I've not seen one," McCauley replied.

Niall considered his feelings. Ordinarily he would concede the safety of the lads to their brother, highwaymen or no. It was purely his concern for Miss Fulton that inflated his apprehension. And yet, he could not quiet his misgivings. He felt that he must find a way to ensure that she was safe. For that, he would need time and access.

"How do you like the horses?" Niall asked the lads.

Charles shrugged. "They are very much the same as yesterday."

"I suppose they are not such a treat after all," Niall said leadingly.

"No, that is why I should like to go into the village with my brother," Charles replied.

"Perhaps," Niall suggested in tones designed to entice, "if you are very well-behaved and request it of the baron with your best manners, he shall allow you to go. Naturally, I ought to go along with you, as well. I have a particular need to restore my supply of candy."

"I want candy!" Christopher interpolated.

"I shall not go without you," Charles soothed his brother. "But the carriage only allows for six and that other lady wishes to go along, so that makes one too many. Perhaps Mr. Doherty needs must stay behind."

"But he is to buy the candy!"

"Do not fret, Master Christopher," Niall said, dropping into a squat to speak in the boy's ear. "I do not believe your brother wishes to take Lady Anne to the village. In fact, I think he shall be more willing to take you along for that very reason. He can offer to take Lady Anne another day since there shall not be room for her."

"We shall see," Christopher said, doubtfully.

"Indeed, we shall," Niall said under his breath. To his delight, matters unfolded precisely as he predicted. Furious at her rejection, Lady Anne flounced into the house. The baron wasted no time mourning her absence, and happily assisted Miss Fulton and Miss O'Sullivan into the carriage. They sat across from one another, followed by Lord Bissell, who took up his seat to the far side of Miss Fulton. This required him to step over the feet and skirts of the ladies, something Niall thought uncouth, though he dared not say as much. The seating arrangement did, however, prevent him from knocking his knees against the baron's during the journey, a circumstance for which to be grateful.

He settled in with one lad to his left and one directly across from him, but as his seat afforded him an unobstructed view of Miss Fulton, he had little of which to complain. As he gazed, he could not help but notice that she had added a charming blue spencer to her ensemble, one that matched her sash, as well as blue kid gloves and half boots. Her hat was a delightful confection consisting of a soft brim and poke that framed her face without obscuring it. It was blue, as well, and deepened the hue of her eyes.

She turned to catch him staring at her. Smiling, she very gently nudged his foot with the toe of her boot.

Hastily, he dropped his gaze and found contentment in the sweep of her gown from knee to ankle.

As the carriage swung into motion, so did Miss Fulton.

185

"Lord Bissell," she said far more gaily than Niall thought wise. "Have you heard the gossip as to the highway robbery?"

"One should not attend to tittle-tattle, Miss Fulton," the baron objected. "It does not become a lady."

Niall burned to correct the baron, but was powerless to speak until invited.

"Oh, 'twas not one of your guests who told me of it," Miss Fulton said so sweetly that the baron seemed to miss the implied barb. "It was Mr. Doherty. He had it of the physician whom he drove into the village to fetch for Mr. Wilkinson."

"Is this true, Doherty?" the baron demanded.

"Of course, it is. Why should Miss Fulton wish to deceive you?" It was a timid reply compared to the scathing retort that first leapt to his tongue.

"Miss Fulton is none of your affair," the baron said tersely. "However, should the need arise, there is a pistol between the squabs and the side panel next to the door. Do you know how to use it?"

"Yes, of course," Niall replied.

The baron's eyes narrowed at what he doubtless deemed a presumptuous response.

"I fear for the lads so near to the gun," Miss O'Sullivan said, drawing the baron's attention from Niall. "Perhaps it would be better if they each sat as far from the coach door as possible."

Niall did not wait for the baron's approval. "That is a sensible suggestion. Lads, quickly, do as she said."

They were small enough that there not too much pitching back and forth of the carriage as they made their ways

186

to the far seats. As it brought Miss Fulton directly across from Niall, he could only be glad of the new arrangement.

"I am grateful to know we shall be safe with you guarding the door, Mr. Doherty," Miss Fulton said in tones meant to distract attention from the true reason for her delight. "And your tender concern for your charges does you credit, sir. What a splendid father you shall make one day."

Niall, who nearly came undone at her audacity, pressed a finger against his lips to forestall the threat of outright laughter. He nodded in what he hoped was an appropriate response to such a remark. Certainly, there was no written guide that revealed the correct reaction to such a remark.

"Mr. Doherty, sir," Christopher asked, "might we purchase a toy pistol in the village?"

"I want one too, Mr. Doherty, but one of my own," Charles whined. "I don't wish to share with my little brother."

Niall opened his mouth to serve Charles a gentle reprimand, but was interrupted by the baron.

"Indeed, you may both have your own toy," he said loftily.

Niall quelled his indignation; if the baron wished to spoil his brothers, it was his affair. He felt mollified, however, when he noted the glance of consternation exchanged between the ladies.

The remainder of the journey was strained. The lads, encouraged by their brother's attentions, became increasingly cross and demanding, the baron increasingly frustrated, and the ladies increasingly dismayed. At one point Miss Fulton, biting back a smile of amusement, looked to Niall for rescue. He very slightly shook his head to indicate his powerless state.

All were delighted to emerge from the carriage once they had safely arrived at their destination. As Niall was closest to the door, he had the privilege of offering his hand to the ladies. It suited him very well to walk off with them, one on each arm, whilst the baron lifted his brothers to the ground. It was a pleasant reminder of a not so pleasant fact: gone were the days when Niall would order out the family coach or tool his Phaeton, the spokes of its wheels picked out in yellow.

He missed his horse, as well, and their frequent gallops along the surf along the Dublin seashore. His melancholy would do him no good, however, and he thrust the thoughts aside. When the baron claimed the ladies, Niall fell back a few paces as befitting his lowly status. He watched dolefully as the lads cavorted about; he knew the baron would only upbraid Niall if he were to properly take the lads in hand. To his chagrin, it was he who would be required to cope with the lads' imperious behavior once they were returned from the village.

He trailed along behind his betters for a tedious three quarters of an hour as they pointlessly deferred to one another. He nearly cheered aloud when the decision was finally taken to enter the premises of the circulating library. The moment Miss O'Sullivan emerged with her books wrapped in brown paper and tied up with string, the wishes of the boys could no longer be delayed.

"Please, Arthur!" Christopher implored his brother. "We want our guns!" This cry was followed by a slightly more sedate request from Charles.

"Very well, you rascals!" the baron said with a self-conscious grimace for the ladies. "They are good lads," he said in hearty tones for all to hear, "but their tutor does not seem to know how to take them in hand."

"They are indeed sweet lads," Miss Fulton said loudly enough for Niall to discern from his place in the rear. "I have never known them to be sweeter, however, than when Mr. Doherty is sole overseer of their conduct. And they are so swift to learn under his tutelage! I believe they are well onto French."

Lord Bissell grunted. "Be that as it may, they have not learned how to conduct themselves when in the company of others." The baron turned to look at Niall over his shoulder, his brow raised in disdain.

Indignant, Niall stopped and looked back the way they had come. Realizing that they had passed the only shop in the village to offer toys for sale, he returned the way they had come. He cherished hopes that the time spent waiting in front of the shop would be sufficient to cool his anger. Miss Fulton, however, seemed alive to his every movement and insisted that the baron turn around to enter the shop.

"Here it is!" Charles eagerly said as he bounded to his tutor's side. "Mr. Doherty, have you found the toy pistols already?"

"No, Master Charles, I have not yet been inside."

The baron scowled and elbowed his way past both to enter the shop. The rest of the group followed, with Niall in the rear. Upon entering, he blinked in the dim light to find the baron inspecting a table full of items for children. "Where have the guns gone?" he asked, turning this way and that in search of assistance.

Christopher ran to his side. "There are no guns!" he wailed.

"It seems we have chosen the wrong day to favor this establishment with our presence!" the baron announced whilst the shop girl wilted under his scorching eye. "Why have you no guns?" he demanded.

The girl immediately disappeared through the doorway to the back room, and a gentleman, ostensibly the proprietor, greeted them.

"My lord, how good of you to honor us with your presence," the man said with an effulgent bow.

"Do you have toy pistols for the lads here?" the baron asked genially enough.

"No, my lord, we do not. They have all been bought up, though I am expecting more within the month."

"That long?" the baron cried, eyeing the crestfallen faces of his brothers. "That will not do at all. These lads are after a pistol today!" He looked about again, as if expecting wooden guns to magically appear in each location upon which his gaze fell. "Well then," he capitulated, "what other play things do you have for young lads?"

The proprietor scurried to the table to suggest one toy after another: a carved rocking horse, illustrated books, a set of Spillikins, but Christopher only wept and shook his head. During the fracas, his brother crossed to the other side of the room and closely inspected an item he held in both hands.

Niall caught Miss Fulton's eye, and the two of them approached Charles to learn what he had discovered. It appeared to be a miniature hammer, the handle carved and expertly planed just as a full-sized one would be.

"Look, Mr. Doherty, look Miss Caro! Miss Fiona!" the lad exclaimed. "It's small so that it is easy to use."

"Yes, I see that," Niall said as he placed himself between the lad's line of vision and a small hatchet lying on a nearby shelf, it's blade as sharp as a full-sized one might be. He again caught Miss Fulton's eye and drew her gaze to the wicked little instrument.

Her eyes grew wide when she spotted it, and the two of them exchanged another glance over the lad's head. "Master Charles," she began, "it appears as if the candy jars have been recently restocked. Let us go and see what might be new," she suggested.

"I shall, just as soon as Mr. Doherty stands aside and hands over that hatchet," Charles replied.

The baron turned to observe Niall, who steadfastly refused to move. "Do as the lad says!" Lord Bissell bellowed.

Niall, suppressing a sigh, very reticently did as he was told.

"There 'tis!" Charles cried. "I knew I had seen it! May I have it, Arthur?"

"Oh, but it looks so dangerous," Miss Fulton interjected as Charles held the sharp blade up to his eyes for inspection.

"Is it truly meant for a child?" Miss O'Sullivan asked in strident tones.

"Let us have it," the baron commanded with a crook of his finger. Charles handed the hatchet to Arthur, who turned the cunning object around and around in his hands. "Dangerous it might be, now that the tutor has failed to keep him from the thing, I suppose there is nothing for it but to let the child have it."

Miss Fulton's gasp was only outdone by Miss O'Sullivan's.

"Lord Bissell," Niall said, unable to withstand the urgency

191

he felt, "I do not believe it is an appropriate toy for Master Charles."

The baron gave Niall a look of extreme displeasure, but he retained some control of his voice. "I do not agree. The child shall have it and his brother, this very solid hammer," he insisted as he picked up both of the miniature tools and handed them to the lads.

"Thank you, Arthur!" they cried in unison.

"It does not take much to encourage young boys to behave themselves, now, does it?" the baron asked in congratulatory tones, his face beaming. "They shall be as good as gold now, see if they won't."

Niall knew not where to look or what to say. He suspected that the ladies felt much the same.

"I want candy!" Christopher called out as the hammer slipped from his grasp and clattered to the floor.

The baron's jaw dropped in so comical a fashion that it was with great difficulty that Niall restrained a bark of laughter. He looked to Miss Fulton, who covered her mouth with her hand, her eyes dancing with levity.

"Shall I wrap these for you?" the proprietor asked as he scurried to retrieve the abandoned toy.

"But of course!" Lord Bissell turned to Charles, who studied his hatchet with great interest. "Do hand that over to the gentleman."

Niall forced away a fit of pique. He was a gentleman by birth, whose father could have once upon a time bought out the entire shop. And yet, the proprietor was given more respect than Lord Bissell had ever afforded Niall. He retired to the corner of the shop nearest the door and watched as the lads selected their candies.

By the time the proprietor had poured the candy into twists of paper, Niall had gained control of his anger. He stood aside and held open the door as the baron swept by on his way out, followed by his brothers and the ladies, Miss Fulton last of all.

She looked up at Niall as she passed, her eyes filled with compassion. She doubtless dared not say what she thought any more than he. Indeed, the journey home was silent save the sighs of longing from the lads. They eyed the parcel containing their purchases with devotion and seemed to know that one wrong word might result in its disappearance.

When Oak View hove into sight, the atmosphere became less oppressed, and the ladies began to speak of trifles amongst themselves. Niall was content to listen; the rise and fall of Miss Fulton's voice was as lyrical as any melody. Once the carriage had come to a halt at the top of the drive, the tension had nearly dissolved. Niall exited and offered his hand to the ladies. He even dared to give Miss Fulton's fingers a squeeze. In return, she clung to his longer than she ought. His heart soaring, he deemed the outing time well spent.

The baron, however, radiated discontent. "Miss Fulton, Miss O'Sullivan," he instructed. "I would be obliged if you were to take the lads into the house and wait with them in the ante chamber until Mr. Doherty comes to claim them."

"Yes, of course," Miss O'Sullivan said. Miss Fulton managed a tight smile before they walked away.

Niall was relieved she would not be witness to the reprimand that was sure to come. Before he rendered the baron his full attention, however, Niall allowed himself the luxury of watching Miss Fulton disappear through the doorway of the house. He was rewarded for his constancy with a final backwards glance over her shoulder.

"Drive on, McCauley," Lord Bissell directed, a command that was promptly obeyed with a grinding of the wheels against the gravel of the drive. The baron paused a moment for the noise to subside before turning to Niall with an imperious lift of his brow. "Mr. Doherty," he said pleasantly enough. "Your impertinence these past few days has not gone unnoticed. I like to think that I am a fair man, one who treats his servants with the equity befitting their stations. What can I have done to deserve such a breach of my trust?"

Niall longed to riposte with a question of his own: what had the baron *not* done? He knew, however, that such a reply would result in immediate dismissal. "My lord, I must beg your pardon if I have been impertinent," he offered. "However, my only desires have been to protect the ladies during the jaunting car race and my young charges from their youthful folly."

"You forget yourself, Mr. Doherty, it is I who allowed them the toys. Therefore it is I whom you have accused of folly, and I who must be, if appropriate, censured. However, not by you, a servant who should know better than to speak when he has not first been spoken to."

Niall felt his face flush with the heat of his disgrace. "I am certain I never accused you, my lord, of any folly, whatsoever."

"It was hardly required for you to do so. What you have said is sufficient to sink you below reproach. As to the race, how was a reprimand in the hearing of all my house guests to rescue

Miss Fulton and Miss O'Sullivan from any danger whatsoever? I employ a gatekeeper for the very purpose of keeping the gate, though I suppose you have an impertinent response to that, as well."

Niall carefully considered his reply. He dared not say anything that should indicate his feelings for Miss Fulton. "I do sometimes forget myself," he conceded with a bob of the head. "However, despite the fact that I am paid a wage, I am hardly in the same class as Mrs. Walsh or the butler."

"Your lack of proper deportment speaks to an important truth," the baron retorted. "When you allow servants privileges that are above them, they forget their place entirely. From this moment on you are not to dine in the dining room, guests or no, nor shall you be seen in the house when not in the company of my brothers at any time whatsoever, not for any reason. I shall inform Lady Bissell of my edict."

Niall endured the wash of heat that suffused his entire form. He did not trust himself to speak. He focused, instead, on the pain in his head which was no doubt due to the manner in which he clenched his teeth so as to stifle his tongue.

"Do you have nothing to say for yourself?" Lord Bissell asked in the benevolent manner adopted by those who have won their arguments.

"No, my lord," Niall managed with a sketch of a bow.

"Very well. Now, enter the house via the kitchen door. Go and collect your students from the ante chamber. At the end of lessons, I shall be up to question the boys as to what they have learned today. Please inform them that they shall then receive their toys and sweets, should I be pleased with their progress. It is about time someone took them in hand and did away with their appalling behavior through the application of proper encouragement."

Mortified, Niall forced himself into a deep bow, one that gave him a grand view of the baron's boots.

"Well done, Mr. Doherty, well done. And to think that m'father always maintained that the Irish are too simple to learn much of anything at all," the baron said with a sniff before he took himself off to the house.

As Lord Bissell marched away, Niall did himself the service of airing one silent argument after the other. In the end, he determined that none were worth the breath he longed to expel on them; it was unrealistic to expect reason from such a man.

He made his way to the kitchen door, his knees stiff from having been locked tight in indignation. Once he had collected the lads, he led them up the staircase with perfect circumspection. Leaving them to their own devices in the school room, Niall went to his chamber and scrawled a brief note of explanation to Miss Fulton. She must know why he would not be to dinner, why he would not be allowed to sing with her, or to even see her for the duration of the house party.

He tied the note to the string and lowered it to her window as he had the others. "Goodbye, Miss Fulton," he said to no one at all.

Chapter Thirteen

Caroline sat at the escritoire in her chamber and tapped the end of her feathered quill against her cheek. The strength of her feelings for Mr. Doherty required that she justify them to her father, and she intended to give him the whole of it in a letter. He was of such an excitable temperament that she dared not speak to him of it whilst in company, and it seemed they were never alone. Finding the right words still proved difficult, however. With a sigh, she lowered the quill to the parchment when she heard the light reverberation of footsteps from the room above.

Assuming it to be one of the boys in the school room, she returned again to her letter. She had just completed a lengthy list of Mr. Doherty's desirable qualities when she heard a tapping at the window. Delighted by the prospect of a message from him of whom she wrote, she lost no time in collecting the letter. It was with dismay, however, that she learned its contents.

Now that Mr. Doherty had been banished from the house party, a letter to her father would serve little purpose. She knew it was time in Mr. Doherty's presence her father required in order to form a favorable opinion of his own. Realizing that she had counted on the singing of the duet to serve that very purpose, her hopes plummeted. In its place rose the possibility of an offer of marriage from the boorish baron. It was a thought that did not bear contemplation.

She passed the time until dinner in her room. Whatever it was that the other guests were up to, she hadn't a care. When Fiona arrived to change, Caroline found that she had little to say, and was grateful to find Fiona full of news.

"Mr. Wilkinson is the kindest man I have met," she said, her face aglow. "He is in such considerable pain. His countenance is white with it, and yet, he never complains."

"There is much to recommend the man," Caroline said dully.

Fiona seemed not to notice Caroline's lassitude. "He continually expresses himself as grateful for the books I secured for him at the circulating library. But, do you know," she asked eagerly, "he has read more pages aloud to me than I to him. What do you say to that?"

"I confess I can only assume him a man smitten." Caroline was grateful her countenance was not visible, as it was doubtless less pleasing than her words.

"Smitten? Do you truly believe it?" Fiona asked happily. She gave one last tug to Caroline's tapes and sighed. "I have finished," she said as she turned around for her own gown to be tied. "I wish you might sit with us on occasion and then you shall be capable of an informed opinion."

"I should like that," Caroline said in all truthfulness. "It seems I shall have much time on my hands. I do not mix well with the English ladies, as you well know."

Fiona held her thick red hair away from the tapes that secured her pale green evening gown. "And," Fiona prompted, "quite naturally, after tonight, you shall ignore the attentions of Mr. Doherty, an action I have been pleading with you to take from the outset."

"Yes," Caroline said, shortly.

"Caro," Fiona said, a question in her voice, "you are very quiet this evening. Pray tell; you do not have feelings for Mr. Doherty, do you? It would grieve me should your heart not be unscathed."

Caroline had thought she would keep the truth from Fiona, but found that she yearned to speak of it. "Indeed, my heart has been wounded, and I am unhappy."

Fiona turned around and took Caroline by the hand, her expression downcast. "I blame myself. I ought to have been firmer in my convictions in regard to him."

"You are not to blame, Fiona, not in the least," Caroline asserted. "I shall tell you all, and then you shall see who is the villain in this matter."

Fiona's eyes grew large. "Do not say it is your father? Caro! No! Surely you cannot have expected him to countenance such a match."

"Of course not. But I had hoped that Papa would come to know Mr. Doherty as I have; to see that he is so much more than a tutor," Caroline insisted. "When he takes my hand in his, just as you have done, I do not see a servant who is beneath me. I see an educated gentleman, one with vast knowledge and intelligence, one who plainly cherishes the same hope for a family as do I."

"Caroline," Fiona began.

"No, my dear, do not say it," Caroline warned. "Hear what

I have to say, and then you may tell me what you think. Shall that do?"

Fiona nodded in agreement and Caroline continued. "I believe you would agree that Mr. Doherty should make an excellent father, especially after that scene today in the village. I have no doubt that he would treat me with respect and honor, as well. However, I am persuaded that the baron should not."

"I do believe you are correct. As to the baron, in particular, I should not like to see you wed to such a yahoo. But you need not marry the first man with dark curls and remarkable eyes who woos you so as to escape your father."

Caroline *tsked*. "You rather make it sound as if my care for him is entirely due to his outward appearance."

Fiona sighed. "I confess, I prefer Mr. Wilkinson, but your tutor is precisely the sort of man you admire. Having said so, the more time I spend in the company of Mr. Doherty, the more attractive he becomes. He is indeed wonderful with Charles and Christopher. But these are not arguments that should persuade your father to consider him as suitable, nor should they persuade you."

Caroline pulled her hand from Fiona's grasp. "Can you not see? No amount of persuasion is required. I love him. I love him more than I have ever loved anyone; more than I can express. I have known him for less than a se'enight, but I cannot imagine my life without him."

"Oh, Caro," Fiona asserted, "forgive me. I did not know. Truly I did not. I believed you to be merely infatuated."

Caroline dropped into the chair at the dressing table. "It was my purpose to allow you to believe it was so," she said, staring at her reflection in the mirror. She could not say when she had ever looked so drab. "It hardly matters now. The baron took exception to Mr. Doherty's impertinence in regard to the toys and has refused to allow him to attend the house party, not even so as to make up the numbers for dinner. As such, Papa shall never become acquainted with the gentleman I have come to know."

Fiona sank onto the bed, her face a mirror to Caroline's misery. "Poor Mr. Doherty! I do not know what else to say, unless it is that Lord Bissell is abhorrent!"

Caroline smiled in spite of her anguish. "I am grateful for your empathy, though I wish it had come about by some manner more pleasant." She struggled in vain to blink away her tears.

"My dear," Fiona said as she rose and went to Caroline's side. "I believe I know some of what you feel. I am more than infatuated with Mr. Wilkinson myself, and I believe he feels the same. That I should fall in love with such a man is nothing at which to wonder. For him to believe himself attached to me when London is full of far more suitable matches is inconceivable. And yet, love transcends such things, does it not?"

Caroline took Fiona's hand in hers. "Yes, it does."

Dinner, however, did not transcend superstition. Mrs. Walsh refused to continue her preparations once she learned there would only be thirteen to dine. The pall over the party was greatly exacerbated when the guests learned that one of the kitchen girls had succumbed to a sudden illness early that morning. The remainder of the kitchen staff, aided by Miss Deakin and the parlor maids, did as well as one could expect, but it was a grim meal, to be sure.

As they entered the drawing room, Caroline leaned close to whisper in Fiona's ear. "I am indeed sorry for the poor kitchen maid, but I find that I am more relieved than is strictly proper; I shall sleep without the wail of the banshee tonight."

"Banshee!" Fiona hissed. "Who has said anything of a banshee?" she asked with a shudder. "Put it all from your mind; I know I shall." She looked around the room and frowned. "Should you be too bereft if I went to read to Mr. Wilkinson?"

"Not so that it signifies in the least," Caroline said with far more equanimity than she felt. "You must go. I believe that I shall retire early, as well."

As Fiona took her leave of Lady Bissell, Caroline found a seat on the sofa from where she watched the English ladies settle themselves on the other side of the room. Mrs. Knight, being the last through the door, had only a place next to Caroline from which to choose. To her astonishment, Mrs. Knight preferred to stand.

"You may have my chair," Lady Bissell said pleasantly as she rose and seated herself beside Caroline on the sofa. "I should like to spend more time with Miss Fulton. Perhaps," she suggested, turning to Caroline, "you would sing for us."

Caroline wished to demonstrate her gratitude for her hostess' kindness, but found she could not. To sing without Mr. Doherty was too sad a notion. "I must thank you, Lady Bissell, for your kindness, but I have developed a headache and should like to go to my room."

Lady Bissell nodded. "I do understand. It has been a difficult day for all of us."

Caroline smiled her gratitude, executed a full curtsey, and left the room without a backward glance for any of the others.

Upon opening her chamber door, she went directly to the escritoire in order to pen a blistering note to the baron. She felt it the best letter she had yet written. Indeed, it was a relief to defend Mr. Doherty, as well, but she knew she did not have the courage to have the letter delivered.

With a sigh of defeat, she tossed her quill to the desktop. It came into her mind to write a note to Mr. Doherty, instead, but she did not know how she could have it delivered with no one's knowledge. Pushing back her chair, she rose and went to the window. It was not yet fully dark, but there was no sign of the string that he had used to lower his letters. As she opened the window for a fuller inspection, she was startled by the wails that came from the edge of the park. They were much the same as she had heard before, except that the unearthly wails frightened her even more.

She endured a night every bit as disastrous as the day to which it put an end. Fiona had never arrived to assist Caroline to undress, and she was forced to sleep in her clothes again. Her emotions vacillated between apprehension for her friend and annoyance at her discomfort. The hem of her gown consisted of a double row of ruching that insisted on sliding up and gathering around her waist. Coupled with the ceaseless moaning, she found it impossible to sleep.

Disposing herself as best she could against the wad of silk, she looked up into the blackness and puzzled over the footsteps she had heard before dinner. Recalling that she had often heard footsteps and pacing in the room above, she wondered how much noise such small boys could make. That either of them would be up to wander about in the school room during the night was nonsensical, as well. Suddenly, she knew: the chamber above hers could belong to none but Mr. Doherty, himself.

Tears slid down her face as she contemplated the agony of her situation. She wished so much to see him, to speak with him; to be comforted by him. If only she could rise through the air and travel the short distance between her chamber and his. Briefly, she considered opening her window and calling for him, but there would be too many others who should hear her, as well. The possibility of being discovered whilst doing anything so gauche set her cheeks to burning.

Then a more practical solution occurred to her. Quickly, she sat up in bed and gave three firm knocks to the wall beside her headboard. She waited with bated breath for any response and was rewarded with the faint sound of squeaking bedsprings. This was immediately followed by a muffled series of decisive knocks, three in all.

The tears came again; happy ones. He was there. He had known all along that she was there, as well. She slid down under the blankets, her fear all but gone. He had been aware of her; missing her; wishing for her as she was wishing for him. It was more than she had dared hope.

Come the dawn, she was only too glad to rise. She went immediately to the window in the case Mr. Doherty had left a note. She found nothing, but it was still quite early. She had heard no footsteps as of yet, and she hoped that he was still asleep. She was about to turn away when she saw two small figures as they crossed the lawn; each held something long in one hand. It could only be Charles and Christopher with their new toys. Miss Deakin had most likely been pressed into service in the kitchen or perhaps had overslept and was still in her chamber. Either way, it was left to Caroline to prevent the lads from an encounter with whatever haunted the woods.

Throwing a shawl over her blue spangled silk, she picked up her evening pumps, and slipped out of her room and down both staircases in complete silence. Once she had gone through the front door, she donned her shoes and crossed the park as speedily as possible.

Once she arrived at the row of ash trees, she paused to listen. There was a wood of old oaks, their branches spread wide against the sky, just beyond the ash trees. She knew that any sound she made would echo. The realization made her feel foolish; the wailing she had heard had not been the work of any banshee. Fully alive to the presence of danger, she picked her way carefully into the woods as she looked about for the lads. Whoever was in the wood, she did not wish to draw their attention to the presence of Charles and Christopher.

Unfortunately, they had left no discernable clues as to which way they had gone. As she looked left, then right, she considered which direction two young lads would choose. After some hesitation, she finally went straight back into the darkest part of the woods. After a few paces, the world of sky, water and mountain retreated, and she felt as if she had stepped into a cathedral. Towering canopies of leafy green blocked the sky, obscuring the faint light that shone through the clouds. The ground was soft beneath her feet and dank; the dry leaves of autumn had long ago broken down and been absorbed. All was silent save for the occasional trill of a bird.

She strained her ears for any sounds the lads might make and thought she heard something once, then again, but from different directions. Startled, she spun about and looked back the way she had come, when suddenly the silence was shattered. She heard a plethora of noises in quick succession: the low snort of a horse, the slight jingle of a harness, followed by breath in her ear, hot and foul-smelling.

Before she could turn around, something was shoved into her mouth, muffling her screams. Then her shawl was wrapped tight around her and the ends secured so that she was trussed up like a sausage. The tree branches spun past her as she was grasped in a pair of strong arms, lifted into the air, and seated on a horse.

Unable to use her arms, she nearly pitched into the horse's mane. The man seated behind her pulled her to his chest. Dazed, she saw that his hands were covered in black hair. She looked down at the man who had tied her up and noted the utter lack of mercy in his eyes. He seemed satisfied, however, as he walked to his horse and swung into the saddle.

Caroline tried to speak, to demand the answers to dozens of questions. More than anything, she yearned to know the fate of Charles and Christopher. As they nudged the horses into a slow trot, she felt the air in her lungs freeze with fear. What if the lads had been taken before her and had met some horrible fate? She prayed for their safety, refusing to consider what might lie in store for her.

As they carefully went their way, she could feel the tension ease in the arms around her. After what must have been half a mile, she realized she was being taken so deep into the woods that her screams would remain unheard by the residents of Oak View. Fervently, she hoped there had not been time for these two men to take the lads before they had come across her.

After another quarter mile or so, the men seemed to feel safe and began to converse. To Caroline's surprise, they spoke in French. She comprehended them, but deemed it just as well that she could not speak; she might better learn how to escape if they remained unaware that she spoke fluent French. And yet, she had so many questions. Were they to hold her for ransom? If her father gave in to their demands, would they release her?

"What are we to do with her, eh?" the man with the hairy hands quietly asked of the other.

"How am I to know?" the other replied. He had a light growth of brown hair on his face. "We shall decide when we are arrived back at camp."

Caroline found this exchange encouraging: it was apparent they had not planned on abducting her. It was quite possible they had not taken the lads, either. And yet, they were desperate and faced with a problem upon which they had not reckoned. For the first time, she trembled with fear for herself alone. It was then that she began to hear a faint cry, one similar to that she had heard during the night.

"He is getting worse," Hairy Hands said as a stream of foul breath made its way past her nose.

"He shall recover," Bearded Man said. "It requires time, that is all."

Hairy Hands, seated behind her, grunted. "He was struck more than two days ago, eh? His wound festers. He must have a physician tend to him, or he will die."

"Shut up!" the bearded man said. "He will not!" There was a pause before he added, rather hesitantly, "Perhaps the girl was sent by the fates to help us, eh? We can trade her for the physician."

Hairy Hands behind her laughed. She could feel it rumble deep in his gut. "They will kill us all. We have held up a gentleman and his wife in their carriage! No one shall care that we are starving or that we received nothing for our troubles except a bullet for Pierre."

"Ssst! We cannot allow her to know our names or we will be forced to kill her," Bearded Man insisted. "That gown, that face; she will be missed, and someone will come looking."

"Are we to take her with us, then? All the way to London? Are we not already burdened with a man wounded and dying?" he asked as the moaning increased.

Bearded Man did not respond. Instead, he pulled back on the reins and, with a squeak of his saddle, swung himself to the ground. Leaving his horse behind, he silently made his way into a dense growth of trees and disappeared between two massive trunks. It became evident by the intensity of the moans that the wounded man of whom they spoke was just to the other side of the tree trunks.

"What am I to do with her?" Hairy Hands called. "Am I to sit here all day?"

Bearded Man returned. "He is alone. Let her go," he said with a jerk of his head. "I shall catch her."

Before Caroline processed his command, Hairy Hands had given her a slight push. She knew a moment of terror as she slid from the horse and plunged briefly through the air into the waiting arms of Bearded Man. He lowered her safely to the ground, but her knees buckled beneath her when she attempted to stand. As she sagged into the horse, Bearded Man seized her by the shoulders and stood her upright. Then he put a hand at the small of her back and pressed until she realized that she was meant to walk.

The shawl restricted her movement, but she managed to hobble to the opening between the massive trunks. She attempted to ask for help, but the rag in her mouth made intelligible speech impossible. They told her, repeatedly and in French, to walk on, but she refused to allow them to believe that she understood. The ground was webbed with roots, like veins on the back of an old man's hand. Carefully, she alternately stepped over and around them. When she lost her balance, she bounced into the trunk of the nearest tree. In this manner, she made it into a clearing at the center of a ring of ancient oak trees, enormous in size.

It was darker within the clearing than it had been without, and the eerie tones of suffering reverberated in the air, causing the hair on her arms and neck to stand up on end. Gradually her vision improved, revealing a fire pit in the center as well as personal items: clothing, horse tack, saddle bags, all scattered about. She looked for any sign of the lads, but there was nothing to indicate that they had ever been there. Then Hairy Hands, who she noticed had the same growth of hair on his face as Bearded Man, took her by the shoulders. She jumped in fear that he should hurt her, but he merely helped her to sit on the ground at the base of the tree between two large roots.

The groaning was now very close and her stomach roiled with fear. She looked in the direction from which it came, but could see nothing but leaves and fallen tree branches. Bearded Man came to her side and crouched down close enough that she might have laid her head on his shoulder. He did not spare her a glance, however, as he went to work moving branches and piles of leaves away from what proved to be the face of a third man.

He turned his head and raked Caroline with his eyes. "That is no physician."

"Did you expect us to ride into the village and bespeak his services?" Hairy Hands demanded. "Are our lives worth so little?"

"Quiet!" Bearded Man said as he turned to whom could only be Pierre. "I shall not abandon you, *mon ami*, do not fear."

"I know. I know. Only . . . I am dying."

"Hush, no, you shall be all right, you shall see," his friend insisted.

Pierre sighed, but his moaning had quieted.

"But, truly, what are we to do with her?" Hairy Hands asked.

"I cannot say. Let me think!"

"And what of those boys? I don't like that they are wandering about."

"They are too frightened to come this far. Forget them."

Caroline's felt her fears ease. Every one of her questions had been answered, and the lads were safe. She now had only her own safety to address. To do that, she must be free from her shawl. She peered down at the filthy handkerchief in her mouth and nearly fainted with disgust. Instantly, she did all that she could manage to spit it out.

The three men looked at her in surprise, and Hairy Hands

began to laugh. "She does not like the taste of your handkerchief, Michel."

"Please," she mumbled in English. "I cannot breathe!"

To her relief, Hairy Hands drew the sickening rag from between her lips. Whether he understood Irish-accented English or merely took pity on her obvious distress, she could not guess.

"Thank you," she said. She wondered again if it would not be best to talk her way out of her situation by appealing to them in their own language. As she considered the idea, she scanned the circle of trees for any means of escape. They were astoundingly close to one another, the largest gap being the one through which she had entered. As her gaze swept past it, she was astonished to see a shadowy figure behind one of the trees that framed the entrance.

She thought it to be one of the lads; instantly, her bones turned to jelly in fear for them. Noting that the Frenchmen were entirely absorbed in their conversation, she felt free to study the figure in the darkness. To her vast relief, it was too tall to be either of the lads. Slowly, the figure raised a finger to its lips and silently stepped between the trees. As the shadows on his face lightened, Caroline could make out the familiar features of Mr. Doherty.

She felt her eyes grow wide in mute appeal. Jerking his head in the direction of the men, he held up Charles' little hatchet. She nodded, realizing that he wished her to distract them, and began to think. When a plan unfolded in her mind, she trembled with apprehension; if anything went wrong, it would be on her head. Taking a deep breath, she looked again to Mr. Doherty before executing her plan.

"What was that?" she asked in a voice of terror.

The men looked at her in dismay, even Pierre.

"There is something out there; by the horses!" Her heart pounded in fear that she had perhaps sealed Mr. Doherty's doom.

Hairy Hands cast a doubtful look as slowly he went towards the gap in the trees. He peered into the gloom then slipped between the trunks. Moments later he returned with the little hatchet at his throat and Mr. Doherty's arm around his neck.

"*Bonjour, Pierre et Michel,*" Mr. Doherty said in flawless French as he marched his captive into the clearing. "I regret that we meet again under such unpleasant circumstances, but Étienne has refused to cooperate."

Pierre, from his place on the ground, chuckled. "Have you come to rescue me, Niall?"

"No, it is for the young lady I have come," Niall replied pleasantly, "but I shall do everything I can to help you, as well, Pierre. It depends, however, on your friends."

Caroline listened to their conversation in growing astonishment. It seemed that the four of them were known to one another.

"Have you become a physician since we met you?" Michel asked harshly.

"You know I have not. However, a physician is at the house at frequent intervals to tend to a guest. He could help you, Pierre. Of course, if you are the three who held up the carriage near the village, matters could prove difficult."

"Tell him what he wants to know," Étienne begged. "This thing at my throat is small, but it is sharp as any knife!"

212

His friends remained silent as Michel favored Caroline with a scowl. Alarmed, she noted that there was nothing but a tree root between the two of them. Fearing what he might do, she slid up into a standing position and shrank as far from him as possible.

"Release the young lady," Mr. Doherty repeated, "and I shall see that Pierre receives proper treatment. We shall say that he is a friend of the family, shall we not?" Mr. Doherty asked with a nod for Caroline.

"*Oui*." Caroline replied in French, as there was no longer the need to hide her knowledge of it.

"She understands what we have been saying!" Hairy Hands cried. "She already knows the truth!"

"Indeed, she does," Mr. Doherty confirmed. "She also comprehends that you are not evil men, just desperate former soldiers who have been falsely accused of crimes, ones for which you should be forced to pay the ultimate price should you return to France."

Caroline felt her face crumple with compassion. "*Oui*," she repeated. "I swear I shall not betray any friend of Mr. Doherty."

"Very sensible of you," he replied in the same even, pleasant tones he had adopted from the beginning. "What shall it be, Michel? I can ensure that Pierre gets medical attention, you and Étienne go free; no one dies."

"Let her go," Étienne insisted. "He will do anything to save her. Can you not see that she is his woman?"

Caroline gasped in indignation. "I am no such thing!"

"Proper ladies do not run from the house in the early morn in their evening gowns," Michel said with a sneer.

Humiliated, she looked to Mr. Doherty to defend her honor.

He gave Caroline an assessing stare and said something in French that she did not quite understand. She knew the language as well as any of Mrs. Hill's students, but the direct translation of his words baffled her. It was something along the lines of: a beautiful outside that was more beautiful beneath.

"Mr. Doherty!" Caroline cried. "You shall lead them to believe I am something I am not!"

"Indeed, I do not," Mr. Doherty replied. "She is," he said for the men, "as beautiful as I have said. I should not like to see such beauty destroyed. Now, what shall it be?"

"Do as he says, Michel," Pierre said with a groan. "Perhaps you want me to die, eh?"

Michel rose to his feet with a sigh. "How do I know you will come back for Pierre?"

"You do not, but you have no choice. If you do not do exactly as I say, Pierre shall surely die. Now, this is how it shall be. Michel and Étienne shall mount one horse and ride off in the opposite direction of the house and village."

"You are to steal my horse?" Michel groused. "We have already lost one!"

"I shall need it to transport Pierre to the house, shall I not?"

"Very well," Michel replied, defeated. "What can I do?" he asked with a Gallic shrug.

"Nothing that is not to my liking," Mr. Doherty said. "I shall then do what I can for Pierre. When you get to London, assuming that is your destination, send word to me at Oak View with your direction. I shall then ensure that Pierre is informed of your whereabouts when he is well enough to join you."

"It is a good offer," Pierre groaned in appreciation.

Michel walked over to stare Mr. Doherty in the face. "I should not trust you, Niall, but I do. I know you to be a good man, just as you know me to be one."

"I do, but there is the matter of the young lady. She is innocent in all of this, and I shall not allow her to be harmed in any way. So, if we are agreed, I think that I should like to keep Étienne close by my side until you have mounted."

Michel shook his head in disbelief but, after stuffing their belongings into the saddle bags, he did as he was told. Mr. Doherty then escorted his captive through the gap to the horse. Caroline could see very little of what was happening, but the squeak of the saddle told her that two men had mounted.

"I shall remain here," Mr. Doherty called to her through the gap, "until I am convinced they have gone far enough in the right direction."

Relief washed over Caroline at his words. "Do not be astonished if you should find us gone when you return," she replied, her voice shaking with hysteria and laughter. "You shall never guess what has happened: Pierre has asked me to elope." She smiled down at the wounded man, whose wailing had so often had her quaking in fear.

He gave her a feeble smile in return. "You are not his woman, no! You are *the* woman." He held up his hand and jabbed a dirty finger at the gap in the trees. "The one he has been looking for."

Caroline shook her head. "I do not understand."

"You are the one," Pierre said so faintly she barely discerned his words. "I see it in his eyes when he looks at you. There is a story . . ."

"Yes! He is an excellent storyteller." It was her wish to keep him talking so that she need not fear that his silence meant his expiration.

"*Oui, incroyable!* Has he not told you the story?" he asked so breathily that she knew he would soon slip into unconsciousness or worse.

A tale came to mind; one Mr. Doherty had appeared to love most of all those he had told at Oak View. "I believe he has. Is it 'The Swan Bride?'"

"*Non*," he whispered, his eyes flickering shut.

"Pierre? Please speak to me," she insisted.

It was then that Mr. Doherty returned. He went immediately to her side to untie her, but she twisted away from him.

"Pierre, is he breathing? Please see if he is still alive!"

Mr. Doherty knelt on the ground and held a hand to Pierre's mouth and nose. After a few moments, he nodded. "He has only fainted." He stood and untied her shawl. "We must get him to the house as soon as possible."

"Charles and Christopher?" she asked as she pushed the shawl down to the ground. "Where are they?"

"I saw them from my window," he replied, holding out his arms to her.

She fell into them, reveling in the sensation of being crushed to his chest. Closing her eyes, she sighed in pure contentment. It was the moment for which she had yearned. "But they are safe?"

He rested his cheek against the top of her head. "By the time I had finished dressing and run down three flights of those ghastly narrow stairs, they were nowhere to be seen. I saw you, however, just as you disappeared behind the ash trees. I followed, which was when I encountered my young charges. They were determined to build a fort with their new tools. When they told me that they had heard a faint scream, I sent them back to the house. Charles, of course, refused to go unless I took his hatchet as protection."

Caroline laughed. "That dear sweet, lad; I owe him my life. I owe *you* my life. I do not know what would have happened if you had not seen us. We might have all three of us vanished. No one would have known where to begin to look for our bodies."

He shuddered, and she dared to put her arms around him.

"What if I had not seen you? I cannot bear the thought," he murmured against her hair. "To think that such brilliance might have been snuffed out and made to vanish."

"Which reminds me, Mr. Doherty," she said in mock severity, leaning back in his arms to peer archly into his face. "Why would you have them to believe me a woman of ill repute?"

"My poor Miss Fulton," he said, laughing as he gently pressed her cheek again to his chest. "Who is to say what good men will do when they are trapped and afraid? What if they had heard your name in the village? Is there one in all the land that does not consist of a gossip or two? A visiting heiress, beautiful, and meant for the local lord; that is irresistible fodder for such folk. I should not like the two of them to return in the night and find a way to abduct you again and hold you to ransom."

"You are so very wise," she murmured against his hastily-tied cravat. It gave off a whiff of starch and linen. Nothing had ever smelled so wonderful. "And yet, I found your remark about me to be quite shocking." She felt her face blush at the recollection.

"What is amiss in saying you are even more beautiful underneath this lovely exterior?" he said with a squeeze. "I was merely commenting on your internal beauty, your intelligence, your talents, your wit. If they should choose to interpret it to mean something foul, that is their affair."

"Oh," she breathed, touched. "You are so kind and very clever." She pulled back and looked up into his face that had become so dear. "I had thought I would never see you again, and now this. I find that I am happy to have been dragged into the woods."

He cupped her cheek in his hand and ran his thumb, ever so gently, across her lips. "Not as happy as am I," he said, his voice uneven.

Her heart began to race; surely now he would kiss her. She looked up into his face, but he did not lower his head to hers. Closing her eyes, she waited, but still he did not kiss her. When she opened them, she found that he gazed at her with sorrow in his eyes.

"Mr. Doherty, what is it?"

He dropped his hands to his sides and stepped back out of her arms. "This is the last time that I shall see you. 'Twould only lead to misery were we to meet again. When the house party is over, you shall go home to County Cavan. Unless you have decided to accept an offer of marriage from the baron, you shall never return. If you do accept him, I shall go away," he said, his face white.

"But, Mr. Doherty, do you not see?" she cried. "You have rescued me from certain harm; my father cannot refuse you. You must go to him! Naturally, I shall go to him first, to explain," she said, her excitement growing. "Then I shall insist that he hears what you have to say. It shall clear the way for you."

"And what shall I say to him, my dear Miss Fulton?" he asked, his eyes full of anguish. "That he should give his daughter to me, a man with no money, no prospects, no home of his own?"

"What does that matter?" she asked insistently. "If my dowry is sufficient to set up the baron as a mutton farmer, it is enough to keep the two of us anywhere we choose to live."

"Yes," he said, "but that is not what your father wants for you. Upon reflection, I am astonished that he should wish to part with you at all. You are all that he has. It shall take everything the baron has to offer, possibly more, for your father to endure even the thought of his separation from you."

She knew that he was right, but she could not bear it. "I love my papa and do not wish to hurt him. But is it right that I should be miserable for his sake?" she asked, the tears sliding down her face. "How am I to be without you?"

He brushed away her tears and placed his hands on her shoulders. As he pulled her towards him, she thought that he had reconsidered; that he meant to take her in his arms and deliver the kisses for which she longed. Instead, he put his mouth to her forehead. "No matter what happens," he said through lips that clung to her skin, "no matter where you go, I choose you, Caroline Fulton, now and forever."

The heat of his tears on her face, the pounding of his heart, the effort of his trembling restraint, none of it said as much as the fashion in which he dragged his quivering lips across her forehead.

"We must make haste," he said, stepping away from her. "The physician most usually calls directly after breakfast."

Caroline sniffed, her breath shuddering in her lungs. "Yes, poor Pierre! I shall help you get him onto the horse."

It was with difficulty that they succeeded in the transference of Pierre from the clearing to his mount. Mr. Doherty swung himself up into the saddle behind the wounded man to give him the support needed. Taking the reins in his hands, he turned to Caroline. "Follow me to the end of the woods. Once we emerge at the edge of the park, you shall be safe, but then I needs must go as fast as I can, for Pierre's sake."

"Yes, she said sadly. "I understand."

Quickly, they picked their way through the trees, and when they emerged from the woods, he turned and gave her one last, long look.

She smiled at him in hopes it would say all that she could not. Then he galloped away, chunks of the lawn flying into the air in the wake of the horse's hoofs.

Caroline waited until there was no chance of his overhearing before she fell to her knees and sobbed. She looked up through her tears to see Mr. Doherty, off in the distance, navigate the horse around to the back of the house, and then he was gone.

Reluctantly, she considered her possible fates. She could choose to marry the baron, or someone like him, bear his children, and have someone to care for her. Or, were she to remain unwed and live with her father, she would one day inherit all that he had and be forever on her own.

She thought about Charles and Christopher, their dear freckled faces and eager embraces. She thought of the infants born by Fiona's sisters and how Caroline never failed to wish for one of her own whilst holding them in her arms. She had already bid adieu to the man she loved; she found it to be every bit as difficult to say farewell to motherhood. She had fallen to her knees a sweetheart, but rose from them a determined spinster.

As she walked slowly back to the house, she watched a flood of horses flow past along the edge of the park: the baron and his guests. She turned quickly away in hopes she had not been identified; she had no wish to explain the events of the morning. There was little she could do once she entered the house, however, but run up the stairs as quickly as possible.

To her chagrin, she was met just inside the door by her father, along with Lady Bissell and Fiona. Each bore an expression of varying degrees of shock. Neither of the ladies was as disapproving as her father, however.

"What ha' ye been up to, young lady? Yer hair is disgraceful! T'ere is dirt and grass stains on yer gown! Could it be the same ye wore to dinner last night? Where ha' ye been?" he demanded.

"Papa," she begged, "I want nothing more than to explain it all to you, but I should prefer it to be in private."

"We shall discuss it in the carriage on our way home!"

"Home! We are to go home?" she asked in dismay.

"You don't believe the baron shall marry you now?" her father demanded.

"Well, at least there is that," she murmured as she brushed past her father and started up the stairs.

Chapter Fourteen

Niall longed to laugh. He was certain someone would, someday, when he heard the tale. It would be Niall telling the story, the one having to do with the man who deserted the woman he loved in order to rescue a highwayman.

There was no laughing, however, when so much as a breath taken too deeply seemed to pierce his heart. It was just as well; he would have never found the strength to part from Miss Fulton if Pierre were not in need of immediate rescue. When he approached the house, he realized there was no repenting his actions. It was with sharp resignation that he drew his mount to a halt and rapped at the kitchen door.

Mrs. Walsh, her face white with strain, opened it. "What is it?" she demanded in cross tones.

"Mrs. Walsh, I beg your pardon, but I am in need of assistance. A friend of mine is hurt and requires a physician. Is there a place he might rest until I arrange for the physician to see him?"

"It's plastered, is he?" she asked, inspecting Pierre where he lay sprawled along the neck of the horse.

"Not drunk, no. He is meek as a lamb and very tired. He needs a place to rest and a physician before he can resume his journey."

"Where's he bound?" she asked doubtfully.

"London, I suppose. I realize it is an inconvenience, particularly when you are short of help, but 'twould be a great service to me. He would be happy to pay." The words slipped easily from his tongue though he doubted Pierre possessed so much as a farthing.

"No, no, t'ere is no need for t'at," she said, satisfied. "If he's a friend of yours, t'at is more t'an satisfactory. Take him down from t'ere and he shall have my room for the time bein'."

She watched with interest as Niall negotiated the wounded man into position to be hefted over his shoulder. He knew it would exacerbate Pierre's pain; if he were fortunate, he would again lapse into unconsciousness. Following Mrs. Walsh into a small room next to the kitchen, Niall noted a carefully made bed against the wall.

"Ye just lay him right t'ere." Mrs. Walsh indicated.

Niall needed no further encouragement and slung Pierre onto the bed. A foul stench rose into the air when Niall pulled away the man's boots, but Mrs. Walsh didn't seem to notice. As she studied Pierre's face against the pillow, the lines of her face were softer than Niall had yet seen them.

"Go! Fetch the physician," she instructed. "I'll do what I can for the poor fellow until ye return."

"You are a saint, Mrs. Walsh," Niall said gratefully.

"We shall see Mr. Do'rty, we shall see," she said with a sad smile.

Niall pounded up the steps to the ground floor, the first, and finally to the second floor where Mr. Wilkinson's chamber was most likely to be found. When Niall reached the baize door, he opened it slowly and peered around it to ensure the passage was empty. He knew the baron had taken his male guests on a shoot whilst most of the ladies should all still be at breakfast. Seeing that the way was clear, he went to the first chamber door and, placing his ear to the polished wood, intently listened. Hearing nothing, he opened the door. The room was empty. Doing the same at each door, he came nearly to the end of the passage.

Suddenly, a door opened, and a maid appeared. She stared at him, her eyes wide with surprise. Niall hardly noticed; his gaze was drawn to the large windows that framed a familiar view of the park. There was no doubt that he gazed upon Miss Fulton's room. "Can you tell me," he asked with some difficulty, "the location of Mr. Wilkinson's chamber?"

"Indeed, it is to the other side of the passage, nearly to the landin'," she replied as she stepped out of the room and shut the door behind her.

Niall waited until she disappeared into another chamber before he drew open the door to Miss Fulton's. He knew it to be wrong, but he could not resist the opportunity to touch what she had touched; to breathe the air she had breathed; to see the sky from where she had stood.

He went to the window just below the one from which he delivered his letters and stared across the park to the row of ash trees. Then he looked about and noted that her bed was indeed placed just below his. He went to it and ran his hand along the headboard. Supposing he had located the spot where she had knocked to him just the night previous, he placed his hand over it and pictured her kneeling on the bed and knocking.

When his eyes began to fill, he knew he must be leave. As he turned to go, his gaze fell upon a crumpled piece of parchment addressed to Mr. Fulton. Niall assumed it to have been written by Miss Fulton and, based on the number of times his name appeared, on the subject of himself. Consumed with a curiosity he hadn't the time to indulge, he took it and slid it in the pocket of his jacket. Then he opened her chamber door a crack so as to determine if the passage were empty.

A couple of ladies were making their way into another chamber. The moment they shut their door, Niall stepped into the passage, opened the door to Mr. Wilkinson's chamber, and slipped inside. He was gratified to find the physician at Mr. Wilkinson's bedside, though a bit abashed at the manner in which they both stared at Niall in consternation.

"I beg your pardon," he said with a bow, "but when you have finished here, there is another who is needful of your services," he explained.

"Not another like the kitchen maid, I hope," the physician said, shaking his head. "That was a sad case."

"No, I am certain it is not the same ailment," Niall replied. "I shall wait in the passage until you are free," he said, in the case Mr. Wilkinson wished for privacy.

"There is no need," he said kindly. "Take up a chair; it is no trouble."

Gratefully, Niall sat and watched with interest as the physician examined Mr. Wilkinson's injured foot and dispensed a bottle of laudanum for the pain. "When the first is gone, here is another," he said. Niall hoped he had more in his black bag for Pierre.

"I am Dr. O'Brien," the physician said as he snapped the sides of his bag together. "Where are we to go now?"

After executing a bow for Mr. Wilkinson, Niall led the physician out to the passageway. "We shall take the servants' stairs to the kitchen," Niall explained. "I pray that you shall not mind that I do not request your services for a guest, but for someone laid low in a room next to the kitchen."

"You need not apologize," Dr. O'Brien said. "I attend to people from all walks of life, in all sorts of circumstances."

Niall silently wondered if the physician had ever before tended to a gunshot wound. If he felt obligated to report such occurrences to the authorities, there could be troublesome consequences. Niall decided that he would worry about it later, after Pierre's life was saved.

"He is through here," Niall instructed, indicating the doorway through which the physician must go.

"Ah, and what do we have here, Mrs. Walsh?" the physician asked.

"This poor man has a wound in his shoulder," she said fretfully. "I have cleaned it up as best I could."

Niall gazed at Mrs. Walsh in amazement. More surprising than her concern for this stranger was the fact that she had, in addition to washing his wound, washed his face and hands, removed his shirt, and tucked him up under the blankets. Niall looked about the room, but there was no sign of his clothing, much of which pointed towards Pierre's identity as a French soldier.

The physician pulled back the cloth Mrs. Walsh had pressed to the wound. "It would seem that your friend encountered a bullet."

"Yes," Niall replied shortly. Silently, he wondered how much he dared say about how Pierre had come by such a wound.

"'Twas simple, really," Mrs. Walsh said. "The poor man was hit when one of the baron's guests accidentally fired off his gun. T'ey were out to shoot birds and t'is poor man got the worst of it, didn't he Mr. Do'rty?"

"I am persuaded he had no wish to be shot," Niall agreed, grateful he was not required to lie. Impressed with Mrs. Walsh's storytelling, he decided he ought to come below stairs more often; perhaps she knew a tale or two that he had not heard.

"Well, he is very fortunate." Dr. O'Brien examined the wound more closely. "The bullet went straight through; only muscle was damaged."

"I am glad to hear it," Niall said in relief.

"Tell me, when did this happen?" the physician asked.

"'Twas several days ago," Niall hedged. He felt certain the psychiatrist knew full well the wound was not a fresh one.

"Why did no one fetch me at the time?" Dr. O'Brien demanded.

Niall frowned. "I couldn't say. I came to find you the moment I was made aware of the need."

The physician nodded. "You have done well with the cleaning of the wound, Mrs. Walsh. However, it has become inflamed. Will you make a poultice of herbs and honey?"

She cocked her head and arched a brow. "I dare ye to name any who could make one better!" she insisted as she stood and quit the room.

Dr. O'Brien turned to Niall. "A few days with frequent applications of hot poultices should draw out all of the infection. Then I shall be able to stitch up the wound, after which he should heal in good time."

"Thank you," Niall said. "Would you be so kind as to address the bill to me, Niall Doherty? I shall pay it when I go into town on my next afternoon off."

"Very well, Mr. Doherty," the physician said as he walked to the door. "I shall return later this evening to check his progress."

Niall sketched the physician a bow and turned to Pierre. He did little but groan before Mrs. Walsh returned with the warm poultice. She applied it with such loving attention that it made Niall wonder.

"I must thank you," Niall insisted. "You are kind to him."

"He is too pretty to die," she said softly. "He puts me in mind of me brother when he were young."

"I do not know how I can repay you," Niall said.

"Ne'er ye mind," she insisted. "He shall remain here 'til he's well. Ye need not fear t'at I shall tell any of the high and mighty above stairs," she insisted.

"Mrs. Walsh, you are a treasure. I shall be down to see how he does when I can."

"Indeed, ye shall. Now, ye had best go and see to t'ose lads. I need Miss Deakin to help in the kitchen again today."

"Of course," Niall said, the picture of calm despite the throb of anxiety that assailed him. He ran up the three sets of stairs and burst into the school room just as Charles had neared the end of his tale. It was about a beautiful maiden in the forest who was captured and screamed at length until the handsome prince ran to her rescue with his magic ax.

229

"That is a fertile imagination you have," Niall said briskly.

"It is what happened," Christopher insisted. "I was there."

Niall could not prevent his gaze from flying to the nursery maid's face in alarm, but she only smiled. "Thank you, Miss Deakin." Niall waited until she had left the room, far more reluctantly it seemed than in the past. He could only assume she preferred caring for the children over working in the kitchen. "Now, my lads, it is best if we do not share the story of your adventure this morning with others. Your mother and brother should not be happy to learn of it, should they?"

"My brother was most displeased with us yesterday," Christopher observed, "but he gave us the toys and candy anyway."

Niall suppressed a groan. "Perhaps, but you were not meant to leave the house on your own. If he were to learn of it, I am persuaded the baron should be quite angry. He would most likely remove your little tools altogether." Niall did not wish to encourage dishonesty, but he had Pierre's life to protect, as well as Miss Fulton's reputation. If only she were present in the school room, she would contrive a means to turn the lads' attentions to their lessons.

"I hear horses," Christopher said.

Charles jumped to his feet and ran to the window. "Someone has come to Oak View," he observed as he gazed down at the drive below.

Christopher ran to the window, as well. "Oooh, pretty horses," he murmured.

"Lads, it is time for lessons," Niall adjured as he went to the bookcase. His finger lingered over the binding of *Castle Rackrent*, but he quickly decided it, with its wry depiction of

230

Anglo-Irish landlords, would only do the lads an injustice. "Masters Charles and Christopher, I must insist that you return to your chairs," he said as he went to the window.

He saw that a traveling coach did indeed wait at the front of the house. "Perhaps your mama has a new guest arriving for the party." He put a hand on each lad's shoulder to direct them to face the school room. "Please be seated."

Charles and Christopher did as they were told, but Niall soon found they did not benefit from it. His thoughts so continually drifted to how he might arrange to catch a glimpse of Miss Fulton that he hardly knew what it was he said. After twice offering the incorrect date during the history lesson and failing to discover a mistake in Christopher's mathematics, Niall allowed the lads to return to the window.

"Look, Charles," his brother said. "The coach is still there."

"Look! Isn't she lovely?" Charles replied. "She has such a beautiful hat."

"Yes, but she looks so sad," Christopher remarked.

"Is it your mama?" Niall rose and went to the window. He looked down just as a lady disappeared into the carriage. He noticed that there was now luggage strapped to the top but did not feel any alarm until he realized that it was Miss Fulton and her father, who stood in conversation with Lady Bissell.

"She is going away," Niall said in disbelief.

"But she can't!" Christopher cried.

"Not without saying goodbye!" Charles insisted.

It was all he could do to refrain from opening the window and calling down to her. He could not abstain, however, from staring down at her in apprehension. The lads tapped

231

frantically at the window and, looking up, she saw them. She smiled and waved quite merrily as if she anticipated a happy journey. In point of fact, she seemed perfectly content. It smote him to the heart.

Mr. Fulton also looked up, scowling. Instinctively, Niall stepped back, almost as if to dodge a blow. He watched with growing devastation as Miss Fulton was handed into the carriage. As it pulled away and moved down the long drive, the old man ran out of the gatehouse to open the gate and shut it behind them with a resounding thud. Miss Fulton was gone. Forever.

"I fail to comprehend," Fiona hissed into Caroline's ear, "why it is we have taken our leave so abruptly. Certainly there was time for me to bid a proper adieu to Mr. Wilkinson. He shall believe I do not care for him."

"Nor was I allowed to so much as to dash off a note to Mr. Doherty," Caroline whispered in return. She brushed away a tear. "I am persuaded that Papa wished to be gone before the baron returned to witness my disgrace."

"At least you were able to wave to Mr. Doherty in the window," Fiona pointed out. "How you managed to smile is something I shall never understand."

"I did not wish to upset the lads." Her voice trembled. "I would not have them remember me as sad, but rather as happy to have known them."

"And Mr. Doherty?"

Caroline nodded, her eyes filling with tears. "And there was

Lady Bissell," she said as she dabbed at her cheeks. "To have Papa carry me off in disgrace was bad enough. I did not wish to add to her burdens by behaving as if I were dreadfully unhappy." The fact that she was, indeed, dreadfully unhappy, was neither here nor there.

"Lady Bissell was truly gracious," Fiona returned quietly. "I do believe she was sorry to see you go."

"Poor Papa," Caroline mused, sadly. "He might have had a baroness for a daughter."

"Whatever is in store for you now, it must prove preferable than to be the new Lady Bissell," Fiona said bleakly.

"I do not know, my dear." Caroline felt as if her heart had turned to stone and lodged in her throat. "Papa is so very angry. I am delighted that you, at least, shall be free to correspond with Mr. Wilkinson."

"Why should you not write to Mr. Doherty, as well?" Fiona asked.

"I suppose I might, but it should avail me naught. Papa shall never allow me to know Mr. Doherty any better than I do this moment." She recalled that Pierre had called him Niall; Niall Doherty. It was a perfectly splendid Irish name. "I do not wish to allow Mr. Doherty hope when there is none. I have never known Papa to be so angry at me," she said with a heavy sigh. "I am persuaded he shall not allow me to go out of the house for months."

Fiona reached over to take Caroline's hand. Neither of them dared to lift their gazes to the face of Mr. Fulton. He had said so many dreadful things already and had no wish to invite another of his awful tirades.

They broke their journey for the night at the same inn they

had stayed at on their outgoing journey. This time, however, Caroline was not allowed to dine in the public room nor walk about the garden. Her father arranged for dinner to be brought to her chamber, where she remained until their departure in the morning.

By the time the carriage drew to a halt in the drive of Fiona's home, Caroline felt as if she had been away for a year. Her distress was heightened by her father's determination to put her in mind of his humiliation at every turn. Rather than stop for a dish of tea with Fiona's mother and father, Caroline was not permitted to alight from the carriage. When she saw how it would be, she put her arms around her friend and held her close. "Goodbye, my dear. Please write to me," she murmured before the tears constricted her throat.

"I shall!" Fiona replied, leaning back out of Caroline's arms to search her face. "I shall write to you every day and bring the letter to your doorstep in the case that I am not allowed to see you."

Caroline nodded, but she could no longer hold back the tears.

"He cannot keep you shut up forever," Fiona whispered.

Caroline again nodded her agreement, as speech was impossible.

Fiona gave Caroline's hand a final squeeze, then she moved out of the shadowed carriage into the daylight without. Her mama and papa were standing on the drive, waiting to take her in their arms whilst their pack of dogs cavorted up and down the drive.

Caroline leaned forward so as to view the happy scene

when, with a snap, Mr. Fulton shut the carriage door. She bit back the hasty words that came to her tongue as she stared into the gloom of the empty carriage. It was punishing in the extreme to be reduced to a mere eavesdropper of the joyful reunion of Fiona's family. The tears flowed faster as Caroline realized what a trial was yet to come. Somehow she had forgotten how much she looked on Fiona's mother as her own. To not be allowed to consult Mrs. O'Sullivan on the fit of a new gown or, most particularly, matters of the heart, seemed too cruel a fate.

Thoughts of Bess, Caroline's abigail, next came to mind. Hopefully, she was returned from tending to her sick mother. The young maid was possessed of a listening ear upon which Caroline could count to be in full sympathy with all that she said. But when they finally arrived at The Hollows, she was dismayed to learn that Bess's mother was still gravely ill. A kitchen maid was sent to help Caroline out of her gown and stays, but she was not one Caroline wished to trouble with her private musings. *Papa has robbed me of everything*, she thought.

Come the morn, the same girl arrived to assist Caroline to dress. She almost chuckled aloud when she thought on how what she wore hardly mattered. She might remain in her night rail all day; no one but the kitchen maid would be the wiser. When the girl left, Caroline sat at her writing desk and wrote a letter to Fiona.

Once that task was completed, she picked up a book and attempted to read. Her thoughts continually wandered, however, to the stolen moments with Mr. Doherty by the little spring; the instant she first knew that he loved her; the fervent kiss he had pressed to her forehead within the circle of oaks in the woods.

With a sigh, she went to the window that looked out over the back garden. How she longed to be out among the green. It was a color she would always associate with Mr. Doherty and their time together at Oak View.

Listlessly, she passed the day in such idle pursuits until, late in the afternoon, a rap came at the door. She pulled it open to find the housekeeper, who regarded her with impertinent curiosity.

"Beggin' yer pardon, miss, but yer father is wishful to see ye in his study, ta sooner ta better."

"Thank you," Caroline said as she went to her writing desk to retrieve the letter to Fiona. Then she made her way to her father's study and rapped on the door.

"Come in," her father said in tones so cross she knew he had not softened his stance to any degree. Indeed, it sounded as if he were angrier than ever.

As she lifted the latch, she was dismayed to see how her hand shook. She had never before been afraid of her father; he had always been the one to spoil her, to capitulate to her, to fulfill her every wish. Somehow he had transformed into the very one responsible for the loss of her every comfort in life. She could not imagine what remained for his taking, but the very notion made her tremble.

Slowly, she opened the door and looked into the room. Her father sat in his favorite chair by the fire, reading the periodicals. Apprehensive, she entered quietly in the case he found himself angered purely at her existence. He lifted his head and saw her, grunting an acknowledgment of her presence. Then he returned his attention to his reading.

Caroline knew not what she should do. She stood for so long in such a state of trepidation that her knees began to ache. To be alone in her bedchamber suddenly seemed a far more welcome prospect. Finally, she could bear it no longer. "Papa? I was told you wished to speak to me for some reason."

He jerked his head up and glared at her. "I have not forgiven ye, if t'at is what ye believe!"

Her lips fell open in astonishment.

"I shan't tolerate such behavior, ye hussy! Ye shall catch cold at t'at, see if ye don't!"

Caroline stifled a sigh and bowed her head. "If you are not to tell me what is wanted, I shall return to my room."

"Ye shall not go to yer room 'til ye are told to go to yer room!"

Caroline nodded. "Yes, Papa."

"Ye shan't speak 'til I tell ye to speak!"

Caroline bit her lip and said nothing.

"T'ere is not one t'ing ye shall do unless I have commanded it!"

Tears stung her eyes as she considered her father's lack of charity. He had never even allowed her to explain. It seemed now he would never know the truth. She sniffed as the tears began to fall.

"Is sniveling all ye have to say for yerself?" he demanded.

"If by that you mean to grant me permission to speak . . ." she started before he interrupted.

"Not if t'ere is to be tears! I cannot abide 'em! When ye are

237

prepared to answer me questions wit'out weepin', I shall hear ye."

Silently, she held out the letter for Fiona.

He gave her a stony stare then returned his attention to his periodical.

Caroline allowed the letter to flutter to the floor in hopes the butler would collect it and see it delivered. Then she picked up her skirts and fled to her room. It was not until the key was turned in the lock that she began to weep in earnest. Wracked with anguish, she wondered if she would ever be able to speak of Mr. Doherty without weeping.

The following morning she heard the sound of wheels against the gravel of the drive. She ran to the window that looked out over the front of the house to behold Fiona as she stepped down from her jaunting car. She looked up at the window and smiled, putting her hand to her brow to shield her eyes from the unusually hot sun.

With a surge of gratitude, Caroline greeted her friend with a wave. She waited as Fiona rapped and the door, followed by the sound of it opening and the faint murmur of voices. The tones of her friend's voice, however dim, was so very welcome! To her dismay, Caroline heard the butler deny Fiona entrance and the snap of the door snapping shut. She no longer smiled as she looked up again at Caroline's window.

"Wait!" Caroline called as she turned the window latch. To her surprise, the window would not be moved. At first, she thought it to be stuck, but as she pushed and prodded, the panes of glass merely rattled in their frames. At last, she shook her head as she gazed sadly down at Fiona. She seemed to understand, her head hung low as she climbed aboard her jaunting car and drove away.

Caroline waited with great misgiving until the jaunting car disappeared from view before she dashed to the window that overlooked the garden. Frantic, she turned the latch of that window, as well, and found that it would not open, either. Her skin flushed and her heart raced as she realized the truth: her papa had ordered the windows nailed shut from the outside. It was with a great sense of betrayal that she realized he must have had it done whilst she was with him in his study the day prior.

She fell across her bed and contemplated her choice to live with a man who possessed no honor. If she were to endure such selfishness, she ought to have done so as the baron's wife and mother of his children. Tears would have been welcome, but to her astonishment they would not come.

The day after and the next were like the first. When, by the fourth, she still could not weep, Caroline felt ready to speak to her father. Each time someone came to the door with food or to pointlessly help her in and out of her gown, Caroline sent word to him. To her dismay, there was never any response. More days passed and Caroline grew desperate. Bess was never restored to her, so the letters Caroline wrote to Fiona were given to the kitchen maid in hopes she would see them carried to the O'Sullivans. However, in spite of Fiona's daily visits with her letters clearly in hand, none of them made their way to Caroline.

After a fortnight of almost total seclusion, a folded parchment was slipped under Caroline's door. In disbelief, she took it up and turned it over in her hands. The seal had been broken, leading her to believe her father had read it. Surely he had read all of the others, as well. She wondered what was different about this one that she should have the chance to know its contents. She spread wide the parchment and was immediately disappointed by the brevity of Fiona's words. It told only of her invitation to return to Oak View. Mr. Wilkinson was still in residence, and he would not leave Ireland until he saw her. She was to depart the following morning.

Caroline read of her friend's happy news with joy, even as her loneliness increased in equal measure. She suspected she would soon hear of Fiona's betrothal to Mr. Wilkinson. Caroline did not know when she could hope to see Fiona again; Mr. Fulton was not likely to allow his daughter to attend the nuptials.

Another week passed, one of very little rain, and her chamber became unbearable. As she could not let in fresh air, the unusually hot weather was a misfortune rather than a treat. How she would have loved to be outside basking in the sun! And yet, she did not enjoy her view of the garden as it slowly browned in the heat. She moved to the window that overlooked the front of the house in hopes of observing a passing carriage.

To her astonishment, she saw an unfamiliar vehicle roll along in the dust of a distant road. "Let us make a wager," she said through the window glass to the pigeon that stood on the sill. "If that carriage turns down the lane to my house, come supper, I shall give you a parsnip."

The pigeon cooed, a piece of brown grass in its beak as Caroline watched the progress of the carriage with growing anticipation. "Huzzah!" she cried when it turned into her lane.

"I wonder who has come to call. It is not the O'Sullivan carriage, of that I am certain," she said by way of informing the pigeon. "Nor does it bear a crest, so it might very well be a hired carriage."

The bird tilted its head, but it did not fly away.

"You are after that parsnip, are you not?" she said with a smile. "Naturally, no one from Mullagh need hire a carriage to call on us. Therefore, whoever is in the carriage hails from somewhere far." She watched the bird as it regarded her with an unblinking eye. "How delightful if it should prove to be Fiona with her Mr. Wilkinson. They had best hurry; it looks as if it shall finally rain. Then again, perhaps the driver has mistakenly turned down our lane and shall only circle the drive and go on his way."

She had decided this to be likely, but waited, along with the pigeon, to ensure her accuracy. She had never been more surprised or delighted in the whole of her life when the carriage drew to a halt, and Mr. Doherty alighted. He looked extremely dapper in an elegant hat, a charcoal jacket, and buff pantaloons. He wore snow white gloves and in his hand he carried a proper cane which he employed to rap on the door.

It was not until she heard the butler's muffled greeting that she fully realized the import of Mr. Doherty's visit. He had traveled a great distance; surely it was not purely a social visit. He must have come to ask her papa for her hand in marriage. Her feelings were a mix of joy and alarm as she ran to the pier glass. It reflected a girl with cheeks grown pale, her hair half undone and falling about her face. The white muslin gown she had found eminently suitable for the warmth of the day now seemed decidedly drab.

241

Heart pounding, she ran again to the window to note that the carriage yet waited. She knew it to be a miracle that he had been allowed into the house; that he had come at all was a notion incomprehensible. Even as she frenziedly pinched her cheeks and smoothed her hair, she knew her father would refuse to allow her to speak with the man she loved. Still, Mr. Doherty was a clever man. Surely he would contrive a speech suitable to mollify her papa. If not, wouldn't he, at the very least, leave her a message?

In too short a time she heard the front door snapped shut. Her heart lurched as she ran again to the window. Mr. Doherty stood on the drive, his hat and gloves in his hands. Slowly, he turned and looked at the door as if astonished to find himself chased out of the house.

As he lifted his hand to the carriage door, Caroline sprang to life. Forgetting that the window would not open, her hand slipped on the latch. Frantically, she rapped on the window, prompting the pigeon to burst from the sill. At the same moment, the clouds parted, and water poured down upon the parched earth. It was through a sheet of rain that she saw him slap his hat to his head and open the carriage door.

In desperation, she pounded on the window. "Mr. Doherty!" she cried in hopes he would hear her voice above the torrent. She thought perhaps he hesitated, but it seemed he did not hear her. Unwilling to give up, she banged on the window even after he had climbed into the carriage. Exhausted, she watched as the carriage drove away, out onto the road, and out of sight. He had never even looked up.

Thoroughly dismayed, she slid against the unyielding

window to the floor. He was gone, never to return. Something inside of her broke so painfully that it made her gasp, and yet she could not weep. Instead, she sat beneath the window and entertained trivial thoughts: the carpet required sweeping; a mouse had made its home in the wainscoting; her feet were cold. She tucked them beneath her gown with such care it made her laugh. It no longer mattered what happened to her. The hope she had been so foolish to entertain had been rent asunder and fled away.

It was another se'enight of such hopelessness before a second letter was slipped under her door. Fiona was to marry Mr. Wilkinson. They would travel together to London for the wedding. Caroline was invited, but she knew her papa would not allow her to attend. She would be surprised if she ever were to see Fiona again. Naturally, it did not hurt; nothing did. Caroline threw the letter on the fire; the old life was gone.

As she lay upon her bed that night, she doubted sleep would find her. There was never enough to do in order to induce the proper amount of fatigue; and then there was the ceaseless drum of the rain against the house. Once it had begun, it seemed it would never stop. It was if the sky wept the tears she could not. It served as a constant reminder of the moment she had learned not to care.

At some point she must have slept, for she had a vivid dream. She was in a large city, surrounded by a great number of people. They seemed mostly to speak with Irish accents, but there were other languages spoken, as well. She realized that she was in Dublin, a city she had known well when she attended finishing school. The area was unfamiliar, however, and she looked about with great interest. She crossed over a bridge and walked down a street, then turned into another and another. The streets surrounded a square and were filled with leafy green trees and rows of black railings.

Then she turned onto a street that she knew; it was the location of her finishing school. She opened the gate and went up the walk. As she rapped at the door and waited to be allowed inside, she looked down at her gown. It was the dull red that she had not ordered until after leaving Mrs. Hill's. On her hands was the pair of blue kid gloves she had purchased for her stay at Oak View the month prior. The door opened, she entered, and woke with a start.

In the morning she understood: the old life was over, but she must return to Dublin for the new life to begin. Her father, quite naturally, would never allow such a thing. She must do it on her own and, for that, she would need money. She had a few of her mother's things she could sell, but first, she must be released from her chamber. That would never happen until she earned her father's confidence.

She went to her writing desk and scratched out a note to her papa, telling him how very sorry she was for the distress she had caused. It sounded like a confession, of what she could only guess, but she found that she no longer cared what her father thought of her. Hoping it would induce a reaction from him, she slid it under her door, and waited impatiently for the result.

Late in the afternoon, Mrs. Cadogan rapped at the door and escorted Caroline, as if a guest in her own home, to the door of the study. More anxious than frightened, Caroline lifted the latch and entered. Her father sat in the same chair, but he held nothing in his hands. He seemed too weak for that. He appeared to be extremely fatigued, and she was persuaded that she had never known him to be so thin.

"Papa, are you well?" she asked, certain he had lost at least a stone in the past few weeks.

He gathered what strength he had to sit up and glare at her. "Ye have somet'ing to say to me?"

"Yes, Papa. I am sorry for what happened. I would never wish to give you pain. Please forgive me."

"Very well, t'en. That was all t'at was required of ye, me girl."

She rather doubted that was the case, but she refrained from airing her opinion. Instead, she walked to his side and took his hand in hers. It felt frail and the veins on the back more pronounced, like the roots of the oak trees in the wood. "I have always been sorry to have hurt you. It is only that you never gave me an opportunity to explain."

He lifted his eyes to her with great effort. "Ye may tell me now."

"There is nothing to tell, really," she said. "I have done nothing of which you should be ashamed."

He nodded, weakly. "T'at is good. I hear t'at Miss O'Sullivan is to be married."

Caroline marveled at the ease of her confession. "Yes," she said slowly. It seemed her papa was too weak to quarrel. "We are, of course, invited, but I suppose London is too far to go."

"We shall see, we shall see . . ." he mumbled.

That night before she went to bed, she tried the door. It fell open at her touch. She was free.

Chapter Fifteen

"Why are you going away, Mr. Doherty?" Christopher asked.

Niall tucked the blankets tighter around this young lad who had wound his way round his heart. "I have a new position at Trinity College in Dublin. I am to replace a man who fell ill and cannot return to his duties."

"Shall you like it there better than you like it here?" Charles asked.

"If by that you mean shall I like my students better than I like you, then the answer is no," he said with a fond smile for both lads.

"Then why are you leaving?" Christopher repeated, his lower lip trembling.

"It is difficult to explain," Niall replied, his own feelings doleful. "I suppose it has most to do with having a home of my own so that I may one day marry and raise sturdy lads such as you."

The two of them gazed at him in silence, their eyes glowing in the light of the lamp Niall had brought to the nursery from his bedchamber.

"Mr. Doherty," Christopher said very softly. "Will you tell us a story?"

"Of course," Niall replied, pleased to have been asked. It

246

was the last opportunity he would have to speak to the lads before his departure in the morning. "Let me see . . ." he mused, sitting upon Christopher's bed. "I have told you so many, I do not know that there are any remaining."

"There must be one," Charles pointed out in his usual prosaic manner.

"Very well, have I ever told you the story of Connla, son of Conn of the Hundred Battles?"

Both lads shook their heads, their golden curls dancing along their pillows.

"Well, Connla was the best sort of son," Niall said quietly, thinking on the sons he was about to lose. "He was tall and strong, and very courageous. He was also handsome, with red hair that flowed down his back. One day he and his father stood on the mount of Usna when Connla saw a young maiden approach him."

"Did she have ruddy hair like Miss Fiona or golden hair like Miss Caro?" Christopher asked.

Niall felt his heart constrict. "Golden, like Miss Caro's," he said softly. "And she wore a long, white gown. Still, she was somehow different from any maiden Connla had ever seen, and so he asked her from whence she had come. She told him that she was one of the Hill Folk of Mag Mell where they live together in peace and happiness, feast without end, and no one grows older or dies."

"I should like to live there," Charles interjected.

"As would I," Niall said, not realizing until that moment how true were his words. "Only, it is a place that mortals cannot dwell unless invited by one of the fairy folk. Now, Connla's father could not see or hear the maiden, so he asked, 'To whom are you speaking, my son?' But it was the maiden who answered and suddenly the father could hear her say, 'Connla speaks to me, a beautiful young woman who shall never die. I love your son and shall take him away to Mag Mell where we shall live in joy and peace.' Then she turned to Connla and said, 'Oh, come with me, Connla of the ruddy hair and kingly form, come where thy beauty shall never fade.' This speech frightened Conn so much, that he called upon the Druid, Coran, to save his son from such a fate.

"Coran appeared and chanted in the direction from whence the voice had been heard. Suddenly Connla could not see or hear the fairy maiden, but just before she disappeared from his sight she threw to him an apple."

"I like apples," Christopher said.

"As did Connla, which was a very good thing, for he ate nothing but that apple for an entire month."

"How could he eat just one apple for so long?" Charles asked dubiously.

"That is an excellent question. It was because every time he took a bite of the apple, it became whole again. But that was not the most extraordinary feature of this apple: it represented the love of the maiden and with each bite it made him long for her until he could think of nothing else. When a month had passed, Connla was with his father when the fairy maiden again appeared to him. 'Leave the world behind, my Connla, and come to Mag Mell, a place where you are eagerly awaited by the fairy folk. They have learned of you and your brave deeds, and long to see you numbered among their dear ones.'

"Though he could not see her, Connla's father heard the maiden's words and it frightened him, for those who went to live with the Hill Folk never returned. So he called again on the Druid Coran, who appeared at Conn's bidding. But the maiden would not be banished. 'You have no power over me and never shall,' she said calmly to the druid. Connla's father watched his son, however, and saw that he clung only to the words of the fairy maiden.

"Then he said to his son, 'Do you wish to go with her?' Connla heard his father's voice and turned to him. 'It is hard on me to leave all of those whom I love, but I am seized with a longing for this maiden, and it never ends.'

"When the maiden heard this, she spoke to him and said, 'Connla, come with me in my crystal Curragh to join my people. Though the sun is sinking, we shall yet be there before the light is gone. We can live there together in joy and our days shall have no end.' Connla spoke not at all, but ran to the crystal Curragh and leapt inside. And then could his father see all. He stood and watched the gleaming canoe glide away until it disappeared into the setting sun."

There was a palpable silence. Niall thought that perhaps the lads were asleep. Then Christopher stirred and spoke in a small voice. "I know why you are leaving us: you wish to be with her."

Niall quelled a bitter laugh. "No. Indeed, I should be surprised if I were ever allowed to see her again."

"Why should you not?" Charles asked in astonishment. "She is your friend!"

Niall rather agreed. "It is not Miss Caro's choice. At least, I do not believe it to be." He was reminded of the letter he had found in her room, the one to her father that spoke of Niall's qualities. He would never have gone to Dublin to seek his new position if it weren't for what she had written of him. He owed her much.

"Then whose choice is it?"

Niall pondered the question before saying, "I shall answer your question with another story. Will that do?"

Charles nodded, and Niall moved to sit on his bed.

"A year and a day ago, a man met a maiden, just as Connla did. However, this man's name was Sean, and it was not Sean's father who did not like the idea of their marriage: it was hers. He did all that he could to keep them apart; he even found a new husband for the maiden. But she did not love him; she loved no one but Sean. This made her father so angry that he took her to a land far away."

"Did she bid him a proper goodbye before she left?" Charles demanded.

"She was not allowed to speak to him. However, she did wave to him in farewell."

"But wasn't she sad to leave him?"

"Of course! But she loved him so much that she did not wish him to be apprehensive for her. The father was so cruel, you see. But, she left behind a letter," Niall said, his voice faltering. "One that expressed all of the reasons she loved him so."

"And what were they?" Charles asked.

Niall hesitated, reluctant to laud himself. "Let us say that she saw in him qualities he had not seen in himself, ones that, knowing she believed them, made him want to live up to them. So, one day, he went to the city and found work to do that would be worthy of the maiden. When all was arranged, he wished to call on her, but her father was still angry and did not allow them to meet."

"That is unjust!" Charles burst out.

"Indeed, it was," Niall agreed, his heart full. "So Sean spoke to the father and said that if he were not allowed to speak with her, perhaps the father could convey to her a message. The father agreed, and Sean pondered on what his message should be. For you see, he had sent letters to the maiden, and she had never replied. This made him wonder if perhaps her father had kept them from her, and he realized she must believe he did not love her. Surely it was the father who interfered, so the message he had for her must be one the father could never understand so that he did not withhold it from her. So he told the father this: 'Please tell her that the water in the spring has run dry.'"

"The water in our spring has run dry, as well," Christopher said sleepily.

Charles ignored his brother. "Why did Sean say that?" he asked, his nose wrinkled in bewilderment.

Niall could not help but think on the day he had spotted his father's watch face down in the mud of the spring. The memory still caused his heart to ache. "It means that it was the father who stood in the way of their happiness, but that Sean still loved her."

"Did she know what it meant?"

Niall nodded. "She ought to have well enough."

"What did her father say? Did he give her the message?"

"Sean certainly hoped that he did. The father was not clever enough to know what it truly meant, so he would not see any harm in doing so."

"Then, has Sean given up?"

Niall considered the question. If her father had indeed given her the message, it had prompted no response. It had been months since the house party; an acquaintance of five or six days, no matter how close, was easily forgotten. "He loves *her* still," he insisted. "Is that what you wish to know?"

"No. What I wish to know is, did Sean give up fighting for her?"

Niall mustered a smile as he placed his hand on the lad's head. "Let us hope you shall be luckier in love than have I," he said. "Now, your brother is asleep, and you must soon join him. Miss Deakin has promised to be certain you are up and ready come the morning to meet me out front, so that we may take a proper leave of one another."

"I am glad," Charles said as he turned on his side and burrowed into the mattress. "Good night."

"Good night, Master Charles. Good night, Master Christopher," he added in the case the boy was yet awake. He did not respond. Taking up his lamp, Niall quit the nursery through the school room and looked about. The bookshelf had been cleared of his personal property, but he had not yet located the volume of Shakespeare Miss Fulton had held in her hand the night she graced them with her presence. Spotting it on a table in the corner, he retrieved it as Banquo's words came to mind. Were the matchmaker's sweet words half-truths? Or were they the truest words of all? Even if they were, he doubted he

252

should ever be ready to stand on the Wellington Bridge to seek out his true love.

With a sigh, he ran his fingers over the cover of the volume last touched by Miss Fulton. Then he went to the door and left the Oak View school room forever. As he walked along the passage to his chamber, he thought how he was about to spend his last night in that particular bedchamber. It had lost a good deal of its charm once Miss Fulton no longer slumbered in the one just below.

Upon entering the room, he placed his book and lamp on the writing desk next to the coil of string he had used to lower his notes to her. A wave of melancholy assailed him at the memory it induced. He picked it up, full well knowing he should discard it, and put it in his pocket. Then he went to bed and slept without dreaming.

His parting from the lads the next morning was every bit as treacherous as he hoped it would not. For some reason Niall could not conceive, Lord Bissell had chosen to see him off. He treated Niall to the selfsame behavior that had prompted him to quit the premises in the first place. Lady Bissell, however, kindly attempted to remedy the baron's clumsiness.

"The lads shall certainly miss you, Mr. Doherty," she said. "They have never had an instructor they liked so well. I must thank you; they have become much better behaved since you arrived."

"Thank you, Lady Bissell. I hope that I have done well by the lads, as well as you," he said, with a bow. He sketched a bow to the baron, as well, but he had turned away to berate the lads over some trifle.

Niall waited until they had politely endured their brother's admonishments before calling them to his side.

"Goodbye Mr. Doherty," Charles said with a grave look into his tutor's eyes. "I shall miss you."

"And I shall miss you," Niall said.

"I wish that you did not have to leave," Christopher said sadly. "But since you must, please tell her that I asked after her."

Niall affected surprise. "To whom should I relay this greeting?" he asked with a hand on the lad's head.

"Why, Miss Caro, of course," Christopher said matter-of-factly.

Niall did not wish to disappoint him, nor did he wish to lie, so he merely shook the lad's hand and boarded the carriage. It would take him as far as the nearest coaching inn, where Niall would then board a public coach and resume his journey to Dublin. He would be required to spend the night at more than one inn, but it was a journey he had made once before, and it would not be too arduous. Rather it was the state of his heart that threatened to sink him.

Just before the carriage reached the gatehouse, Niall lowered the glass and put his head out the window. The lads waved goodbye, their expressions woeful; it was a hard thing to leave them behind. They were not the reason for the black despair that assailed him, however. It was the gurgling brook, the wide, green park, and the towering row of ash trees to which his gaze clung. To quit the very place where he had met and known Miss Caroline Fulton was a wrench to the heart from which he felt he would never recover.

Dublin, July 1816

The River Liffey lay just to the north of Niall's lodgings at Trinity College. However, since he had arrived in Dublin, he had studiously avoided the quay along the river. Whenever he went out, he turned south towards the gracious, less congested, neighborhoods where the once-upon-a-time Doherty townhouse was found. It was a far more compelling lure than the metal footbridge that had finally been made available to the public the spring following his arrival. Despite the widespread excitement that none need ever again cross the river on a decaying ferry, Niall could not bring himself to go anywhere near.

A visit to the townhouse, however, one large enough to house Niall's longed-for future family as well as his mother and sisters, had become a daily ritual. That his father had lost it in a game of cards was a circumstance Niall had never fully accepted. It wasn't that his father was too irreproachable to gamble; rather it was that he was far too skilled to lose.

By winter term, Niall had become consumed with the notion of owning the home of his youth. It wasn't only to recoup what had been lost or to possess a key that would allow him to enter the green in the center of the square; it was as much about living in the very rooms in which he had envisioned Miss Fulton. To that end, he requested from a colleague a recommendation for a solicitor.

However, it wasn't until his students had returned home for the summer that Niall fully turned his attention to the matter of the house. He set off on foot one fine summer day, the solicitor's address in his pocket. Before long, Niall realized that the route he must take would bring him in view of the Wellington Bridge. In spite of the hollow pit the notion made of his stomach, he forced himself to walk briskly onward. Yet, when he discovered that he must indeed cross the river, he hesitated.

He considered paying the toll to walk across one of the larger bridges meant for carts and carriages. People walked along them, as well, but, it seemed to Niall, at their peril. He recalled a tale from his youth about a poor lad who was crushed under the wheels of an English traveling coach. It seemed suddenly ridiculous to go out of his way to walk along a perilous bridge when the footbridge lay before him.

He ascended the metal steps that led to the long expanse across the water, and once on the bridge proper, he paused to take in the double length of wrought iron railings. There were a dozen people on the bridge: several gentlemen like him, a few wizened individuals, and a clutch of children accompanying three women. Whether they were married mothers or eligible nursery maids, he could not say; he refused to study them closely enough to determine the details.

With a determined step, he walked on, refusing to meet the eye of any on the bridge. He nearly laughed aloud at his apprehension, whilst questioning himself as to the reason for his absurd behavior. To his surprise, the answer came to him immediately and with great force: he feared to learn that anyone other than Miss Fulton was the one of whom the matchmaker spoke. This time, he allowed himself to laugh aloud; he had never had a thought more ridiculous. Had he not long ago accepted that Miss Fulton was not within in his reach?

A quick succession of thoughts followed: if she once loved him, she did no longer, the letter of hers that he so cherished had been written when she was in the midst of a passionate infatuation; and finally, an acquaintance of five days could not possibly forge a lasting love. And yet, he could not deny his love for her had made its home in his heart forever.

It was not until he encountered the steps on the far side of the bridge that he recalled why he had ventured north of the river in the first place. Referencing the scrap of parchment with the address, Niall continued his quest to locate the offices of the solicitor. Once he found the building, a tall, narrow affair along the quay, he realized that the main of the structure housed a fish restaurant.

Further analysis revealed that he was meant to go up a set of rickety stairs to a door on the top floor. As he climbed, accompanied by the drifting scent of decaying fish, he began to doubt that this particular solicitor could be of service. However, he had no wish to inform his colleague that he had not met with the man, so he went to the door and rapped upon it. It was opened by a clerk and Niall was asked to wait in the ante chamber. The wait seemed interminable and was long enough for Niall to determine that he should be happy never to see a dish of fish for the remainder of his life.

When he finally entered the inner office to discuss the matter at hand, the solicitor listened carefully. Niall outlined the details as he knew them in regard to the loss of the house, including his suspicion that his father might have been cheated. He also requested that the solicitor determine whether or not the owner of the house would consider selling it to Niall, and at what price. The solicitor promised to look into it, and added that he would inform Niall of anything that he learned through a letter sent to Niall's lodgings.

Encouraged by the outcome of the meeting, Niall had forgotten about his return journey across the footbridge until he was once again on the rickety staircase. He considered taking a meal at a pub on the north side of the river, but the odor of dead fish had done away with his appetite. With no sound reason to do otherwise, he took the steps to the bridge and again paused to investigate whom he might chance upon.

There were the usual women and children, gentlemen and vagabonds, but this time, he espied two fashionably-attired young ladies walking towards him. This was precisely the portion of the population he wished to avoid. So quickly that he was again tempted to laugh at himself, he ran back down the steps and strode off along the quay. Despite his haste, a fragment of their conversation drifted his way as they descended the bridge.

"It is still difficult to comprehend you are a married lady," came a voice that was half carried away on the breeze.

"Soon it is I who shall be saying the same of you, Caro!" said the second.

There was no mistaking this voice; it belonged to Miss Fiona O'Sullivan who, it seemed, had married. And the first could belong to no other than Miss Caroline Fulton. The moment he realized it, he whirled about, but the ladies had turned left off of the bridge where he had turned right, and were soon lost in the crowds along the quay.

Slowly he returned to the bridge and walked across it

without a qualm, the matchmaker's promise momentarily forgotten. His thoughts were consumed with questions: How was Miss Fulton in Dublin? How did she escape her father's tyranny? What was the meaning of Miss O'Sullivan's remark in regard to Miss Fulton's marriage? Was she soon to be married as well?

It seemed only a few minutes had passed before he looked up and found himself again on the grounds of the college. The brisk walk had done nothing to repair his appetite, so he went straight to his rooms. As he sat at his desk and worked on lessons for the following term, he found he was required to continually force his thoughts away from Miss Fulton. In exasperation, he rose to his feet, crumpled the parchment into a ball, and threw it into the fire with such force, he was taken aback.

Dropping into the chair by the fire, he watched the parchment turn red around the edges, then black, and finally ash gray. As his temper mellowed, he was astonished to realize he was angry. He had no right to be, of this he was certain. And yet, he could not deny the fury that swelled his veins. Miss Fulton was to marry another. It felt like a most unwarranted betrayal.

He knew he was wrong to begrudge her happiness. Did he truly prefer that she waste away in her little village for want of him? With a laugh of derision, he realized it was precisely what he had pictured. He had built for himself a new life, but he expected her to live forever with the consequences of her father's domineering ways.

Most every night since they had parted, Niall had lain

259

awake pondering on whether or not Miss Fulton would even now be his if he had only had the courage to speak to her father. This thought was always followed by unbidden reminders of his powerlessness. For Niall to have requested a private audience with Mr. Fulton would have been an act of indefensible irregularity. He would have been carried off by a pair of footmen and shown the door simply for deigning to ask.

But now, having beheld her in Dublin, Niall was doomed to a thorough examination of his every action in regard to Miss Fulton. Of one thing he was certain: he had behaved with honor. He had done all that he possibly could, nothing less. Once he had acquired his new post with new freedoms, he had gone to her home to speak to her father, but Mr. Fulton was not in the least interested in what Niall had to say. He refused to so much as allow his daughter to meet with her suitor.

How, then, did she come to be in Dublin with plans to marry? Niall would have wagered all he had that Mr. Fulton would prove reluctant to wed his daughter to anyone. It was a puzzle that proved only to haunt Niall.

He spent a sleepless night during which he adjured himself to forget her. When he awoke, however, he could think of nothing but seeing her again. Departing his rooms at the same time as the afternoon prior, he retraced his steps to the metal footbridge in hopes he would encounter her. It was only as he crossed it that he realized he had not taken into account the time he had spent with the solicitor.

In order to pass the time, he walked up and down the quay for nearly an hour when, quite suddenly, he saw the two young ladies just as he had the afternoon prior. Longing to know of what they spoke, he quickened his pace until he fell in step behind them as they moved off of the bridge and onto the street. He slowed his pace and strained his ears so as to overhear any inkling as to Miss Fulton's marital status. To his delight, he was rewarded with a comment from her own lips.

"I long for those few treasures of my mother's," she said in a voice that bore no laughter.

Had he not known it was she who spoke, he would not have recognized her voice at all. It was if she were a different person that the Miss Fulton he knew. It could only be her, however; she wore the same dull red gown and blue gloves, hat and boots she had worn the day they had gone to the village from Oak View the summer previous. To his chagrin, they once again walked along so quickly that he was unable to hear anything more.

Waiting for their possible return, he gazed into the water and soon became lost in his reflections. He looked up only to discover that Miss Fulton had passed him by and had already crossed nearly half of the bridge. He quickly followed but was unable to catch her up until they had both reached the south quay. Trailing her, he saw with some surprise that she headed east towards Trinity College.

As he did not wish to be seen, he paced a safe distance behind, wondering again what had brought her to Dublin. Perhaps she had a relative who was sponsoring her *entre* into Dublin society. Or she might have chosen to stay with the family of the man she planned to wed. Neither supposition pleased.

As he rounded a corner, he was astounded to find himself

on a street not far from his old home. Several houses down from the corner, she opened the front gate, went up the lane to the door and rapped. It opened and a maid, who seemed to expect Miss Fulton, ushered her inside. He made a note of the address and determined to learn the identity of the occupants as soon as possible.

He lingered at the gate for longer than was strictly wise before reluctantly returning to his lodgings. Over a meal of bread and cheese, he mused on the remark she had made concerning her mother's treasures. He supposed any young woman about to be married should be wishful of having her mother's things. But why did she not possess them? Had she left them at home? Had they been destroyed in a fire, perhaps? Is that why she was in Dublin? Her home and perhaps even her father were gone, and she was free? Then why had she not responded to his message?

He spent another sleepless night as he puzzled over such riddles. By morning he had reached a conclusion: he must make a journey. This time, however, when the butler presented him to Mr. Fulton, Niall would refuse to depart until he received answers to his questions. He arrived at The Hollows the following afternoon, and was greeted politely enough by the butler.

"Mr. Fulton is not at home," he said as he stepped back to shut the door.

"Wait!" Niall cried urgently, prepared to wedge his foot in between the door and its frame if required. "Perhaps you remember me. I am Mr. Doherty. I was here to call on Miss Fulton last summer."

The butler nodded, and frowned as if Niall's words pained him.

"When shall Mr. Fulton be returned?"

"I cannot say," the butler replied.

"Then I shall wait," Niall insisted.

"I am afraid he shall not return today." The butler seemed reticent to divulge more.

"I know better than to ask for Miss Fulton," Niall said leadingly. "I saw her in Dublin only yesterday."

The butler's face fell as his eyes lit with joy. "Dublin! Did you speak to her? Is she well?"

"She seems very well, indeed, though I am sorry to say we did not speak. Had you not known where she has gone?"

The butler hesitated, then, with a sweep of his hand, said, "You had better come in."

Niall doffed his hat and crossed the threshold into the front hall. Aside from an air of listless vacancy, it looked much the same as it had the summer prior.

"Mr. Fulton is away in search of Miss Fulton," the butler explained. "She left a letter stating that she was going to the city. He had supposed she meant London."

"Poor devil! His apprehension must know no bounds," Niall said, aghast. "You must send word to him, but only say that she is safe. As to why she has left here, I can only hazard a guess as to her motives, and have no wish to betray her. I swear that when I return to Dublin, I shall see to it that she writes to her father."

The butler nodded as tears filled his eyes. "I am that grateful. 'Tis good to know she is safe. The horrors we have been imagining . . ."

"I assure you, she is indeed safe. I have come, though, to learn more about her circumstances. Will you tell me how long ago she left?"

"It has been since the autumn."

Niall reeled with the knowledge that she had been in Dublin nearly as long as he had. "Do you have any reason to believe she left home to be married?"

The butler betrayed his shock, his eyes wide. "No! Her father did not allow her any letters, save a few from Miss O'Sullivan. He refused to post any of the letters she wrote and burned most of those she received."

"Including those of mine," Niall observed tersely.

"I am afraid, 'tis true," the butler replied, discomfited. "I assumed the young miss ran away so as to attend the wedding of Miss O'Sullivan in London. I never had thought 'twould be Dublin that she went."

"Very well then; she did not go to Dublin to meet a man. Can you think of anyone she might know there?"

"The family moved from Dublin near on ten year ago. 'Tis doubtful that she would remember any she might have known there. However," the butler said, his voice taking on a more hopeful tone, "she attended a Dublin finishing school."

"Of course!" Niall replied. "She had told me so herself."

"Do you believe that she went to Mrs. Hill, then?"

"I do not know," Niall replied, though the house she entered could very well have been a school for young ladies. "I have reason to believe she has plans to marry." He went over the small store of words he had heard from her lips in Dublin, each one full of sorrow. "However, I do not believe her entirely

264

happy. I will do all in my power to help her if she will allow me."

"Thank you, Mr. Doherty," the butler said with a bow. "How might I be of assistance?"

"I have seen her but twice, both earlier this week, both times in the company of Miss O'Sullivan. They were speaking, I believe of Miss O'Sullivan's nuptials."

"Indeed, Miss Fiona was married in London shortly before Christmas. Miss Fulton had already gone away. However, when she did not return after the festivities her father became concerned."

"Of course. And yet, if she had gone to London before arriving in Dublin, how has she paid for such journeys?"

"That is a mystery," the butler intoned.

"I happened to overhear a portion of her conversation with Miss O'Sullivan. She said how she longed for her mother's treasures. Can you make anything of that?"

"I am afraid there is little I can tell you in that regard. The maid who attended her has long since been dismissed. I cannot say what any of those treasures might have been. If it is your wish to restore them to her, I am afraid I can be of no assistance."

"Is there anyone in the house who might know what these treasures are?" Niall asked in tones loud enough to be heard by the servant partially obscured behind a door to another room.

"I am not certain," the butler began, but was forestalled by the emergence of the old woman, feather duster in hand.

"And who might you be?" Niall asked kindly.

"I'm Mrs. Kiernan. I ha' been with the family since Miss

Fulton were a babe. I know exactly what she were talkin' 'bout, but she must have took t'em with her, for I not seen t'em since afore she left."

"Since *before* she left?" Niall asked. "Are you very certain?"

"Yes," she said in a fearful manner, her eyes wide.

"Then it seems she has sold them to acquire the funds for her journey," Niall pointed out. "Will you make me a list, Mrs. Kiernan?"

"I canna write," she replied.

"Perhaps, if I were to have a pen and parchment."

"Of course," the butler agreed. "If you would, please follow me into the study."

"Mrs. Kiernan?" Niall indicated that the maid should follow, as well. Like her, he entered the study with no small amount of trepidation; it had been the scene of his greatest blow since the death of his father. Looking about, he realized it was far less threatening minus its domineering inhabitant.

As he sat at the desk, he was overcome with a curious feeling. To sit in the same chair as Mr. Fulton when he denied Niall his only happiness in life was unexpected in every way. Picking up the pen from the desk, he dipped it into the well. "Mrs. Kiernan, tell me, please, which items once belonging to her mother disappeared prior to Miss Fulton's departure."

"Well, 'twere a set of coral-studded combs and a silver brush with a matchin' mirror, the sort ye hold in yer hand."

Niall wrote them on the list. "Was there any jewelry?"

"T'ere might ha' been; I don't know. I dust and clean in t'ere; I didn't go pawin' t'rough her box o' jewels. If she had t'em, she not often wore t'em."

"Thank you." Niall recalled the ring of blue-green rhinestones Miss Fulton claimed to be her mother's and added it to the list. "Is there anything else?"

"Yes, a perfume bottle; 'twas empty, but it still smelt o' flowers, and lastly, a porcelain figger; a shepherd and a lady with a lamb in the folds o' her skirt."

"Excellent, Mrs. Kiernan," Niall said, a smile spreading across his face. He was about to proclaim the three of them geniuses when a shadow fell across the room.

"What are ye doin' here?" a voice bellowed. "Out with ye!"

"Sir!" the butler cried in astonishment. "I have had no word of your arrival!"

Niall noticed that Mrs. Kiernan shrank in fear against the wall as he rose hastily to his feet. "Mr. Fulton, I beg your pardon. I have news for you of your daughter, very good news indeed."

Chapter Sixteen

Caroline looked down at the box of watercolors in her hands. It was not as ornate as the one she had sold to pay for her journey to Dublin, but it would do. Her students had other thoughts to occupy their minds. Those who had not returned to their homes for the summer were to go to the seashore for the day. Caroline would supply the lesson, a lecture on seascapes, whilst Mrs. Hill would provide transport for the six of them, as well as a hamper of food. It was just the sort of excursion Caroline had adored as a student at the school. This morning, however, she had not the heart for it.

Placing her paint box into a hamper, she added parchment and canvases, as well as several small easels. The hamper would prove heavy, but she had arranged for the coachman to carry it to one of the carriages. She considered requesting that one of the footmen accompany them; it made her anxious to be so many females attended only by two aged coachmen. However, Mrs. Hill did all in her formidable power to discourage the intermingling of youthful males and her charming students. As such, Caroline supposed her request would be denied.

She could not recall when she had felt so anxious, and supposed her concerns stemmed solely from the fact that a man had recently taken to following her about the city. She never dared look directly at him, so she had no notions as to his age or appearance. He was, perhaps, entirely unexceptionable. Nevertheless, it was passing strange that she should catch a glimpse of him on three different occasions in the course of two days. And there was the remark made by the maid who opened the door to her after her latest outing: she claimed that a man had followed Caroline to the gate and stood watching for some time after she had entered the house. The very idea made her flesh tingle.

Whilst the girls were upstairs donning bonnets and gloves, Caroline made her way to the front hall. She noted her appearance in the mirror with no small amount of surprise: her face was wan and thin despite the healthy appetite she had maintained since arriving in Dublin. Fiona, who had recently passed through Dublin on her way to visit her parents in Mullagh, claimed that the fault lay in the fact that Caroline no longer smiled. Perhaps, she thought as she grimaced in the mirror, Fiona was correct.

Forcing her lips to curve upwards, Caroline studied her reflection from various angles. To her chagrin, she caught the reflected expression of an appreciative footman as he stood guard in the hall. She had just opened her mouth to deliver a reprimand when someone rapped at the door. It felt almost as if Fate had come to call. Astonished at the shiver of anticipation that coursed through her at the sound, she slowly pivoted towards the door. .

The footman pulled it open to reveal a tall man wearing a hat of glossy beaver, York tan gloves the same shade of yellow as his pantaloons, and a cravat that gleamed snow white against the immaculate cut of a deep blue jacket.

Caroline did her best to feign disinterest in spite of the man's appealing elegance; it would not do if it were said in the hearing of Mrs. Hill that Caroline had ogled a male visitor. She could not, however, refrain from stealing a glance into the man's face.

"Miss Fulton?" he asked, his expression a mixture of delight and something akin to regret.

"Mr. Doherty?" she echoed, her heart hammering in her chest. Surely she stared at a ghost, one who was ever near but had somehow transformed into someone she never expected to see again in this life.

"Miss Fulton," he repeated, as if he expected those two words to say everything he had not.

She knew she ought to send him away immediately, but she could not do it, not for any amount of money, love, or happiness. "I shall speak with him outside," Caroline murmured for the footman as she swept past him. "Do shut the door after me," she added.

"What is this?" Mr. Doherty asked as she took his arm and led him a few paces down the lane towards the gate. "Am I to be denied entrance?"

Caroline heard the words 'yet again' in his voice and felt her skin turn hot with mortification. "Pray, do not take offense. Mrs. Hill expects us to adhere most rigorously to her stricture against gentlemen callers. But tell me, how come you to be in Dublin?" She hungrily took in every feature of his face: the firm jaw and sensitive mouth, the fantastical, pale, blue-gray eyes fringed with sooty lashes, the startling contrast of black curls against his high-pointed collar.

"I have been here since the start of the autumn term. I was

fortunate to have found a position teaching history at the college."

"At Trinity! Mr. Doherty, how wonderful!" she cried in genuine delight. "I knew you were capable of more than teaching small lads. And how do *they* fare?"

"I have not seen nor heard from them since I left Donegal," he said wistfully. "I hope they shall soon learn to stand up to their brother."

Caroline smiled. "That is not likely. They are such charming lads; I should be grateful for a few such as they. Girls are astonishingly difficult."

He smiled, his expression bemused, as if he entertained thoughts that carried him far from her words. His reply was perfectly appropriate, however. "Am I right to assume you are teaching here?"

"Yes; Painting and French. I have been in town nearly since the beginning of term, as well." She speculated as to her own abstracted appearance as she briefly pondered on all that had occurred to bring her to Dublin.

"I wonder that we have only now encountered one another," Mr. Doherty said. "I should have liked to stop you when first I saw you, but you moved away too quickly. You were with Miss O'Sullivan, only, I believe she is now to be called otherwise."

Caroline looked up into his face in disbelief. How she had longed to see herself reflected in those eyes that stirred her very soul. "Indeed, she is now Mrs. Wilkinson. I only regret that I was unable to attend her marriage."

He seemed to hesitate. "Your father?" he asked knowingly.

"As always," she sighed. "Oh! There is so much to tell you!

Unfortunately, I must take my leave. I am to escort the girls on a painting excursion. They are doubtless all assembled and waiting for me in the mews."

His lips curved into a smile, but it did not reach his eyes. "There is much that I would like to tell you, as well," he said. "However, I understand that you are not entirely . . . free," he added, his tone inscrutable.

Caroline paused, thinking of what she might manage. "I am free this Sunday. Is there somewhere we could meet?"

"Truly?" he asked, with a doubtful smile that betrayed his disbelief. "Would you be inclined to meet me at the college? There is much of interest to see there."

Quickly they agreed on a time and place to meet, and she lingered by the gate, her feelings in a state of confusion, until he reached the corner. To her delight, he turned and doffed his hat to wave it in the air. "Until then!" he called so joyfully it made her blush.

She responded with a demure smile that belied her excitement. Mr. Doherty was in Dublin! It seemed too impossible to be true. She walked up the path to the house as if in a dream. As she mused on what it was he wished to tell her, she entered the house and followed the sounds of girlish voices out through the back door and into the mews. Seeing that the painting supplies and food were strapped to the back of the carriage, she counted heads to ensure that all of the girls were in attendance. All of this was done with competence, though her mind was far from her deeds. It was as if her body occupied an entirely different sphere than that of her spirit.

As the carriage rattled along the quay towards the shore, she wondered how Mr. Doherty had come to find her. Then she realized that which ought to have been unmistakable: the man of whom she had caught glimpses, the one who had evidently followed her to the house and stood at the gate had been Mr. Doherty. It was his proximity that made her skin tingle, though she hadn't the least idea that he was near. Suddenly, an afternoon of painting at the seashore seemed the dullest of pastimes.

When the day of their engagement to meet finally arrived, she considered her ensemble with great care. There had been no funds for new gowns since leaving home, nor had there been room in her solitary trunk for more than her most suitable outfits. After careful consideration, she chose a straw-yellow gown and a periwinkle-blue velvet spencer. With the addition of a *Gros de Naples* hat tied smartly under her chin, she felt as fashionable as she could wish.

Her afternoon away from the school was not one of which Mrs. Hill would have approved. Though Caroline had often gone out, most recently on the arm of the new Mrs. Wilkinson, it had never been to meet a man. Mrs. Hill had made it more than clear that she did not approve of her female instructors meeting with gentlemen of any stamp. Caroline suspected this had most to do with the inconvenience of replacing those who traded teaching for marriage. And yet, as Caroline slipped out the front door, she felt nearly as censurable as she did when she had sneaked out of the house to meet Mr. Doherty by the spring at Oak View.

She wondered if it would always be thus; if they were doomed to a clandestine alliance of which no one approved, one that could never be deepened nor fully acted upon. And yet, their circumstances had altered since she had watched Mr. Doherty through her rain-pelted window. He now held an honorable position at Trinity College, whilst Caroline was the penniless teacher. Perhaps he would finally find it acceptable to make her his wife.

At the same time, she marveled that he had not yet married another. Surely the maidens of Dublin were queuing up for such a man. He was honorably employed, charming, intelligent, and highly attractive. She was tempted to believe it was his love for her that encouraged his single status, and yet, he had always seemed convinced that they did not belong together. Even if time had softened his doubts, so it would have his love. An acquaintance of five days could not be expected to endure a parting of a year. But, truthfully, she loved him more than ever.

As she pondered such incompatible notions, she noted the turbulence of the sky above. The rain began to fall before she had covered half the distance between Mrs. Hill's and the college. Opening her umbrella, she quickened her step until she arrived at the entrance to the old library. When after five minutes he had not appeared, she began to fear that he had changed his mind.

And then she saw him; he was in company with a very distinguished gentleman, doubtless another teacher at the school. They seemed to be discussing a matter of great import as they walked towards where she waited. As she looked from one to the other, she realized Mr. Doherty was every bit as distinguished as his companion. Gone was his country attire of corduroy jacket and low straw hat, replaced by this elegant man in breeches, high-crowned hat, waistcoat, and smart jacket. It was the same gray coat he had worn the day he had come to her home the previous summer. She wondered what course her life might have taken if they had been allowed to meet that day. Quickly, she dismissed the thought as Mr. Doherty bid farewell to his companion and, seeing her, broke out into a smile of gladness.

Her heart beat faster as he approached; she had always found him the most handsome of men, but when he smiled is such a way, it made her positively breathless. She hoped her admiration was not as discernable to bystanders as it seemed it must. She longed to throw herself into his arms and cling to him despite the blush that rose in her cheeks at the thought.

He said nothing at first. Rather, he stared at her as if he doubted her presence whilst being enchanted by it. Finally, he held out his arm to her and said, "You have come."

"But of course I have," she replied as she put her arm through his. She thought he restrained a start of surprise at her familiarity, but there was nothing in his manner that would lead her to believe it was unwelcome. "Did we not agree to?"

"Yes, it's only that I . . . Well, I don't know what I thought," he said as he led her into the long room of the library. "I suppose I believed it too much good fortune to see you again so soon after having been so long parted."

She looked up into his face and smiled. "It seems rather like a dream."

"Indeed, it does. For us to meet was always displeasing to one person or another. It now seems somewhat laughable, does it not?" he asked with an unwarranted intensity.

Caroline nodded in agreement despite thoughts of Mrs. Hill's opinion, if she but knew, on the matter. However, Caroline would not have Mr. Doherty guess the reason for her blushes. "Allow me to beg your pardon for the sake of my father," she said. "He remained angry for so very long. It is why I was forced to leave. I could not contemplate being trapped in that house for the remainder of his life. There was a time when he even kept me locked up in my chamber! If I had not seen you through the window, I would never have known you had come to call."

He looked down at her in surprise. "Would you not? I left for you a very particular message, one he promised to deliver."

Her heart again began to hammer in her chest. "A message? May I know what it was?"

Looking down into her face, he smiled, though his eyes were tinged with disappointment. "It no longer signifies," he said shortly. "Ah! Behold one of the wonders I wish for you to see." He stretched his hand towards a harp. It was made of a lustrous wood and stood on a plinth at the end of a row of tall bookshelves.

"It is beautiful! Are any allowed to play it?"

He shook his head. "It is far too old and precious. It is said to have belonged to Brian Boru, himself, the last High King of Ireland. But that is not what I find most interesting about this harp; it bears the coat of arms of the O'Neill family."

"But you are a Doherty," she replied, somewhat bewildered.

"My mother is an O'Neill by birth," he said proudly. "My given name is in honor of her family. The O'Neill's are descendants of Niall Noígíallach of the Nine Hostages. Have you heard the tale?"

"I should like to hear it from your lips, at any rate," she asserted with a smile.

"Well, you see," he said cheerfully, "Niall was the only son of Eochaid's second wife, Cairenn. His first wife, Mongfind, mother herself to four fine sons, was so envious of Cairenn that she gave all of the heavy work to her so as to cause her to lose the child. When he was born, Cairenn was afraid for him, for the cruelty he should doubtless encounter, so she left him high in the rocks to die. Happily, he was found and raised to adulthood by a poet who told him of his true parentage. When Niall grew to a goodly size, he returned to Tara to rescue his mother from the cruel Mongfind."

Caroline willingly fell under the spell his voice wove. She did not want it to end. "But what of the nine hostages?"

"It is not a pretty tale," he said with a woeful shake of his head.

She supposed the truth was that it was a story that did not speak well of his ancestor. "Tell me, then, about the coat of arms. I wonder what this red hand signifies."

"'Tis an old legend, yes?" he said in the lyrical voice of his origins. "It tells of a promise made that all of Ireland would belong to the first to swim or sail across the sea and touch Irish soil. There were many contenders, including O'Neill, who somehow fell behind the others. But, the land was to be given to the first to touch the Isle of Eire, so O'Neill devised a cunning plan. Once he drew near enough, he cut off his hand and threw it to the shore, thereby being the first."

"I suppose that is why the hand is red," she said with a laugh. "Though, 'tis rather shocking."

"Yes, and very likely a pack of lies. The story seems to originate hundreds of years after the coat of arms, complete with the red hand, first appeared."

"We Irish are canny, are we not?" She smiled her pleasure. "Truly, 'twas a lovely story; one that demonstrates the nobility of the O'Neill family; and the harp is beautiful, but 'tis the rows and rows of books that entrance me!"

"I had hoped they would," he admitted, his eyes dancing. "Believe this if you can; 'tis rumored that a second floor is to be added, one which shall also contain as many books as this entire room. 'Tis astounding."

"I had never imagined there could be so many books in all the world," she breathed.

He held out his arm, which she took as warmly as before. Together they strolled up and down the gallery, pausing to examine a book as often as they liked. When she grew tired, he suggested they sit on a bench in one of the window embrasures with a view of the grounds.

Caroline had so many questions, but hesitated to ask the ones closest to her heart. "Tell me of our friend Pierre," she asked instead. "Pray tell that he survived!"

"Indeed, he did! The bullet passed through him, so once Mrs. Walsh rid the wound of the infection, the physician stitched it up. He was off again to London within a fortnight. I wrote to tell you of it, but I have been told that you were never given my letters."

"No, I was not," she said sadly. "I wished to write to you, as well, but I knew my letters would never find you. One of the questions I should have loved to ask is how you came to know our three Frenchmen in the wood."

"That is, indeed, a tale!" he said with a smile. "Professor Luce had taken me off on a grand tour of the Continent, just as I would have had my father lived. We were abroad for two years and were glad when Napoleon was finally conquered at Waterloo. We were ready to go home. It was then that we met Pierre, Etienne, and Michel on the road from Edinburgh to Stranraer where we took ship to Larne. They had somehow escaped being sent home to France after having been shut up at Edinburgh Castle for a good deal of the war. They had been pressed into serving in the military in exchange for delaying a prison sentence, but they doubtless felt they had been imprisoned long enough."

Caroline shivered. "So they were, indeed, criminals."

"They claim to have been innocent of the crimes of which they were convicted. It never mattered to me whether or not they were guilty until it was your life that was at risk," he said as a shadow crossed his face.

"That was a day like no other," Caroline observed. "And now we are both here. I seem to recall that you moved from Donegal to Dublin when you were still young. Have you enjoyed living here again?"

"More than I thought possible," he said, with so frank a look that her breath froze in her lungs. "I am a Donegal man to be sure, but Dublin has unexpected charms. And," he said, breaking off his gaze to look out through the window, "I have only yesterday learned that the man who cheated my father at cards has agreed to make reparation. The townhouse shall soon again be in my possession."

"Oh, Mr. Doherty!" she cried in delight. Perhaps now he would ask her to grace his home as his wife.

279

They sat in silence for a few moments before he quietly spoke. "There is a matter of importance that I must confess to you."

His words gripped her chest in alarm. If he admitted his attachment to another, she was persuaded she would be unable to prevent herself from weeping in view of all assembled.

He hesitated. "The occasion when I came to your home last summer," he said slowly. "That was not the last time I was there."

"Was it not?" she asked, trembling with elation that her worst fear had not been realized.

"No. I imagine you have arrived at the correct conclusion; that I had seen you when you were out with Miss, er, Mrs. Wilkinson. I was amazed," he said candidly. "I could not work out how you came to be in Dublin. I knew your father would never allow it. I confess it made me concerned for your welfare. So, I went to The Hollows to inquire after you."

"You journeyed to County Cavan?" she asked in astonishment. "To ask after me?"

He nodded. "Your father had been in London looking for you. I could not refrain from easing his fears for you, though I did not tell him precisely where to find you," he insisted. "He lives in expectation of a letter from you, however."

"It is good of you to tell me," she said for his ears alone. "I must thank you for not providing my father with my direction."

His expression softened as he leaned back against the bench. "It was my good fortune to have discovered it."

Self-conscious, she smiled and bit her lip. "I had been told that I was followed home one day last week."

"I dared not make myself known to you," he said, his cheeks reddening, "until I had learned more of your circumstances." He drew a breath as if to speak further, but a frown appeared between his thick, black brows, and he fell silent.

"What is it?" she said with a bright smile contrived to hide her apprehension.

"I was thinking of the visit I paid to your little shrine in the back garden," he said, his smile wry.

She felt her skin burn a fiery red. "Oh! No one was to see it; I thought I had hidden it so well." She told herself it was impossible for him to know she had built it in hopes of making an offering that would bring him again to her side.

"I regret to say that this washed up," he said as he reached into his pocket and pulled out a small object. "As it was doing little good there, I thought you might prefer to have it once again in your possession."

"Oh!" she said, startled. It was her mother's ring, the one she had sacrificed at the shrine; somehow it had brought him back to her. "You are so kind to restore it to me. I have been missing it."

He regarded her in some surprise. "You do not regret the loss of that for which you made the sacrifice?" His words were light, but his eyes were heavy with shadows.

"Indeed, no. That is to say . . ." She paused, unsure of how much she dared reveal. "There is time yet," she finished with a hopeful smile.

He looked long into her eyes then turned away. "I have been given reason to believe it had all run out," he said in low tones.

She could not discern his meaning until she remembered his own offering: the pocket watch of his father's. "I am sorry," she said, her heart aching. She had thought she knew what he had wished for that day at the spring. So, why did he not speak?

He continued to look off into the distance. "'Twas a dry summer."

She cast about for a suitable reply. "'Twas, but this summer has been different. We have had so much rain."

He turned to her and smiled. "I wonder that you did not sacrifice the little swan we found at the spring, rather than an item as precious as your mother's ring."

"I . . ." she said, hesitating as she searched his face. There was something of the old Mr. Doherty, the one she met when she first arrived at Oak View, in the cast of his eyes and mouth. Suddenly unsure, she refrained from telling him that the swan was her best-loved possession. "It is of no consequence," she said dismissively.

He looked down at her hands in her lap as if he would take them in his own. "Might I ask what it was you wished for?"

"You may ask," she riposted.

"However, you shall not say." He smiled, seeming to have recovered from whatever dark thoughts had beset him.

"One must have one's secrets," she replied, her smile demure.

"I shall confess a secret if you do," he offered as he drew a long, thin object from his pocket.

"It's a piece of string," she said in some confusion.

"Not a piece of string; *the* piece of string," he said with a furtive smile.

"No! Say it is not so!" she gasped through her laughter. "You could not have kept such an ordinary item for all this time."

"Indeed I have! Such work this string was set to; it should be preserved forever, like Brian Boru's harp, should it not?" he asked merrily.

She held out her gloved hand, and he coiled the string into it. "It is a bit soiled and frayed at the ends," she pointed out, "but I am persuaded it could yet bear the weight of as many letters as one could wish."

He cocked his head. "I suppose so. It only lacks a pair of windows." He offered her a curt smile as he retrieved the string and returned it to his pocket. "I would invite you to join me for supper at one of the pubs along the quay, but I am convinced you are otherwise occupied."

"I wish I were free to accept, but I fear to be seen," she replied. She trembled at the possible forms of chastisement that should fall upon her head if Mrs. Hill learned of such an outing.

"It is as I suspected." The light faded from his eyes. "Might I at least escort you home?"

She smiled. "I would like that." How she hoped it would give him further opportunity to speak. "However, I must ask you to accompany me only as far as the corner of the square. If anyone were to see us . . ."

"Yes," he said sadly. "But do say you will see me again, at least once more before . . ."

"Before?" she asked, perplexed.

He looked at her quizzically. "Is there a place we could meet that shall not condemn you to stricture?"

She considered, but could not call to mind a place in Dublin that one of the other instructors might not visit at any time. "No, I do not think so, not a place in particular. However, no one could possibly object if we were to merely come across one another," Caroline mused.

"No one?" he echoed doubtfully.

"No one that signifies," she said, her face heated. "I have made a habit of leaving the house most afternoons to venture out across the river and back."

"Yes," he said with a sardonic smile. "That is where I first saw you here in Dublin."

"Of course," she said with a laugh. "How could I have forgotten? You may find me there any day that suits."

"Thank you," he said as he rose to his feet. "I cannot say precisely when it shall be, only that it shall be soon."

"That is perfect," she said brightly, despite her misgivings as to his intentions. Did he wish to offer for her hand or tell her that they shall never meet again? "Should anyone known to me be close enough to observe us together, my surprise shall be genuine."

"I have long admired your capacity to turn every negative into a positive." He held out his hand to her and, taking it, she stood. Again, she put her arm through his so that her hand rested on his upper arm, up against his heart. He covered her fingers with his; she could feel the heat of them through his gloves and hers. They started out on their return journey to Mrs. Hill's, their steps in time with one another.

As they walked, the gray sky dissolved. Patches of blue appeared between pure white clouds, and rays of sunshine

284

sparkled in the droplets of water that clung to every leaf and blade of grass. Birds appeared in the sky, warbling sweet songs. Caroline felt it a symbol of hope for her and Mr. Doherty. Looking up into his well-loved face, she pondered on how she might bring up the subject of marriage.

"I fear I gave you a disgust of my manners when we first met at Oak View," she ventured.

He seemed taken aback. "Why would you say such a thing?"

"Now that I am returned to the sensibilities of Mrs. Hill, I am reminded that there are social conventions one ought to observe. I have come to realize that my behavior in pressing you to speak with my father was improper."

His arm tensed beneath her hand, and he frowned. "You regret that you were so free with me at Oak View."

She felt stung, rebuked. "Only if it has proven to lower me in your esteem."

He sighed, but the frown disappeared. "Your Mrs. Hill is English, I believe."

"Yes, why do you ask?"

"You are Irish; I am Irish. We do not stand on ceremony to the same degree as the English. Their ways are not always preferable, are they? I found the too-staid conventions at Oak View to be suffocating. I was very lonely there, and then you arrived," he said, his voice thickening. "You were so ingenuous, so artless, you nearly sparkled." He looked down into her eyes. "Every day before you came and every day after you departed were ones of desolation."

Caroline felt her heart rise on wings of hope. Perhaps this

was the moment when he would declare his intentions. She gazed back at him, her smile tremulous.

He slowed his pace and drew her round to face him. Looking into her eyes, he brushed his fingers against her cheek then took her hands in his. "It is I who must beg your forgiveness."

"Pray tell, for what?" she asked in bewilderment.

"For the liberties I took," he said quietly. "You need not fear it shall happen again."

Caroline tried and failed to remember the liberties to which he referred. If only he kissed her now, she might be his bride by autumn. "I can recall nothing you have done or said that should require my forgiveness."

"Now that matters stand as they do, was it not wise that we did not give too much of ourselves to each other?"

Caroline felt her face fall. "It is true that my circumstances are not as they were," she began.

"You need say no more, Miss Fulton," he said in tones too formal for contentment. "We have walked together as far as you have wished me to go. There is someone in the house you would not wish to see us together, am I right?"

"Well, yes," she readily admitted.

"Then let us part as friends and say only that we shall see one another once more."

Tears sprang to her eyes. He had only just reappeared in her life. "I beg you to understand; I do wish to see you more often! It is only that we must be cautious."

"Of course," he said, exactly as if he understood nothing at all. "Until then." He lifted his hat, exposing his head of black curls, and bowed.

"Goodbye," she said doubtfully. This time, she did not wait until he disappeared from view but made her way immediately to Mrs. Hill's. If he turned to look for her upon reaching the corner, she did not wish to know of it. As she walked through the doorway, Caroline studied each face she encountered. If anyone knew of her tryst, they did not betray themselves. She took dinner with the other instructors who, like her, had no other home for the summer. To her relief, Mrs. Hill was in a spirited mood. In the end, it was a merry meal despite Caroline's lack of appetite.

That night she lay in bed, clutching her mother's ring in the palm of her hand. He had promised she would see him again. "Oh please, let it be soon," she whispered into the dark.

Every day that week she made her way to and from the river, slowly, so as to be easily seen. She could not help but look for Mr. Doherty, though she hoped she was discreet in her manner. She had not guessed such subterfuge should prove so exhausting. Finally, almost a se'enight after they last met, when she had nearly given up hope, she saw him at the foot of the metal footbridge, a parcel in his hands.

He saw her nearly at the same moment and broke into a smile. They moved towards one another when, without warning, a young nursery maid who chased after a child ran directly into Mr. Doherty. The parcel he held fell from his grasp and he bent to retrieve it.

Caroline's impulse was to hasten to his side, but she was forced to turn away when she noticed one of Mrs. Hill's instructors nearby. Her heart raced with apprehension as, silently weeping, she retraced her steps as quickly as possible.

When she arrived at the bench where she rested before returning to the school, she sat down, pulled out her handkerchief and wiped her eyes. As she did, the ring she wore flashed in the light, demanding her attention.

Caroline considered the row of bluish gray rhinestones on the simple gold band and wondered what good her sacrifice had done. It seemed she had wished for the wrong eventuality. This time, she would cast the ring into a pool of greater depth. This time, her sacrifice would amount to something. This time, she would wish that Mr. Doherty would ask her to be his wife.

Quickly, she rose to her feet and moved towards the bridge; if she were late to Mrs. Hill's, there would be unwanted questions. As she hurried along, she gazed intently into the water in search of a suitable place to cast her ring. The bridge was much occupied, and when her gaze fell on a bit of water bluer than the rest, she found she must push her way past several people to make her way to the rail. Then she pulled the ring from her finger and cast it into the River Liffey.

With a sigh of satisfaction, she looked up to realize that farther down the bridge stood Mr. Doherty, parcel in hand, his eyes fixed to the water. She felt almost overcome with joy, but as she drew near, she realized something was amiss. She had known Mr. Doherty to be lonely; she had seen him full of regret; she had looked into his eyes when they brimmed with sorrow. She, however, had never seen his face bear a look of such devastation, as if he had a moment ago learned of his own demise.

She made her way to his side. "Mr. Doherty." She put her hand on his arm. "What is it?"

He turned, his eyes lifeless. When he saw that it was she, he swallowed hard, his eyes over bright and moist. "I met her," he murmured, "just a few minutes ago, here, on the bridge. She is a Miss Lynch." He blinked his eyes rapidly as if to hold back tears.

"Who?" Caroline asked, bewildered. "That nursery maid who collided with you?"

He shook his head. "No. Someone more unexceptionable. Only she," he said and paused. "Pray, forget that I spoke." He mustered a melancholy smile. "This is for you," he said, thrusting the parcel at her. "I am pleased that you returned, as I have been longing for you to have this."

"For me?" she asked in astonishment. "If I had but known . . . But truly, I could not approach you, then. There was someone from Mrs. Hill's," she stammered. "I could not have him see us together."

He frowned and looked studiously away. "Let us speak of other things, such as what is in the parcel."

She had so many questions she wished to put to him, but he did not look as if he were inclined to answer a one. Carefully, she reached into the package and removed the first wrapped bundle. As she drew away the paper, the item flashed in the sun. "My mother's perfume bottle! Mr. Doherty, how came you by this?"

"There's more," he said, his eyes less stricken and a smile playing about his lips.

She opened the second bundle, which contained her mother's brush and comb. Her heart squeezed with gratitude. "But you must have stopped at the local pawnbroker's after you visited The Hollows," she said in wonder, unsure as to its meaning.

He was smiling in earnest now. "Just open the rest," he urged.

The third packaged contained the coral combs that her mother had worn in her hair the day she married. "Oh! How I have wished for these! But this is no accident. You cannot have stumbled upon all of my things by chance."

"There's one more." He looked into the parcel, his eloquent blue-gray eyes dancing.

The last was larger than the rest and took up the entire bottom of the parcel. She knew what it was the moment she took it in her hands. Eagerly, she pulled away the silver tissue to uncover the beautiful water color box. "My father made a present of this to me when I was very young. I have treasured it, as I did all of the rest. I was forced to sell them to pay for my journey here to Dublin. But, somehow, you already know this," she said in wonder.

"Pray forgive me; the shepherdess with her little lamb shattered when it all went tumbling to the ground," he said, his brow furrowed with anxiety.

"Pray, do not concern yourself! I expected never to see any of these things again!"

Wordlessly, he took the paint box from her hands and placed the entire parcel with its contents on the ground at their feet. Then, taking her hands in his, he looked steadily into her eyes. "When I learned from the servants that you had sold these treasures, I wanted nothing more than to restore them to you. I knew I ought not to have brought them to Mrs. Hill's, nor was the college the appropriate place."

"You were quite right," she replied. "Is it for this, only, that you wished to see me again?" she asked in tones she hoped did not reveal her blighted hopes.

He swallowed and looked away as if he were ashamed. "It seems I need make another confession. On your last day at Oak View, I was looking for Mr. Wilkinson's room. I knew that was where I would find the physician for Pierre. When a maid opened the door to a room, quite naturally, I seized the opportunity to look inside. I knew immediately that it was not Mr. Wilkinson's chamber, and as soon as the maid had gone, I went inside. It was *yours*," he said looking up to gauge her reaction. "I knew that I would feel closer to you there than I would ever be again."

"What does any of that matter?" she asked, dismayed. *We are together. Now. On this bridge*, were the words she dared not add.

"There is more," he said, gently squeezing her hands. "I noticed a letter you had written to your father, one in which you informed him of my 'fine qualities,' as you put it. It was crumpled as if you no longer wished him to read it."

She felt a wave of humiliation wash over her. "I did so wish to tell him how very admirable you are; how worthy you are of his daughter. Then I realized it would do no good. I thought I had thrown it out."

"I am so grateful that you did not," he said in earnest. "I cannot express my gratitude for your words, for the good they did me. I should never have had the courage to speak to anyone about a position at Trinity if it weren't for that letter. It wasn't so much that I recognized myself in your compliments; it was that I knew I would never be happy until I became the man you described."

"You were that man!" She tightened her fingers around his. "You are still."

His answering smile was a happy one. "I am grateful to know you believe it to be true."

"It is for that you purchased my things," she said, failing to disguise the lifeless tones in her voice.

"Yes," he said, squeezing her fingers in his. "I wanted so much to thank you."

It was not what she wished him to say. She dropped her gaze to her hands so that he would not see her tears. "I am grateful, as well," she replied in a voice that wavered. "I fear that I shall never be able to thank you properly. You cannot know how much it means to me." She took a deep breath and looked up at him, praying he would comprehend what she hoped to imply. "I have always imagined I would be wed wearing those combs as did my mother."

To her astonishment, his face fell as if he had just heard the worst news of all. Sighing, he dropped her hands and turned to look out over the water. "I had meant to ask you," he said, his voice dull. "Shall you inform your father? I imagine he would make the journey to witness the marriage of his only daughter. When is it to be?"

"I? To be married?" She felt as bemused as if she had returned from supping with the fairies to learn that a hundred years had passed.

He turned to look into her eyes. "You are not betrothed?" he asked listlessly, as if he did not know how he ought to feel.

Nearly overcome with relief, she smiled and put a hand to

his cheek. "No, Mr. Doherty, I am not. And yet, I very much hope to be before the sun sets on this day."

His smile spoke of a joy difficult to restrain. "I had thought . . . Rather, I heard something that led me to believe . . . Well, it doesn't matter now, does it?"

"No, it does not," she said, holding back tears of happiness.

"But, wait!" he cried as he looked wildly about. "I have just met Miss Lynch," he said, his eyes wide and his brows beetled in agitation.

"Mr. Doherty," she said, putting her hand again to his face so as to draw his gaze to hers. "I do not know where Miss Lynch might be. However, I am here, standing before you."

He looked into her eyes and swallowed hard. "Miss Caroline Fulton," he said as if he intoning the spell of a druid. "I choose you." His eyes shone like water in the sun as he took her shoulders in his hands and lowered his mouth to hers. He kissed her tenderly, his lips warm against hers, until she knew the last shattered piece of her heart to be finally redeemed.

It was over far too quickly, but Caroline had no wish to be disagreeable. "Very well then, Mr. Doherty," she said with a sigh of contentment, "if you shall insist on bestowing kisses in full view of all and sundry, it is only right that you should know my true name."

"True name?" he asked, searching her face in unaccountable alarm. "Your name is not Caroline Fulton?"

"It is not as if I set out to deceive you," she explained, nearly as alarmed as he. "Caroline is my name, but it was not well-favored by Papa. Once my mother had died, and my brothers also, he began to call me as he pleased."

293

"Yes! What? What is it?" he demanded urgently, his fingers pressing into her shoulders.

"It is only a nickname," she explained. "He has called me thus all my life, though Fiona does insist on calling me Caro which infuriates Papa to no end!"

"Miss Caroline Fulton," he implored, the look in his eyes such a mingling of love and hope, fear and misgiving, that it set her entire frame to trembling. "Tell me your name this instant!"

"Lina," she gasped out around her uncertainty. "I am called Lina."

He stared at her in such disbelief she feared he condemned her for a liar.

"Pray, believe me," she asserted, "for what reason would I prevaricate about such a thing?"

"You believe me to be angry?" he exclaimed. Before she could reply, she was in his arms, bonnet askew, her face pressed into the linen of his cravat, her ear against the wild staccato of his heart.

"My darling Lina," he murmured into her hair, his words rumbling in her ear. "It was you. From the very beginning, it was you."

She could not remember when she had felt so safe, so loved; so at home. When he loosened his arms, she felt more bereft than she could recall. Then he tugged at the ribbon under her chin until her bonnet slipped down her back. Whatever its fate was a matter of indifference to her. She could not look away from his fascinated gaze. It was as if she were a loathly lady, a hag who had transformed into a beautiful young woman in his embrace.

Finally, he gave her a smile of such sweetness, one that utterly banished the lonely Mr. Doherty of Oak View. "I was desolate when we parted; I have been desolate each day since," he revealed, his voice rough, his breathing ragged. "Say that I need never be desolate again."

In reply, she lifted her lips to his and closed her eyes in anticipation of another tender kiss. To her astonishment, he swept her into his arms, lifted her off of her feet, and pressed his lips to hers with a breath-taking urgency. This kiss was hot and demanding, as if he were the sun above and she the only river that had the power to quench his thirst. When he lowered her again to her feet, she felt as if she had been made his, irrevocably and forever.

With a sheepish smile, he retrieved her bonnet and placed it on her head, tying it under her chin with a bow. She stared up at him, unable to wholly believe that he wanted her for his wife. "Am I to be Mrs. Doherty, then?" she asked with a smile that spoke of all of her hopes and dreams.

"It could never be anyone but you, nothing doubting." His eyes shining, he took her arm and turned towards the water. She leaned her head upon his shoulder and watched as the vibrant sun settled into the cool waters of the River Liffey.

"Before you escort me home," she murmured, "you must answer me one question. How can the name I was given as an infant be of any consequence whatsoever?"

"Ah, well now," he said, looking down at her in delight, his eyes gleaming in the light of the setting sun. "'Tis a story for the tellin'!"

By the same author

Via Montlake Romance ~
Miss Delacourt Speaks Her Mind
Miss Delacourt Has Her Day

Via Dunhaven Place Publishing ~
Lady Crenshaw's Christmas
Lord Haversham Takes Command
The Lord Who Sneered and Other Tales
Miss Armistead Makes Her Choice

Via Mirror Press ~
A Timeless Romance Anthology: Winter Collection: It Happened Twelfth Night

A Midwinter Ball: Timeless Regency Collection: Much Ado About Dancing

About the Author:

Heidi Ashworth is the award-winning author of numerous regency romance novels, including the Miss Delacourt series. She lives in the San Francisco Bay Area with her husband, three children and two dogs.

of the

Matchmaker
—SERIES—

November 2015... *Power of the Matchmaker*
(A prequel novella of the Matchmaker's story)

January 1, 2016

February 1, 2016

March 1, 2016

April 1, 2016

May 1, 2016

June 1, 2016

July 1, 2016

August 1, 2016

September 1, 2016

October 1, 2016

November 1, 2016

December 1, 2016